BROKEN

BROKEN

C. ARLINGTON BLAKE

Copyright

Ballbreaker Productions

ISBN: 978-1-7358949-0-4
Library of Congress number TXu 2-222-901
Edited by Mariah Jackson
Cover Art by Jun Aceres

Contents

Friendship is like a delicate flower. It needs water and sunlight to flourish. A little love and attention will also always go a long way.

Prologue

Seven and a half years of employment comes to an end as Isabella Maldonado celebrates her resignation from North Mutual Insurance Company (NMIC). Late Thursday, on a mild spring night in May, several employees of NMIC gather at Isabella's favorite watering hole, the Pink Stain Pub located in the East Village section of New York City. Isabella has secured on a new role as a Senior Underwriter at the Plante Insurance Group located in close proximity to NMIC in the Financial District in lower Manhattan. Her very close friends, Kimberly Richardson, Camille Bauman, Monica Moore, and Thomas Banks, are amongst several other employees celebrating with Isabella. The Pink Stain Pub on any Thursday night is packed to capacity. This Thursday night is no different.

Chapter 1: A Fresh Ending

Patrons of the bar sing along to classic rock music from the retro-styled jukebox making it difficult to communicate amongst themselves. The group of several NMIC employees congregate at the very rear of the bar. They spend the entire time laughing, drinking, and telling whimsical stories about Isabella's tenure at North Mutual Insurance Group. Kimberly, a twenty-nine-year-old African American Boston native, wears a white Boston Red Sox t-shirt. Monica, an African American/Asian who is the youngest member of the group at twenty-six years old, has both hands raised above her head with a bottle of beer, dancing to the music next to dear friend Kimberly.

Camille Bauman, one of the senior members of this group in her late forties, is a strikingly attractive Caucasian woman. She relates well with Thomas, who is another senior member of the group in his mid-forties. Thomas is an African American ex-police officer who works for the Special Investigation Unit (SIU) at NMIC. Isabella, or Izzy as everyone calls her is a serious career-driven mid-thirties slender Dominican woman. Everyone huddles together at the rear of the bar as Monica playfully dances next to Kimberly. Isabella looks at her watch before looking over the crowd to the front of the bar. She is waiting for her friend Oliver to arrive as he promised that he would try to stop by for a drink and meet her coworkers for the first time.

As patrons exit, the extremely crowded bar, Oliver Reed and Justin Hughes enter the crowded establishment. Oliver, a mid-twenties African American man, wears a white New York Yankees Jersey with a pair of Blue jeans. Oliver attempts to look over the patrons for Isabella; instead, he catches a glimpse of Kimberly and Monica dancing in the crowd. He smiles, shaking his head side to side as he leans in to talk to Justin. He gathers that it will be extremely tough to get through the bar to find his friend. "It's 9:30, and this place is already packed.".

"You're not kidding. I guess Thursdays really are the new Friday." Justin replies.

Justin looks over at the Kimberly and Monica playfully and seductively dancing together. Monica catches his eye immediately. He's able to get a good look at her face and takes a moment to observe her carefully. Her mulatto complexion with strong Asian facial features makes her stand out from the rest of the women in the bar.

"That Asian looking chick is hot." He says, pointing at Monica.

Oliver looks over at the girls shrugging his shoulders. "She looks a little on the young side, though. But hey, whatever floats your boat."

"If she's here drinking, chances are she's old enough."

"I hope so."

Oliver slowly slithers through the crowd of patrons to the bar, where he orders two beers. Oliver continues looking through the crowded bar but can only see silhouettes of patron's heads from the dimly lit rear portion of the bar. The bartender hands Oliver two bottles of beer.

"You want me to start a tab?" asks the bartender.

Oliver reaches for the beers shaking his head yes to the bartender before walking back toward Justine. He hands Justin a bottle noticing that he is still looking over at Kimberly and Monica hysterically laughing together. Justin points over at Kimberly

"Hey. She's pretty cute too."

Oliver turns to look at Kimberly, getting a good look at her face. "Oh, hell yeah."

"So, what time are you supposed to meet your friend here?" Justin asks.

"She said to be here around seven. It's after 9:30 now. I doubt they're here?"

"Dude, it's like 9:40. They probably left already. This place is pretty busy, but it's still Thursday. Tomorrow does happen to be workday."

Oliver nods in agreement. "We're already here, man. Let's just make the most of it. Plus, I didn't promise I would make it."

Oliver takes a chug of his beer before unlocking his cell phone. He opens to a sporting app that allows him to see current major league baseball scores in real-time. Justin looks over at Oliver, staring at his phone.

"What's up? What are you looking at?"

"Just checking the score. Yankees dropped two in a row, and Boston is already up two games this early in the season."

Justin shakes his head side to side, rolling his eyes. "It's still crazy early in the season. I can't believe you're stressing over a two-game lead right now."

Oliver reluctantly nods in agreement while still looking at his cell phone.

"You need to relax, man. Put the phone away. You've been working on this project for three months straight. We came out tonight to take a break. Which means you need to take a break from the scores too."

"Alright, alright. Putting it away." Oliver locks his phone before placing the phone in his pants pocket. Justin smirks while placing his hand on his shoulder.

"Now, doesn't that feel better?"

Oliver sarcastically looks at Justin, nodding in agreement. "Yeah, yeah, yeah," Oliver replies as he thinks about Justin's earlier statement. "And it's we, by the way."

"What?"

"You said a moment ago that I've been working on this project. We've both been working on this project for the last six months. I could never take all the credit."

"Yeah, but still. This is your baby. I'm just helping."

Oliver shakes his head side to side. "Well, if anyone asks, I'm gonna tell them that you were instrumental with putting it together. As a matter of fact, I'm gonna place your name on the itinerary. You deserve a just as much credit."

Justine smiles, looking at Oliver as he raises his bottle of beer. "Thanks, man. Cheers."

They tap their bottles together before taking a swig of their beer. Oliver leans toward Justin, "Once we present this cost analysis initiative to the owners. And they really take a look at this budgetary model. It'll be a total game-changer. AUA will see triple the profits in the first quarter..."

"And we'll get one hell of a bonus and hopefully a corner office."

"Hey. As long as they take it seriously. We're golden."

They both polish off the first round of beers and head toward the bar for round two. As the evening progresses, the boys consume a few bottles of beer. Oliver's beer works through his body. He makes his way through the crowded bar toward the restroom. Monica and Kimberly are still in the middle of the crowded bar celebrating as Isabella looks at her watch. Isabella realizes that she has stayed out longer than she anticipated and is making the decision to head home. "I'm gonna miss the hell outta you guys."

"So why the fuck are you leaving us then?" Monica exclaims.

"You and that mouth," Kimberly says to Monica.

"What did I say?"

Camille hears the exchange between Monica and Kimberly, turning to Thomas. "She's so drunk she's not even remembering what she's saying."

"These kids today." Thomas laughs as he replies to Camille loud enough for Monica to hear him. "She better not throw up on me again."

"Shut up, grandma and grandpa." Monica sarcastically fires back at Thomas and Camille.

"I'm serious. You drink like that shit's going out of style, and one of us has to carry you home." Thomas says to Monica.

"One of us is going to have to take this trick home." Isabella leans in addressing Thomas.

Thomas points toward Kimberly. "Yeah. You."

"Nah, I'm good, cuz," Monica says to everyone. "I'm gonna catch a cab home and go fuck my man."

Kimberly burst out laughing as the liquor has slightly altered her mood to a jovial state. "Woohoo! Now we're talking!"

Isabella smiles, shaking her head side to side. "Oh, this one is lit too." As she points at Kimberly.

Kimberly rolls her eyes, looking at everyone holding up both of her hands. "No, I'm good. Monica and I are heading in the same direction, so I'll take her home."
Camille looks up at Thomas, smiling. "You know she's not coming in tomorrow, right?"
Kimberly looks over at Camille, no longer smiling. "She better bring her ass in if she knows what's good for her."

"They're bringing pizza tomorrow. Trust me; she'll be in." Thomas laughs.
Monica continues to dance, avoiding eye contact as she talks at everyone who is talking about her. "Y'all know I'm right here, right? I can hear you. I'll be in tomorrow. Don't worry. So, shut the hell up."

Isabella fights laughter, shaking her head side to side. "Some things will never change."

"Shut up, Izzy." Monica playfully fires back.

Everyone laughs at the exchange as Isabella looks at her watch again. Her eyes widen as she notices the time. "Ok. Guys. I gotta get home to my hubby and the kids. This was so awesome, and I want to thank you guys so much for celebrating my last day North Mutual."

Camille walks over to Isabella, wrapping her arms around Isabella. They share an affectionate hug for a moment before Monica intervenes, wedging herself between Camille and Isabella. "My turn. Stop hogging her Cami."

Camille is pushed aside and looks over at Monica with disdain. “Such a little twat.”

Thomas fights laugher covering his face.

“I heard you, grandma,” Monica says to Camille.

Camille takes a deep breath before taking a step toward Monica. Kimberly and Camille make eye contact as Kimberly nods her head side to side, gesturing for Camille to pay Monica no mind. Isabella releases Monica and steps toward Kimberly, pulling her in for a hug. While hugging Kimberly, Isabella notices Oliver approaching and whispers in Kimberly’s ear. “Hottie for you at six o’clock.”

Kimberly releases Isabella spinning around, quickly forgetting about the drink in her hand, spilling it on Oliver’s shirt. A shocked Oliver looks down at his shirt before looking at Kimberly. Kimberly, who is slightly inebriated, burst out laughing at the mishap. “SHIT! I am so sorry.”

Oliver moves his eyes toward her shirt, which reads “Red Sox” on the front. He smiles at Kimberly. “I get it. you see a Yankee fan coming, and you spill your drink on my shirt?”

“No. I swear. I would never do something like that.”

Isabella interrupts Kimberly. “Hi, Oliver.”

Oliver looks over at Isabella. “Hey, Izzy.” Oliver points at Kimberly. “Is she with you?”

“Yeah. I'm here with a few of my friends from work, and Kimmy here is one of my coworkers.”

“Your friend is lucky she's so cute

“Or what?” Kimberly says to Oliver

Oliver smiles, playfully getting in her face. “It would be on.”

“Oh, really. And by “on,” what would that mean?”

Oliver playfully raises his fist, mocking urban street dialect. "It would be on like on son. I keep shit real. It would be a straight-up fight in here. I can't have some out of towner from Boston disrespecting my Yankees gear."

Kimberly playfully steps toward Oliver getting within inches of his face. Isabella turns to the other girls raising her eyebrows, entertained by the playful exchange between Oliver and Kimberly.

"I'm not from out of town, bruh. I live right here in New York City. How's that for keeping shit real?

"BED STUY BITCH!" Monica yells from behind Isabella.

Camille leans in, placing her mouth near Monica's ear. "Would you shut the hell up?"

Monica giggles tuning to Camille. "I'm just keeping it real."

Monica turns around to Isabella on the other side of her face, whispering. "Mira. Callate."

"Alright, alright."

Oliver inquisitively looks at Kimberly. "Did she really just say you were from Bed Stuy?"

"Yep."

Oliver smiles, looking at Kimberly who continues looking at him trying to stay in playful character as a hardcore thug. Oliver looks at Kimberly with confusion.

"How is it that you live in Brooklyn and wear Boston gear? I'm surprised no one has ripped it off you?"

Kimberly breaks character before looking around. She leans in to whisper in Oliver's ear. "I wear this shirt under my jacket or at night. Them boys in Brooklyn don't play."

Oliver and Kimberly burst out laughing as the rest of Kimberly's friend watch the pleasant exchange. They both finish laughing as they stare while smiling at each other for a moment. Monica recognizes that they seem to be stuck in awkward silence as they continue to stare at each other.

"Why don't you ask her for her name?!"

Kimberly shuts her eyes, embarrassed by Monica. She drops her head before mumbling. "I swear. This girl."

Oliver extends his right hand. "I'm Oliver."
Kimberly extends her hand, still holding the cup with some of her drink inside. "Kimberly"

Oliver looks down at the cup and chuckles. "No, thanks. It's already all over my shirt."
Kimberly looks down at her extended hand with the glass in it and laughs. "I've had a couple of these, and as you can clearly see, my judgment slightly askew."
"I can tell."

Isabella leans in, taking the glass from Kimberly, so she can shake Oliver's hand. Kimberly looks back at Isabella, smiling while nodding at the gesture. Isabella takes another look at her watch, realizing that she has to head home. "Ok, guys. This was fun. But I really gotta get home." Isabella points at Oliver. "This one got here fashionably late, so I'm leaving him with you guys."

"Oh, we'll take care of him. Get home safe. Text me, so I know you're home safe." Kimberly replies.

"I will," Isabella replied before pointing at Monica. "And make sure she gets home safe."

"I'M GOOD! STOP WORRYING ABOUT ME! DAMN!" Monica yells at Isabella while continuing to dance.

Isabella pays no attention to Monica's outburst turning her attention to Oliver.

"I'll have to straighten you out later for being so late."

"Actually, I've been here for about an hour. I didn't see you, so I just stayed upfront."

"That's such a lame excuse; you know that, right?"

"I know. I'm sorry. I'll make it up to you." Oliver replies trying not to smile. Isabella laughs, playfully punching Oliver's arm.

"I'm just kidding. Don't worry about it. These guys will probably be here for another hour or two. You'll be in good hands."

Monica walks over to Oliver, handing him a few napkins from the bar to clean off his shirt. "Here you go, bro."

Oliver takes the napkins to clean his shirt as Isabella makes what appears to be her final announcement.

"Ok. This time I'm really leaving. Bye, guys."

The group of friends all turns to Isabella waving goodbye. Camille looks at her watch, realizing that she may have also stayed out a little past the time she initially thought she would leave. She watches as Isabella heads to the front of the bar.

"Ok. And that's my cue to get outta here myself."

"Already." Kimberly poutingly replies to Camille.

"If I don't catch the train out to the island now, I'm screwed."

"Alright. Then I guess I'll see you in the morning."

Camille and Kimberly kiss each other on the cheek before she and a few other coworkers cut through the crowd toward the exit. She passes Oliver as he continues wiping his wet shirt. He lifts his head to look at Kimberly. "Are you leaving soon as well?"

Kimberly shrugs her shoulders. "Maybe."

"Well, if you do, I'm gonna need your phone number."

Kimberly impishly smirks, squinting her eyes at Oliver. "My number? Why would you need that?"

"You're gonna pay for this shirt. From the smell of this drink, you had a whiskey sour. That yellow stain isn't going to come out too easily."

"It's a Yankees Jersey. Trust me. I did you a favor."

"Really?" Oliver laughs. "So how about I spill my beer on your crappy Boston shirt, and we call it even?"

"Homeboy, you spill that beer on me, and I'm gonna slap the shit outta you."

"I'm kidding. I would never do something like that. Especially to a woman as pretty as you are."

Kimberly bashfully looks away as Oliver continues to look at her. She turns to looks into his eyes. They both share an awkward silence while still staring at each smiling.

"All jokes aside, though. I really would like to get your number. You don't have to pay for anything. I just want to talk to you."

"I'm right here. You can talk to me right now."

"What about your friends?"

Kimberly turns around, looking for Monica. She spots Monica and Thomas at the bar together, having a drink.

"Well, my friend Monica is in good hands. She's with our friend Thomas who is like our Pitbull, so to speak. Plus, she'll end up spending the night at my place anyway. So, she's good."

Kimberly turns back to Oliver. "You said you were here with a friend, right?"

"Yeah. I'm actually here with a buddy of mine. Maybe he can come join us?"

"Sure. Or, he could just have a drink with my friends already at the bar."

A small table becomes available as patrons get up and exit the bar. Kimberly and Oliver sit at the table, facing each other, spending their time talking, and getting to know each other. Justin creeps up to Monica, who is standing right next to Thomas at the bar. Justin extends his hand to Monica. "Hi. I'm Justin."

Monica slowly turns her head toward Justin, looking him up and down. Justin smiles as he keeps his hand extended as Monica turns her entire body to face him. Justin fights the urge to look at her physique as Monica is extremely curvy. Her top leaves very little to the imagination as her full breast almost pops out of her halter top. He continues looking into her eyes as she raises an eyebrow. "I'm Monica, and THIS is Thomas." She replies to Justin with an attitude.

Justin looks beyond Monica and greets Thomas. "Oh, hey, man. What's up?"

"Sup?"

Justin's eyes veer down to get a glimpse of Monica's breast before looking back into her eyes.

"Can I buy you a drink?" Justin asks.

"A drink?!" She claps back with an attitude. "A drink?!"

"Yes. A drink. We are in a bar?"

"I know we're in a bar, smartass."

Thomas laughs, covering his face as he looks in the opposite direction trying to avoid eye contact with Justin. Justin is unable to comprehend why Monica has become so hostile.

"Did I. . . Do something wrong. Is there a problem?"

"Yeah. You. You're the problem."

"Me?! What did I do? I just offered you a drink."

Thomas places his hand on Monica's shoulder, fighting laughter. "Alright, Monica, relax."

"Nah, see, he's trying to be slick. Thirsty ass coming over here trying to buy me a drink because he wants some pussy. But the polite shit to do would be to offer BOTH of us a drink. You think I don't see through your bullshit?"

Justin's eyes widen as he is shocked at the hostility Monica is displaying towards him.
"Are you serious? You go from 0 to 100 over a drink? Really?"

Thomas leans into view. "Yep. See what I gotta deal with?"

Justin shakes his head side to side. "For fuck sake, man. Ok. Would you both like a drink?" He sarcastically replies as he looks at Thomas and Monica. Monica doesn't say anything as she continues staring at him as a devilish grin creeps on her face. Her devilish grin turns into a full smug smile.

"Sure. I'll have a Ciroc and cranberry. What about you, boo?" She asks to Thomas.

"I'll have a jack and coke," Thomas replies while laughing.

Justin looks over at the bartender, who is hysterical laughing. "What?"

The bartender continues to laugh, shaking his head side to side. "Nothing. Nothing at all."

Justin leans on the bar to order their drinks. "Two jack and cokes and she'll have a–"

"I know. I already heard her," the bartender replies.

Justin looks over at Thomas and Monica, who are smiling at each other, fighting laughter. He can hear Monica snickering as she leans her head on Thomas' shoulder. Justin turns to the Bartender then back to Thomas and Monica.

"Son of a bitch. I just hustled, didn't I?"

Thomas burst out laughing, turning to Justin. "The next round is on me. No worries, man."

Monica jovially looks up at Justin winking her eye at him smiling. "That was so sweet of you to offer us both drinks."

Justin rolls his eyes, turning toward the bar. "Yeah, yeah. Whatever."

Monica turns to speak to Thomas, gesturing toward Justin so he can hear her. "Yo. Ya man came over here trying to smash. He thinks he's slick. No pussy for you tonight, bruh."

Thomas burst out laughing, almost spitting out his drink. Monica hysterically laughs along with Thomas as she peeks over her shoulder, looking back at an embarrassed Justin. The bartender turns his back to grab a few glasses hiding his face from Justin as he laughs. Justin shakes his head as Monica insults him.

On the other side of the bar, Kimberly and Oliver sit face to face leaning as close as they can to each other as they converse. "So, for real.... You live here in New York?" Oliver asks.

"Yeah. My dad was from Boston. When he and my mom separated, I would go up to Boston for the summer. We would go to a few games a year, and it was something we shared."

"And your mom?"

"She's born and raised in Brooklyn."

"Is she a Red Sox fan as well."

"She really could care less about the Sox, let alone baseball."

"My house. Yankees all the way baby."

Kimberly frowns. "I hate the Yankees. Remember when the Yankees were up 3-0 in the playoffs?"

Oliver loses interest and tries to change the subject. "Ok. next topic."
"And the Red Sox broke the Yankees down."

Oliver falls back in his chair, looking away. "I don't wanna talk about this anymore."

"I mean just annihilated the Yankees."

Oliver abruptly turns toward Kimberly. "Why do you Boston fans always hold on to that?"

"Four games straight. Just murdered them."

"And what have they done since then?"

"Kept your asses out of the playoffs ever since. That's what they did."

"Well, the Yankees have a legacy of championships that no other team has."

"Oh, boohoo. Now, who's holding onto something. You talk about us. Yankee fans always bring up pennants from decades ago like they were there." Kimberly looks over at Oliver. "Like Janet said, "WHAT HAVE YOU DONE FOR ME LATELY!"

Oliver takes the lashing from Kimberly, fighting laughter. "Whatever."

Kimberly continues her assault on the Yankees. "That curse of the Bambino crap is over, buddy. How his fat ass got off home plate was a mystery to me anyway."

"You got me there. I still think walking around town with that Boston shirt can't be easy, but hey, it is what it is."

"I always get into some nonsense when I go to Yankee Stadium."

"No doubt. I've seen it get ugly when the Mets play there. But Boston. You're a brave woman."

Kimberly laughs as she plops backward in her seat. Oliver looks down at the table, realizing that they have nothing to drink. "Shit. I'm so rude. Can I buy you a drink?"

Kimberly thinks for a moment. "No...... I'd like to remember this conversation. Plus, now I gotta be an adult while this one is in my care," pointing at Monica.

"Yeah. She looks a little twisted. Good luck with that."

Kimberly nods as she listens to Oliver. "So, what do you do for a living?"

“I'm a project manager for a large Japanese chemical holding firm with offices throughout the United States and Japan. How about you?”

“Wow. That was a mouthful. You know this isn't a formal interview?”

Oliver covers his face from embarrassment. “Overkill?”

“Not at all. I’m just teasing. I'm an underwriter for an insurance company.”

“Very nice. Do you like what you do?”

“It's a boring job but it pays very well. I’m working on becoming a manager. That's my short-term goal. Once I reach that plateau, I’ll work on my next career goal.”

“Sweet. It looks like we are on the same career paths. Justin and I have been working on a cost analysis initiative where the company spends less but can still see serious profit growth. We have a presentation with the big wigs in a few weeks. Today was one of the first days in a few weeks we’ve been able to go out, unwind and get some drinks. I’m actually thrilled that we came out tonight.”

“So, is that normal that you work that rigorously?” Kimberly asks.

“Not usually. This project has taken a lot of time to research. These guys don't want us to just present solutions. They want us to project all the negatives first. We have to be prepared for every contingency. They will come at us with all types of questions, and we’re going to have to answer their questions, or we’ll look like unprepared idiots, and we’ll never have this chance again.”

“That sounds very similar to my work. I get it.”

“Yeah. So tonight, we’re gonna just unwind. Since tomorrow is Friday, we’ll go into the office a little later and work in a conference room. Maybe I'll sneak away and give you a call," Oliver says while smiling at Kimberly.

Kimberly looks into his eyes, smiling back at Oliver. "That was smooth how you just did that. I think I would like that."

"Well, I won't be able to do that without your number." Oliver hands Kimberly his cell phone to input her phone number. Kimberly continues to smile as she picks up his phone and enters her cell phone number. She hands him the phone.

"I look forward to hearing from you."

"I look forward to calling you."

Again, they share an awkward silence before Kimberly looks at her watch.

"Well. It's way past my bedtime, and I have to get up early tomorrow."
Oliver looks at his watch as well. "Yeah. I may have to head home as well. Can I walk you out?"

"Sure. Lemme go and get this one." Kimberly gathers an inebriated Monica before talking to Thomas.

"I'm heading home now, Thomas. This guy is going to walk us out."

"Alright. I'll come out with you.'

"No, no, no. I'm good. I'm gonna hail a cab from outside. Plus, I get the feeling this guy just wants to see me off.

"Are you sure. I'm not feeling you hanging around some strange dudes that you just met"

Kimberly looks behind her shoulder at Oliver then back at Thomas. “I like this guy. He’s sweet. Plus, I’ll be right outside. He’s not coming with me or anything.”

Thomas shrugs his shoulders in compliance with Kimberly. “Ok. You're a big girl.”

Kimberly kisses Thomas on the cheek before she escorts Monica out front. Thomas remains in the bar, watching as the girls exit the bar shaking his head. Oliver hails a cab for the ladies. A yellow cab pulls over in front of the girls. Monica enters the cab before Kimberly. Oliver closes the door behind her and leans in as Kimberly opens the window. He reaches in, taking Kimberly’s hand and kissing it. Kimberly smiles at the sweet gesture. “Au revoir.”

Kimberly is unable to contain a massive smile.
“Au revoir.”

The cab pulls off, driving down the long New York City street. Oliver stands in the street, watching the cab drive off with Kimberly looking back at him through the rear window. Kimberly sits back in her seat, smiling. “Damn. He is so cute.”

Kimberly turns to look at Monica. Monica has fallen fast asleep, leaning her head on the door snoring. Justin walks up behind Oliver. “Hey, man.”

Oliver remains standing motionless, watching as the taxi continues to drive away. Justin taps on Oliver’s shoulder. “Oliver.”

Oliver turns to Justin. “Yeah.”

Justin's eyes widen as he smiles. “She is gorgeous, dude.”

“Did you see how smoking hot she is?”

“Um. Yeah. It was hard not to notice.”

Oliver steps back onto the sidewalk, still looking down the long city street toward the taxi. "She's amazing. My heart is beating a mile a minute."

Justin stands beside Oliver, looking down the street as well. Oliver turns to Justin, standing beside him, looking down the street.

"Hey, man. I'm sorry our night took a turn but man oh man. You are the ultimate wingman."

Justin places his arm over Oliver's shoulder directing him back to the bar.
"Dude. There's no one man above the bro code."

Oliver laughs as they walk back toward the bar. He places his hand on Justin's shoulder. "My man."

Their night doesn't come to an end as they return to the bar and sit together, getting a few more drinks with Thomas.

Chapter 2: The Smell of a First Day

The transition from an old job to a new position at a new company can feel overwhelming for most individuals. Isabella Maldonado is not most people. Being the consummate professional she is, she arrives to work at approximately 8:01 a.m. Monday at the Plante Insurance Group when she was advised that her shift will be from 9 a.m. to 5 p.m. She sits at her new desk on her first day in the office, rummaging through her mobile folding cart filled with personal and professional items. Pictures of her family, friends, and inspirational photos are placed neatly around the cubicle. The cubicles are uniform in size, with some slightly larger based on the occupants' position at the company. Isabella has taken the role of Lead Senior Underwriter, so her desk is larger and higher than the rest of her colleagues. Her large L shaped desk comes equipped with three computer monitors, a computer tower, keyboard, mouse, and a printer.

As she places a large pen holder on her desk, Isabella looks around. The office is bright due to the layout allowing plenty of natural light from outside. There aren't many walls as most of the structures separating many of the offices are covered in glass. Even the conference room is surrounded by glass. The office is furnished with basic neutral colors—tan industrial carpeting with light gray colored cubicles. Inspirational landscaped paintings are placed throughout the office. The stereotypical "hang in there" kitten poster catches her eye as she smiles, shaking her head side to side.

The first shift is eight o'clock, followed by the eight-thirty and nine o'clock shifts. Upon arrival, she had only noticed a handful of employees at their desks. A few employees enter through the glass entrance door one at a time as the clock nears 8:30. As she places an award at the left corner of her desk, Isabella looks over to the desk to her left. The desk is tidy with a picture of a man and his wife on their wedding day and several pictures of the same man with three young children. She smiles, looking at the pictures before taking notice of the name tag which reads, Benjamin Porter. More employees enter the office through the glass doors as a few employees walk toward Isabella. She turns back to her cubicle, placing more pictures on the wall of her desk as she hears footsteps coming closer to her desk. A very jovial Benjamin walks to his desk, looking over at Isabella, who continues hanging up photos.

"Gooooooood Morning Vietnam!" he yells in her direction as he sits at his desk.

"Good Morning." She replies while smiling.

Benjamin waste no time turning on the humor poorly imitating a British accent. He looks over at her desk, noticing all the pictures of her family. "The ol pictures on the desk on the first day, huh?"

Isabella looks at Benjamin from the corner of her eyes and doesn't answer. Benjamin is unphased by Isabella, ignoring him and continues with the early morning sarcasm. "The ol ignore the guy talking to me on my first day at work, huh?"

Getting slightly annoyed, she shakes her head and continues placing items of her cubicle wall.

Benjamin smiles as he is getting a kick out of annoying Isabella. "The ol get annoyed at the guy sitting right next to you on the first day at work, huh?"

Isabella stops what she's doing and turns towards Benjamin very slowly with an intense look of annoyance. "Are you serious?"

Benjamin fights laughter but continues talking in a poor British accent. "The ol exorcist baby turn your head slow look, huh?"

Isabella says nothing as she continues staring at Benjamin, who is struggling to keep a straight face. He smiles at Isabella, then stands up, walking away. She turns her head to follow him as he walks away.

"What the fuck?" She mumbles before going back to her photos. Moments later, Benjamin returns, ambling with a cup of tea in his hand standing in front of her desk. He smiles, looking down at a very annoyed Isabella. *"Hello, chum. Mi names Benjamin. Welcome to the office. Sorry if mi mate Benny was acting a little foolish this early in the mournin, but he sent me ova air to apologize to ya mate."* Still imitating a British accent.
Isabella takes a deep breath and forces a smile. "Apology accepted."

"I'm sorry. I was just horsing around with you. It's Monday. I was just trying to lighten the mood. I see you with your hair pulled back in that super tight librarian bun, and I'm like. Shit. This lady looks serious. So, I figured I take a shot and try to lighten the mood." No longer speaking with a British accent.

"Because librarians are so such sticks in the mud who enjoy sarcasm first thing on a Monday morning?" She replies sarcastically."

"Precisely. . . I mean. . . but not you. You clearly have a sense of humor. You're not rigid at all. See, I walk in and look at you, and I say to myself. This lady is all fun and games." He quips with a massive smile.

"I was under the impression that you wanted to start over."
"Yes. I thought we were?"

"No. You're still being kind of an ass."

Benjamin chuckles. "Look. I'm really just horsing around. I thought even though it's your first day that you might hate Mondays like the rest of America."

Isabella sits motionless, looking at Benjamin. He can feel a little tension coming from Isabella, so he points to his desk. "Ok, great. I'll just go over there then."

"Yeah. You do that." She follows him with her eyes as he walks to his desk.

Benjamin sits at his desk, turning on his PC. He can see Trish, the office manager walking towards them. He leans over and whispers. "Hey. Librarian."

"Hey, dick." She fires back.

Benjamin fights laughter. "Good one. But. I gotta warn you. Trish's breath smells like she ate a bag of asses chased with a splash of wet gym socks that sat in milk for a week in the sun. She's headed right for you. I suggest you don't lean forward. Just saying."

Isabella turns to Benjamin with a look of disgust. "That's a terrible thing to say. What the matter with y—" Isabella is interrupted by a jovial and enthusiastic Trish.

"Hi! You must be Isabella. How are you?! I'm Trish!"

Isabella stands up to greet Trish, extending her arm as Trish leans in.

"Hi. So nice to—" Isabella is taken back from a foul odor coming from Trish. She recovers and continues. "Ahem. . . So nice to meet you."

"Well, welcome to Plante Insurance Group. Mr. Plante will be arriving later this afternoon. He is going to want to say hi and welcome you aboard. Would you like me to take you to the break room for some coffee?

Benjamin sits while smiling, facing them both. “I already told her where the break room was. I’ll take her once she gets settled in. But I think she's wide awake now.”

“Great. That's just great. Thank you, Ben.” Trish gestures two thumbs up.

“If you don't mind. You can just call me Benjamin.”

“Ok, Benny.” Trish continues.

Benjamin rolls his eyes. “Whatever.”

Trish turns back to Isabella. “Well, Isabella. If you need anything, come down to my desk, and I’ll be more than happy to help you out. Oh– I have some forms for you to fill out.”

“Right. I’ll um. . . I’ll come over and pick them up in a moment.”

“Super. Ok. So, I’ll see you in a few then.”

“Sure thing.”

Trish walks away towards her desk at the end of the office. Benjamin turns his back to Isabella, dropping his head on the desk, hysterically laughing. Isabella falls back in her seat with a look of horror. Isabella’s eyes widen as she turns to Benjamin. “Was that for real?”

Benjamin laughs, silently holding his stomach. Isabella fights laughter but gives in laughing with Benjamin. “Shit. Someone should say something.”

“How do you say anything without seriously hurting her feelings? Every office across the planet has at least one person that you can't say shit to about a body order, or they wear the same clothes, or they have severe dandruff and wear black. I’ve seen it all. When I started here, I walked around looking for it.”

“And what happened?”

“Trish happened. She walked right up to me, and I said, good lord.”

“No, you didn't,” she replies in disbelief

“I did. Then I recovered quickly. I said, “are those contacts?” and she said no. But the compliment made her all giddy.”

“You’re terrible. You know that?”

“I’ve kept my distance ever since.”

Isabella smiles, shaking her head, still looking over at Benjamin. He turns to his computer then has a thought turning abruptly toward Isabella. “And you know, she’s married.”

“No way.”

“I often wonder what that poor dude’s daily life is like when she comes home from work. I figure he’s gotta work the night shift at a paint removal factory, and he doesn't wear the necessary safety equipment, so his sense of smell is all messed up.

Isabella burst out hysterically laughing, covering her mouth. An incredibly voluptuous African American woman wearing a tight red mini skirt, red pumps, and black silk sleeveless blouse walks up to Benjamin's desk, attempting to get his attention while he and Isabella continue laughing. “Hey, Benjamin.”

Benjamin tilts his head to the side to see who is talking to him. “Oh, hey, Tammy?”

“How was your weekend?”

“Dance finals Friday, Chuck E Cheese on Saturday, Laundry Saturday night, Boxing match late Saturday night, pool party Sunday, back to work on Monday. And how was your weekend?”

"Boring. I was alone. I didn't do much."

Benjamin points to Isabella. "Oh. By the way. This is Isabella. Today is her first day."

Tammy waves hello, looking at Isabella's outfit.

"Hi, Isabella. Nice to meet you."

"It's nice to meet you too. I love your outfit."

"Oh, thank you," Tammy replies as she points to Isabella's shoes. "I love those shoes. Where did you get them?"

"DSW. Clearance rack."

Tammy smiles, looking at Isabella. "Seriously. Where did you get them?"

Benjamin smirks and turns toward his computer screen to let the ladies continue their conversation. Isabella replies with conviction. "DSW. Clearance rack."

Tammy frowns, looking away. "Oh. . . Ok."

"Where did you get yours?"

"Jimmy Choo."

"They're gorgeous."

Tammy forces a smile turning back to Benjamin. "Thank you."

Isabella turns back to her desk to finish placing pictures on her desk. Tammy looks at Benjamin, who is looking at email.

"Anyway. I'll see you guys later."

Tammy walks off toward the office kitchen. Benjamin lifts his head. "See ya."

Isabella tilts her head down as she looks at Benjamin from the corner of her eyes. Benjamin tilts his seat slightly over to look at Isabella.

“Personally, I love your shoes. It matches your ensemble perfectly. The blouse and the shoes with grey pants. The hint of silver on the shoes match your bracelet and earrings. You obviously know what you're doing.”

Isabella smirks as she looks over at Benjamin. “I’m glad you noticed.”

“Trust me when I tell you, nothing gets by me.”

Chapter 3: Why Do We Do It To Ourselves

It's a tradition for thousands of New York City residents to flock to sporting events after a long day at the office. After all, New York City is home to the world's most famous baseball team, the New York Yankees. On a Tuesday evening at 6:05 PM at the packed Brooklyn Bridge train station, Justin, Oliver, and a coworker Stanley enter the four train headed uptown to Yankee Stadium in the Bronx. The NY Yankees play host to the Texas Rangers. The trio stands at the door of the train. Oliver turns to Stan.

"Hey, Stan. Thanks for inviting us to the game. Your drinks are on me tonight."

"No problem, man. If I had known you'd buy the drinks, I would've invited you more often."

"Do you ever get tickets for the Boston games?" Justin Interjects.

"I'm a season ticket holder, so yeah. Duh." Stanley replies sarcastically.

"Oliver here has just scored himself a Boston fan."

Stanley turns to Oliver abruptly. "What?!"

"Yep. Born and raised in New York. But wears Boston gear." Justin states while looking over at Oliver. Stanley turns to Oliver in disbelief. "Is this true?!"

Oliver takes a deep breath. "Yep."

"Next stop. You gotta get off. I'll buy my own drinks."

"I couldn't believe it myself," Justin adds.

"Oh, gimme a break. So, what if she's a Boston fan?" Oliver fires back at them both.

Stan's eyes widen as he is unable to believe what he's hearing. "SO, WHAT IF SHE'S A BOSTON FAN! ARE YOU INSANE?!"

Justin burst out laughing. Oliver looks over at Justin shaking his head. "What the fuck are you laughing at?"

Before Justin can reply to Oliver, Stan interrupts. "He's laughing at your idiocracy."

"Yeah. Your idiocracy." Justin points to Oliver attempting to antagonize. Oliver shrugs his shoulders, looking away from them toward the crowd of straphangers. "Whatever."

Stan goes on the offensive. "A New Yorker wearing Boston gear. That's blasphemy. Do you like this girl?"

"Yeah. She's pretty cool so far."

Justin continues to interrupt, which is starting to get under Oliver's skin. He looks over at Justin, not saying a word. "They just met on Thursday. Talked for about an hour at work on Friday. Hung out Sunday and even had dinner last night."

"You gonna give him the play by play on my whole life?"

"Yeah, why not?"

"Dude. Seriously. Kinda quick, wouldn't you say?" Stan adds

"Kinda quick for what?"

"Investing all that time in a chick. Not just any chick. A chick that's a Boston fan. This shit can't go anywhere."

"I say different. I like her and yes. If you have tickets to a Yankees Boston game that you aren't going to use, I'd be more than happy to take those off your hands.

"Those tickets are gonna cost you, man."

"I can handle that. Don't you worry."

"Ok. Then I can make that happen."

"Sweet. So, me and you buddy. Sitting behind the dugout." Justin playfully adds.

"Fuck you. You talk too much. I'm taking my lady friend."

Justin burst out laughing, placing his hands on Oliver's shoulder. Oliver turns to Justin.
"Telling people about my business. What if I start talking about you and Rebecca?"

Justin quickly stops laughing.

"Yeah. Look who's not laughing anymore."

Justin turns away. "Alright, alright. Whatever."

An inquisitive Stanley turns to Oliver and Justin. "What's up with Becks. Still suffering from that yearlong menstrual cycle."

"That, menopause, listeria, hypothermia, rigor mortis any fucked up condition you can think of. It translates to an ordinary day for her mood. You sure picked a winner. I'd rather move to Boston and blow the Red Sox starting lineup than have to deal with that clingy psycho."

"Why don't you tell me how you really feel?"

"I just did."

Stanley hides his face from laughter.

Oliver continues on the offensive. "Seriously. What am I saying that you don't already know?"

"Alright, Ollie, I get it."

"Are you seriously getting mad now?"

"No."

Stanley points at Justin's face. "Yes, he is. Look at him. HEY! Put on your big boy draws and man the fuck up, dude."

Oliver notices that Justin is not liking the constant ribbing. "Ok. Ok. I'm sorry. She's not all that bad. She has some good days."

"When are those?" Stan asks.

"When he doesn't see her!" Oliver replies as he and Stan burst out laughing. Justin tries to fight it but is unable to contain himself as he chuckles along with Stan and Oliver.

"Fuck you, man." Justin playfully punches Oliver.

Oliver places his arm around Justin while still excessively laughing. Almost overdoing the laugh to get further under Justin's skin.

"Yo. I'm sorry, man. I had to."

Justin sarcastically smiles while looking at Oliver. “You’re a funny guy.”

“Is she really that bad?” Stan asks.

Oliver looks at Stan then back at Justin. “Shall I tell him?”

Justin pushes Oliver away. “Shut up.”

Oliver bites his lips, fighting laughter. Stan laughs along with Oliver trying not to overdo his enjoyment of Justin getting humiliated. Justin gives in. “Look. She has her moments, but he isn't lying. She's just getting worse and worse.”

“So, gimme an example?” Stan asks.

“I told her about this project Oliver and I are working on. One night, I tell her I'm gonna be in the office late, and that's the night she tries to set up some group date with her friends. And If I miss it, she gives me shit for it. Then she's always talking about her married friends, and how we're just sitting in one place, and if I loved her as much as my job, we’d have kids by now. She just fucking annoying at times.”

“You need to dead that shit quick.”

Stan is unable to comprehend Oliver’s urban statement. “What did you say?”

Oliver realizes that he used street slang and attempts to correct it.

“Oh shit. I went all Bronx for a second. What I meant to say so you could comprehend is, Justin. I think he should end things with this young lady before she takes a proverbial turn for the fucking worse. Was that coherent enough for you colonizer?”

"Ahhh. See. That made a whole lot more sense.” Stan gestures for Justin to continue talking. “Please, do continue.”

Oliver rolls his eyes as Justin continues talking about Rebecca.

"I do think that it's getting to that point. I'm not happy at all. Plus, this project eats up a lot of my time, and I hate feeling guilty."

"Hey, man. Sometimes you gotta go through it to find the right one, but shit. The process in the middle of all that crap just sucks, man." Stan adds.

"Ya think."

"My last girlfriend, Shannon. The nurse."

"Yeah. She was hot." Justin recalls.

"Pain in the ass."

"Wait. For real? Because, like Justin said, She was really hot."

"PAIN IN THE FUCKIN ASS!" Stan yells, not caring about who on the train can hear him.

"Alright. Relax, man."

"Everything I did, she had a problem with. Nothing I did was as important as her nurse's work. Keep in mind I made more money than her."

Oliver interrupts. "To her defense, nurses do have a tough job."

Stanley holds out his index finger. "Yeah...... An ER nurse in New York City. Tough Job."

Oliver and Justin nod in agreement. "Yeah."

Stanley holds up his index and middle finger, counting two. "Nurse working in Rikers Island. Very fucking tough job."

Oliver nods in agreement. “Yeah, I’d have to agree with that.”

“I’ll do you one better.” Stan holds up three fingers. “A nurse at a retirement home. That's gotta be a shitty job. No pun intended.”

“What’s your point?” Oliver asks.

“The idiot landed a job at an insurance company as a telephonic nurse case manager.”

“What’s that?” Justin asks.

“That's what I said. What the fuck is that?”

Oliver and Justin laugh at Stan's statement.

“She worked an eight to three-thirty shift sitting behind a desk. She wore a headset and everything. She just helped to manage injuries for workers' compensation cases.”

“Ok so...” Justin ask

“Ok, so she wasn't working at a hospital with patients. But here’s one that's better.”

“What?”

“She wore scrubs to work.”

Oliver burst out laughing as Stan continues.

“What kind of sick twisted idiot wears scrubs to an office building where everyone is in casual office wear.”

“Ok. I can see where you would be annoyed.”

“No. You wouldn't because I haven't even scratched the surface. She would come home and drop on my sofa and act like she had a tough day while she's reading about injuries. Did you hear me?

READING ABOUT INJURIES! She doesn't even get to see real blood."

Justin and Oliver laugh hysterically.

"Nurse, my ass. Whenever I see anyone wearing scrubs, it pisses me off. It's like a cry for attention."
Justin and Oliver continue laughing while leaning on each other.

"I hate people in scrubs so much that I don't even like going to my doctor's office anymore."

Oliver turns to Stan laughing. "You're insane."

"So, I ended it. And you know what? I love being single now. I'm going to the game tonight, and I don't have to call anyone. I don't have text someone to let them know I'm safe. I don't have to get a text from someone checking to see if I'm alright."

Justin's laughter comes to a halt. "Yeah. I guess it would be nice."

Oliver turns to Justin, "You should have been in his shoes a long time ago."

"He's right, man. If she's that much of a pain in the ass, dump her."

Justin shakes his head in agreement. Stan points at Oliver getting his attention. "And as for you."

"What about me?"

"Tread carefully. Nothing good can come from a Yankee fan dating someone from Boston."

"Time will tell."

"Yeah right. You're already planning to see a game with her. What's next? You gonna date a Redskins fan. An Eagles fan. Or worse. A Dallas fan?"

Oliver says nothing but smiles. Justin laughs, shaking his head side to side.

"Mark my words. You'll see."

Chapter 4: Behind Closed Doors

One of the advantages of living is a large metropolis such as New York City is the anonymity. Most often, a person you encounter on a given day is never seen again. This can be most advantageous for someone seeking to do misdeeds such as a crime or, most often, adultery. With so many corners, alleys, and short-stay motels, anyone can move through the city and be unknown if they choose not to be seen at the same place more than once. Tonight, Kareem Hardaway, a six-foot-two African American with dreadlocks and full beard, sits in his parked car near the Queensbridge Houses in Queens, New York. His tinted four-door sedan affords him the ability to be barely visible as his chair is pushed all the way back. Pedestrians are unable to view the activity in his car due to the lack of visibility. One passer-by crossing the street turns to look in the car and notices Kareem lying on his back in the driver's seat. The pedestrian takes a closer look at another occupant with their head by the steering column moving up and down. It doesn't take long before the pedestrian realizes exactly what he is witnessing before he laughs and continues about his business.

Within moments, the occupant in the car with Kareem lifts her head as Kareem's body convulses from pure momentary ecstasy. The female occupant, Destiny, falls back in her seat, wiping her lips as she lovingly rubs on Kareem's chest. Kareem quickly catches his breath, opening his eyes to look at the roof liner of his car.

"Hmmm. You taste like a vanilla shake, Papi." Kareem ignores the questionable sound of Destiny's voice.

"Damn, girl. Whew. That was some good shit."

Destiny leans on Kareem's shoulder while he pulls up his pants. "When am I gonna see you again?"

"I don't know. If I get time off from work on Saturday, I'll come through."

"Next time we hook up, you should get us a room."

"Yeah, We'll see. Maybe."

"I brought a nice negligée that I want you to take off of me."

"Word?"

"Yeah, baby. I want to give you all of me. Don't you want all of me?"

Kareem, appearing no longer interested, buttons his pants and buckles his belt while she strokes his thigh. "Uhh. Yeah. That would be cool."

"Yeah. I want to be sexy for you, baby."

Kareem pulls the seat upright, avoiding eye contact with Destiny. "Yeah, yeah, yeah. That would be cool."

"Do you want me to do anything else for you, Papi?"

"Nah. I'm straight. This was great, though."

"Good. I can't wait to see you on Saturday."

"Yeah. Well. I gotta head home now."

"Already?"

"Yeah. I gotta take care of some shit, then get ready for work tomorrow. You know how it is."

Destiny slumps in her seat, disappointed. "Alright."

"Seriously. You all sad and shit. Come on. I'll hit you up when I get home."

"Promise?" She responds gleefully.

"Yeah."

"Yay. Alright." She leans over, kissing him.

"Alright. I gotta bounce."

"Ok, sweetie. I'll hit you up later."

"That's cool."

Destiny exits the car blowing a kiss at Kareem as she walks away. Kareem watches Destiny walk away before turning on his car and driving off.

Later that evening, Kareem pulls up to a small two-story house on Terrace Place in the Prospect Park section of Brooklyn. This section of Brooklyn is lined with semi-detached brick houses in a tranquil neighborhood. He parks his car and walks down the block entering a house using his key. He walks through the living room, placing his car keys in a kitchen drawer. He turns around as the bathroom door opens. Monica exits the bathroom wearing a brown silk short nighty and a pair of thongs. The ensemble leaves very little to the imagination as all of her rear end and breasts are visible. "Oh. Hey baby. I didn't even hear you come in."

She runs up to Kareem, hugging him. He unwillingly hugs her before pulling away. "Sup babe?"

Kareem ignores her outfit as he looks away from Monica.

"I didn't cook anything, but I stopped by Indian spice and picked up some takeout."

"Cool. I'm gonna go take a shower."

"Alright. Would you like me to fix a plate for you and heat it up?"

"Cool."

Kareem enters the bedroom, placing his watch, jewelry, and cell phone on the night table before entering the bathroom to shower. In the kitchen, Monica prepares a plate of food for Kareem and places it in the microwave. She lets her hair down and sits comfortably on the sofa watching TV. As Kareem finishes showering, he exits the bedroom heading straight for the kitchen. Monica turns to look over her shoulder at Kareem in front of the microwave. "All you gotta do is press start. I set it up for you."

"Thanks, babe."

Kareem presses start on the stands in front of the microwave oven, waiting for his food to heat up. Monica turns her entire body towards Kareem, kneeling on the sofa. "Why don't you come sit over here?"

"I'm just waiting for the food to cook, babe."

"Well. You can come sit here, and when it's ready, I'll bring it to you."

"Nah. I'm good, babe. I'll just wait here. It'll take a second."

"I know. But I figured you might wanna come sit with your baby for a minute."

"You're funny," Kareem says, looking over his shoulder.

"What so funny about wanting to sit with you. Even if it is just for a minute."

"Because you know I'm about to eat."

"I just figured maybe you come over here and work up and appetite." Monica seductively flashes her eyebrow at Kareem, who ignores her playful flirtation.

"I don't need to work up an appetite. I'm already hungry."

While still kneeling on the sofa, she leans forward, causing the sofa to pull down on her top, exposing her full breasts. She looks down at her breast before lifting her head, smiling at Kareem. "Are you sure you don't want to come over here?"

"Yeah, I'm straight." He laughs.

"You don't want to come over here and make love to me?"

"You know I'm hungry, and you starting this shit now. Why did you even fix me a plate?"

"Why you always gotta make this shit so complicated? It's like you never want to make love to me anymore."

"Why you gotta be so extra?"

Monica becomes extremely irate. "Extra?!"

The Microwave beeps. Kareem turns to the microwave to retrieve the dish.

"Don't turn your back on me. I'm talking to you!"

"No. You're yelling at me."
"You're such an asshole."

Kareem takes a deep breath, aware that the situation is about to escalate.

"Whatever."

Monica storms out of the kitchen and into the bedroom. As she enters the bedroom, Kareem's cell phone lights up from a text message. Monica picks up the phone and unlocks the screen exposing a long conversation between Kareem and Destiny. Her eyes widen while reading the conversation. As she scrolls down, she views selfies taken by both Destiny and Kareem. She takes a screenshot then forwards the picture of Destiny via text to her cell phone. She sees a text that reads, "I love giving you head." She becomes enraged and walks out to the kitchen where Kareem is eating dinner. She stands behind him, staring at the back of his head. He knows she is standing behind him. "What?"

Monica tosses the phone on the table next to his plate, which lands face-up
"Who the fuck is Destiny?"

"What the fuck are you doing looking through my phone?"

"Apparently, she enjoys giving you head." Monica fires back.

Kareem stands up, turning to her. "I told you about touching my phone!"

"Look who wants to face me now? Who the fuck is that bitch?!"

Kareem points in Monica's face. "Yo. I told you, don't touch my fuckin phone!"

"Or what?? What you gonna do about it, bitch!?"

Kareem grabs her by her neck with both hands lifting her five-foot-three frame off the floor. Monica grabs hold of his arms, gasping for air. "You ain't shit! Get the fuck off of me!"

Kareem tosses her backward, causing her to fall to the floor. She nurses her neck, looking up at Kareem. Kareem stands over Monica, pointing at her. "Stupid bitch!"

Monica stands up, unafraid punching Kareem him in the stomach

"Who you calling a bitch, you pussy. Fuck you!"

Kareem clenches his fist, punching her in the mouth. "Shut the fuck up!"

Monica falls backward, knocking over the garbage pail before hitting the floor. The punch to the face disorients her for a moment. She can taste blood in her mouth before as she shakes off her disorientation. She gets up quickly, turning to Kareem, ready to fight.

"Get the fuck out!"

"Shut up Bitch!"

"I SAID, GET THE FUCK OUT! I swear I'm gonna call the cops and tell them that there's a pussy is in here punching mother fuckers in the mouth!"

"Stupid bitch."

"You ain't nothing but a fuck nigga. Fuck you and get the fuck up out my house."

"This isn't even your fucking house. Your daddy bought this piece of shit!"

"Then get the fuck out my piece a shit.'

Kareem angrily walks into the bedroom, gathering a few of his personal items. He walks back into the kitchen, passing Monica, where he takes his car keys from the draw and exits the house. Monica trots behind him, locking the door. She takes a moment to gather herself from the violent encounter before walking over to the kitchen. She picks up the garbage pail and cleans the kitchen talking to herself. "This mother fucker doesn't know who he's fucking with. I will straight fuck his shit up. I'm not the one."

Monica angrily turns toward the door yelling in that direction while pointing at the door. "Don't you ever think you can roll up in here and put your mother fucking hands on me! I will fucking kill you."

She walks into her bedroom, entering the bathroom, switching on the light to look into the mirror. Monica examines her face and neck tilting her head to the side, taking a deep breath, shocked at the presence of her bruises. "Look at my fucking lip, man. Shit. Why do I keep fucking with these dumb mother fuckers?"

As she continues staring at herself in the mirror, she is unable to look away. Her eyes slowly fill with tears, but she wipes away the tears immediately. Monica allows herself no self-pity and turns around exiting the bathroom. She walks out of her bedroom toward the living room sitting on the sofa, breathing heavily, staring at the walls shaking her head side to side. She remains sitting there alone quietly for the remainder of the night.

Chapter 5: Now You're Mine

New York City is like most cities around the world as it lives and breathes a life of its own. Day to day routines in this city is far from ordinary. People from all walks of life travel from miles away to work in Manhattan every day. And once they arrive in the city, they become a version of themselves base on the nature of the jobs and careers they perform.

On a spectacular sunlit mid-morning at North Mutual Insurance Company located on Water Street near Old slip, Monica, Camille, Thomas, and Kimberly are all working on various tasks. Thomas sits in his office, typing away on his computer with a beautiful view of the east river looking into Brooklyn in the backdrop. Camille strolls down the hall from the legal department popping her head into Thomas' office. "Hey, Buddy."

Thomas looks up at his good friend Camille and blesses her with a massive smile. "What's up, Cami?"

"There's something I gotta show you. Are you busy?"

"I'm here in my office. If I weren't busy, I'd be back at your desk where no work gets done."

"Ugh. You and your sarcasm. Come on. Follow me."

Thomas reluctantly follows Camille out of his office toward the legal department. "Where are we going?"

"Shut up and just follow."

They both walk down the hall. Camille walks in front of Thomas, wearing a close-fitting pair of dress slacks. Camille is a little older than the average office demographic, but she keeps herself in great shape. Thomas looks down, observing her rear end.

"The view from back here is wonderful. You should ask me to follow you more often."

Camille turns to Thomas while still walking while laughing. "Aww, thanks, buddy. Keep those compliments coming."

"Anything for you, young lady."

Camille continues to smile at Thomas, bashfully looking away as they continue toward the company's legal department. "Now, get ready for something awesome."

"Cami, come on. Where are you taking me?"

Camille turns around, facing Thomas while walking backward. "It's a surprise."

"It's not my birthday, so what the hell?"

They continue passing the conference room to the next department.

"Ok. So, I know the kind of woman you like."

"Yeeeah. So?"

"So, they hired a new girl. She's absolutely gorgeous. Just your type."

Thomas laughs as he continues to follow.

"Keep laughing. Wait till you see her. She's right up your alley. She's what you would call thick," as she points at Thomas.

"Well. You know I like my...."

Thomas stops in place as he can see the new employee standing by a file cabinet looking through a file. His jaw drops, and his eyes widen. Camille looks up at Thomas's open mouth.

"Yeah, no. You gotta stop that."

"Be still my heart." Thomas mumbles.

Camille giggles turning toward Thomas. "Didn't know you were a fan of poetry, but I digress. Ok, so I'm going back to my desk. You can thank me later."

The beautiful new employee looks up and can see Thomas staring at her. Thomas comes to and straightens up as he continues looking at her. She shakes her head, looking back down at her file.

Thomas checks his breath as he walks up to the new employee, smiling. She has bouncy brown wavy hair flowing to the side. Her long form-fitting red dress has a split exposing all of her left leg. The dress is accented with a soft white elegant short-sleeve blouse. To complement the red dress, her fingernails, earrings, lipstick, and shoes are all red. She looks like a pinup doll circa the 1940s. As he walks toward her, he looks into a glass wall making sure he looks ok. He stops right in front of her. "Hi."

"Hello." She replies.

"I'm Thomas."

"Hello, Thomas. Can I help you?"

"Ahhh. Yeah. What's your name?"

"My name is Phoebe. Again, is there something I can help you with?"

Thomas Doesn't say a word. He looks at her as a smile slowly crawls on his face. Phoebe smiles back, reluctantly.

"Look. I have a lot of work to do, and you're preventing me from completing any of it. If you don't mind."

"I gotta take a shot in the dark here. I walked in and saw you standing here, and I kid you not. My heart skipped a beat."
Phoebe looks toward the files smiling while shaking her head.

"I was wondering if one day I could take you to lunch or something?

Phoebe looks up at Thomas shaking her head no. "No, thank you."

"Really. Why not?"

"I don't date co-workers."

"I didn't say we have to date. It could just be two coworkers having lunch."

"Again. No, thank you."

"Wait. So, if we weren't coworkers, you might say yes?"

"I don't know about all of that."

"Because I'll hand my resignation right now. I'll wait outside till you come out. This way, we could skip lunch and go right to dinner."

Phoebe fights laughter. "You don't have to do that. But the answer is still no. I'm sorry."

"You're sorry. No. I'm the one that's sorry."

"Why are you, sorry?"

"I'm sorry that I can't get you to come to lunch with me."

"You're just gonna have to get over it." She replies sarcastically.

"Nah. If at first, you don't succeed..."

"Try, try, trying again would be considered harassment."

"Ouch. Ok. that's my cue. Sorry I bothered you."

Fearing that he may have gone to far, Thomas walks backward to watch her as he exits. Phoebe realizes that she didn't really want to scare him off. "Look."

Thomas runs back to her. "Yeah, what's up?"

"I have a boyfriend."

Thomas slowly smiles while looking at her. He says absolutely nothing is maintaining his smile. Phoebe can't figure out why he's smiling.

"What?"

"Nothing. But thanks for telling me that."

Phoebe squints her eyes, looking at him, thinking. Thomas takes a few steps backward. "I'll see you around."

"Ok. Bye."

Thomas turns around and slowly walks out of her department. When he gets out of view, passing the empty conference room. He forgets that beyond the conference room is a clear view of Monica's desk when he starts to dance by himself. Monica lifts her head, watching Thomas dance. She looks around to see if anyone else sees him.

"What the hell is this man doing?"

Thomas lifts his head to Monica shaking her head. He stops dancing before walking over to her desk. "Yo!" He says with excitement.

"What?"

"Have you seen the new chick working over in legal?"

"Oh yeah. Phoebe, right? She got a badonkadonk back there."

"Wait. You know her?"

"Yeah. She's cool."

"And when were you going to tell me about her? It's Wednesday."

"Look, when you're at your desk on a roll with something, you don't wanna be disturbed. So, when I came by on Monday, you said go away. So, I went away."

"Stop it. I didn't say that."

"Yes, you did. You were like, 'Monica. Go away. I'll hit you up later.'"

Really?

"YES!"

"Shit. I'm sorry. You know how many dudes are gonna try to talk to her?"

"Yeah. But she has a man already."

Thomas laughs. "You're funny."

"Why do you say that?"

Thomas points at Monica. "That relationship doesn't stand a chance. He should have married her if he wanted me to back off."

"Yes, but she's a hottie, though."

Thomas stops in place, taken aback by her statement. "What's that supposed to mean? Are you saying I can't catch a fine honey?"

Monica shakes her head with an impish grin. "I didn't say that."

"O ye of little faith."

Monica smiles but feels a sting as the cut on her lip slightly opens. The sting causes her to react, and she jumps, shifting her body away from Thomas, who notices the bruise under her cover-up. She can see that Thomas has an inquisitive look on his face as he leans in to get a closer look. She attempts to lift her hand to cover her lip.

"What happened to your lip?"

Monica removes her hand, repositioning her body further so he can no longer see her lip. "Nothing."

Thomas' smile fades as he stares at her.

"That doesn't look like nothing."

"Well, it is, Dad." She replies with a sarcastic tone.

Thomas stands motionless, staring at Monica as Camille exits her office. Monica starts typing on her PC, ignoring Thomas as he continues to stare at her. Camille approaches Thomas from behind.

"Well?" Camille asks of Thomas, who is still staring at Monica. The look on Thomas' face intensifies as he stares at Monica, who keeps looking at her computer screen. Camille taps Thomas on the shoulder. "Well, Thomas?"

Monica slowly turns to Thomas. "She's talking to you."
Camille looks at both Thomas and Monica noticing the tension. "Am I missing something?"

Thomas shakes his head. "No."

"Ok. So, what happened over in legal."

Thomas slowly turns to Camille and smiles. "Nice. Very nice."

"Do I know you or what?" Camille asks.

"You know me plenty. I gotta start picking out the favors for the wedding."

"The moment I saw her, I thought to myself, "Thomas is going to lose his shit when he sees her."

"Thank you for pointing her out. I have to put a plan of attack together to pull this off."

"She has a boyfriend though," Monica Interjects.

"SO?!" Both Camille and Thomas reply.

"Jinx!" Monica quickly fires back.

Camille laughs, addressing Monica. "Boyfriend does not mean marriage. Fair game."

"Plus, she mentioned the boyfriend way late after the conversation had already come to a close. Mark my words. She's mine." Thomas adds.

Monica turns toward her computer smirking, "You ain't never getting that. Sorry."

Thomas points at Monica. “A hundred dollars says, I do. You can afford to take this bet.”

“I have faith in you, buddy,” Camille replies.

Monica turns to Thomas with conviction. “Shit. Five hundred dollars says you don't. Matter of fact. I’ll pay for the honeymoon.”

“BET!” Thomas exclaims.

Camille smiles looks at them both. “Oh. I’m gonna hold you to this, Monica. I’m your witness, Thomas.”

“Oh, It's on,” Thomas adds.

“Ok, good. It’s on.” Monica says with Sarcasm. “Now, can you two old fucks go away and let me work?”

Thomas’ smile fades as he looks at Monica. “Sure thing. But you better lay off that old folk’s crap.”

“Yeah, whatever.”

Thomas and Camille start to walk away when Thomas turns to Monica. “Oh. And we’re having lunch today, whether you like it or not.”

“I can't. I have plans.”

“What plans?”

“Plans! Can I please finish what I'm doing, please?”

Camille watches their interaction and interjects. “What is going on between you two?”

“Nothing.” Both Thomas and Monica reply.

"Jinx. Haha!" Camille adds playfully. Thomas looks back, laughing at her as Monica rolls her eyes at Camille. "She's so Lame."

Chapter 6: Don't Have Another Drink

Promises to stay in touch with a former coworker and friend once they resign is usually moot. Although statements of keeping in touch become the uniform statement for a farewell sendoff, people rarely follow through, out of sight out of mind. A few months pass since the last time the group of NMIC employees has seen Isabella Maldonado at the Pink Stain Pub. The seasons have rapidly changed from summer to fall. The yellow and orange colors of the trees around the city beautify every home near Central Park West.

On a cool fifty-one-degree, Saturday afternoon, Isabella and Sebastian Maldonado celebrate the birthday of their twin girls Grace and Hope. Their home on 76th street Central Park West is filled with family and close friends.

Kimberly and Oliver arrive together by way of a taxicab. They exit the cab carrying gift bags for the children. As they exit the cab in front of Isabella's house, they can hear the tunes of merengue coming from inside the house. "Ok. It's gonna be one of those parties." Oliver adds as they walk up a small flight of stairs to the front door. Before they can knock at the door or ring the bell, Isabella appears, opening the front door to greet them.

"HI. I'm so glad you guys made it."

"You knew I was gonna make it. But I had to bring my baby girl here." Oliver points at Kimberly.

Isabella is happy to see them both waves them in. "Come in, come in."

Kimberly and Oliver enter a packed house filled with Isabella's family and friends. Kim's eyes widen as she leans in to talk to Isabella. "Is this all your family?"

"Yep! Once I mentioned food, it got out of control quickly."

"Yeah. I can see."
Sebastian squeezes through the crowd and greets his friend Oliver with a bear hug. "YO! WHAT'S UP, BROTHER?!"

"YO! What's up, bro?" Oliver replies

"I'm living the dream, man. Just living the dream."

"Yeah. Bills, bills, and more bills. The American dream." Sebastian replies before looking over at Kimberly. He points at her and Oliver. "So, this really happened? You two?"

"Yep," Kimberly replies to Sebastian.

"Yes, sir," Oliver adds.

Sebastian smiles, moving toward Kimberly to greet her with a massive hug. "What's up, Ma?"

"Same old, same old."
Isabella extends her hand out to Oliver and Kimberly. "Gimme your coats. I'll put them in the bedroom."

Isabella takes the coats as well as the gifts from Kimberly. "Come in and sit down. Or come to the kitchen and mingle with the adults."

Oliver walks directly behind Kimberly with his hands on her waist, kissing the back of her head. They enter the kitchen where the adults have gathered to have a cocktail from the kitchen island filled with liquor. Isabella walks in, addressing everyone in the kitchen.

"Everyone, this is Kim and Oliver. Kim and Oliver, this is everyone." Everyone roars a simultaneous greeting as Oliver and Kim do the same. Isabella's mother, Paola, walks over Kimberly holding a full glass of wine in her hand. "We have some sangria over here. Would you like some?"

"Oh yeah." Kim leans back to Oliver behind her. "You want some wine, baby?"

"Yeah. let's get this kid's party started." He sarcastically jokes.

Oliver and Kimberly mingle with the family in the kitchen, drinking and chatting for a few hours until it's time to sing happy birthday and cut the birthday cake. After the twins open their gifts, most of the friends and family leave the party. The twin head upstairs to their room with their cousins and friends to play with their gifts. A few close members of the family remain behind as Isabella turns on the stereo, and the adults begin to have a party of their own. Sebastian and Oliver move the massive coffee table and area rug from the living room, creating a makeshift dance floor. Sebastian selects a salsa playlist and turns up the stereo.

Isabella and Sebastian dance salsa in the middle of their living room, and they kill it. Other family members join in dancing in unison to the beat of the salsa music. Oliver stands up, attempting to pull Kimberly, who is refusing to dance. Oliver begs her to get up and dance. She reluctantly stands up to dance. Oliver is dancing to the music better than she expected. She covers her face from embarrassment as he dances around her. Oliver gives Kimberly a quick lesson on how to move her feet as the family continues to dance around her. Everyone is clapping in approval as she dances and has gotten a handle of the dance steps. Sebastian and Oliver switch places, and now Oliver and Isabella dance in harmony. Sebastian and Kimberly dance, and Kimberly can't stop herself from laughing. Isabella laughs hysterically at Kimberly, who struggles but still keeps dancing. They all have a wonderful time dancing and laughing. They swap partners again, and Oliver dances extra silly with Kimberly, who continues laughing. Kimberly falls back on the sofa, sweating as the song comes to an end. She looks over at Oliver. “Where did you learn to dance like that?”

"I grew up in Puerto Rico."

"No way. You never mention that."

"Puerto Rico is short for Harrison Avenue and Burnside in the Bronx."

"And that translates to dancing?"

"Yes. I used to go to Orchard Beach in the summer to talk to the girls. The more I learned to dance salsa."

Kimberly looks at Oliver, waiting for him to continue. "Yeah."

Oliver realizes he was about to say too much before he redirects his statement. "Um. The better I got."

Sebastian burst out laughing, pointing at Oliver. "Yeah. You know you had to fix that, right?"

"Shut up," Oliver replies to Sebastian.

Isabella burst out hysterical, laughing at Oliver. Paola exits the kitchen holding a large goblet filled to the rim with sangria. "Does anyone want more sangria?"

Isabella jokingly turns to her mother. "Ma. How are you going to get home if you’re drunk?"

"Mira, I’ll just stay here."

Sebastian looks at Isabella seriously, shaking his head side to side. Isabella looks in Sebastian's eyes. "What?"

"She's had quite a few. Actually, more than a few." Sebastian says in front of the remaining guest.

"So, what? It's a party. Relax," Isabella looks at Sebastian with a look of disgust, hoping he'll get the hint and shut up as talking about her mother in front of her guest has gotten under her skin. Sebastian misses his cue from Isabella to drop this topic and keeps talking. "You should go talk to her."

Kimberly fearing that they may get into an argument looks over at Oliver, gesturing to go outside. "I'm hot. I'm going to go outside and get some air."

"I'll go with you," Oliver says to Kimberly. She stands up, taking his hand, leading him outside to the front stoop. Kimberly sits on the stoop between Oliver's legs, enjoying the beautiful fall evening. Oliver leans forward, kissing Kimberly on the back of her head. "Are you having fun?"

"I'm here with you. Of course, I'm having fun."

Kimberly turns to Oliver, kissing him on the lips. "I've been waiting for that all day."

"Well, there were kids in there. I couldn't jump all over you.

"I know, but you were looking all cute and everything."

"I only look this cute for you, ya know. I wake up looking like shit. If I know, I'm going to see you. I cuten up."

"You better keep it that way."

"I'll try."

The front door opens from behind Kimberly and Oliver. Isabella storms out, putting on her white winter coat and walks past them. Kim looks at Oliver and without saying a word. She stands up, rushing to follow Isabella down the street. "Izzy."

"I'm just taking a walk. I'll be right back." Isabella replies, trying to avoid speaking any further."

"Ok fine. I'll just walk with you."

"Suit yourself."

Both walk side by side about one city block until they arrive at the front of a small grocery store. The traffic light prevents Isabella from going any further. She looks up at the light waiting for the signal to change. Kimberly thinks of something to say that Isabella could reply to. "Hey. What happened to Camille and Monica?"

"Well, Camille hates kids."

Kimberly thinks before agreeing. "True."

"Monica had a previous engagement. I think Thomas went to Atlantic City with his father."

Kimberly snaps her finger as she points at Isabella. "That's right! He mentioned that at work. He's a good son."

Isabella half-smiles in agreement. "Yeah. He is."

The traffic light changes and they both continue walking towards the end of the block. Kimberly looks over at Isabella, who appears focused on nothing in front of her. Kimberly decides to try again to gauge her to talk. "You sure you don't want to—"

Isabella stops walking and unleashes what's on her mind. "You know, I set up the party for the girls. Invite all our families over. Prepare most of the food. Pick up the decorations, and I even decorated the house myself. I wrap the girl's gifts because he doesn't know how to do that. And most likely will have to clean up the house after everyone leaves, by myself.

Kimberly stands motionless, looking at Isabella. "Ok."

"His Mom, who is diabetic by the way, loves to eat sweets. So, I have to watch what she eats because she will dig into all of the sweets at the house. Heaven forbid he does that because that's his mother. But I don't complain. His mom didn't even get a gift for the kids. My mom comes over, brings a gift for the kid, helps me with the party, has a good time, and he has the nerve to bitch about her drinking too much. She doesn't get to spend a lot of time with a lot of family. She comes here and has a great time. So, if she drinks a little bit, I'm not gonna freak out."

"Yeah, that sounds about right."

"Then he says that shit right in front of my guest. Now she looks like a drunk who can't control her liquor. Isabella's mother the drunk. That was a real asshole move. I got so fucking mad that I decided to just take a walk, so I don't make a fool of myself in front of everyone."

"Well, you did the right thing. I know how bad your temper is."

"You have no idea. I was gonna punch his lights out."

"Come on. Just a second ago, you guys were having such a great time. You were all laughing. How do you go from that to punching his lights out?

Isabella takes a deep breath but does not reply. She continues looking straight ahead toward the next block. Kimberly senses she should say something.

"Am I outta line saying that?"

Isabella shakes her head no. "No."

"Why aren't you saying anything?"

Isabella turns to look Kimberly in the eyes. "Why did you go outside to get some air?"

Kimberly looks side to side, searching for an answer. "Um, I was hot. I had just finished dancing."

"And the minute you saw what was about to happen, you head out the door. Right?"

Kimberly thinks before she answers. She realized she could potentially add fuel to Isabella's fire. She makes eye contact with Isabella, who is staring at her like a calm angry parent. She takes a deep breath. "Look."

"Yes."

"If I'm being honest. Yes, I thought you were about to escalate, and I didn't think he should have said that while I was in there. I'm not family, so I don't think I should have been in there once that was said."

"So, you see where I'm coming from?"

"Of course. BUT!" Kimberly raises her index finger. "It's your kid's birthday party. I'd be an asshole to say anything to get you more upset. My job is to get you to calm down. Now, would you allow me to keep shit real for a sec?

"It's all I ever ask."

"Put this in the fuck it bucket for now. We're women. You're not going to forget this shit. Bring it up later when he wants some ass, then tell him no. Isn't that how marriage works?"

Isabella finally cracks a smile. "Sometimes."

"See. Someday I'm gonna be a spiteful, bitter wife who knows when to pick her battles."

Isabella laughs. "You're so stupid. But you're right."

"I know, girl. Are you feeling better?"

Isabella gestures between her index and thumb fingers that she is feeling just a little better. Kimberly smiles. "It's a start."

"Better than where I was a moment ago. Thank you."

"And you were about to walk away all by yourself. Couldn't even sit with my man and have a moment."

Isabella smirks, looking at Kimberly. "So, how's that going?"

"I love that man." She says with a smile that could light up a city block.

Isabella laughs as she turns around to walk back to her house. "I can tell."

Kimberly follows Isabella. "Where the fuck has he been hiding?"

"At work, apparently. In the time that I've known him, he has given that job a lot of his time."

"Yeah. He still does, but he gives me all of his time otherwise. We travel a lot on the weekends."

"Where do you guys go?"

"He took me to Camden yards to see the Red Sox play the Orioles."

"That's impressive. Especially for the Yankee fan that he is."

"Definitely. I took him to a Cleveland game to see the Yankees. Then we went to Sanibel, Florida."

"What's in Sanibel, FL."

"It's a sweet little island on the west coast of Florida. A couple of hours from Tampa. It's so beautiful. Perfect beaches. No kids. It's more of an adult resort. It's so quiet and relaxing."

"Sounds perfect."

Kimberly's smile fades as she thinks more about Oliver. "I've been going away so much that I may have to pull back."

"Why?"

"I haven't spent enough quality time with my mom."

"Oh, right. I forgot about that. How is she?"

"She's good. I do go to see her during the week. But getting to the facility and back home on a weekday is a little tough."
"How are you with all of that?"

"Well. I'm educated now. It was hard to deal with at first, but with some coaching from the staff nurses, I can deal a little better now. It just sucks when I go there, and she doesn't know who I am. It breaks my heart."

"Ugh. That's awful. I'm sorry that you have to deal with that."

"Thank you. It's ok. But there are some good days. I went to see her last week,, and you would have thought it's been years. She was so happy to see me. She started crying. She kept telling the nurse, "Look. Look. It's my baby. It's my baby."

"Aww. That is so sweet."

"It was. I was a puddle of tears. I feel so bad for her sometimes, but moments like that actually makes me kind of happy for her."

"Why?"

"Because at that moment, she expresses such an unfiltered love. Kind of like when a mom realizes she's totally in love with her newborn. She felt it to the point that she couldn't contain herself. She almost jumped out of the chair. I felt her love at that moment. It was a very happy moment when the norm has just been heartbreaking."

Isabella listens, remaining quiet as they near the house. She thinks back to holding her twins for the first time five years ago to the day.

"But back to Oliver. I know it's still early and only a few months, but that man is amazing. I feel like he really loves me."

"He's a good guy. I'm so glad you guys found each other."

"When he calls me. I get so giddy. Sometimes I feel pathetic."

"Don't feel that way. It's not often we get to be happy. A lot of times, people end up with partners they shouldn't be with, ending up miserable trying to make it work. At least
you guys are off to a phenomenal start."

"Yeah. I think you're right. Thank you."
As they return to the house, Sebastian stands outside, waiting for Isabella. She looks up at him seriously and continues walking. Kimberly stops talking as she walks up the stairs, pass Sebastian into the house. She nods as she passes Sebastian. He turns to Isabella, who stands in front of him. "Hey, babe."

"What?"

Sebastian can sense that Isabella is extremely irate. "I wasn't thinking about what happened earlier. I just opened my mouth without thinking."

"That seems more and more normal these days."

"What do you mean?"

"You react to shit and just open your mouth without thinking. I do what I can to not let it get to me, but you had no right to come out of your face like that. Especially in front of our family and friends. You know how private I am, and you run your fucking mouth."

Sebastian humbly takes a step toward Isabella. "I have no excuse, baby. But I'm sorry. I really am. I didn't want to ruin the girl's party."

"That's why I left. I didn't want the kids to hear me flip out on you."

"I'll make it up to you."

Isabella laughs, looking away from Sebastian. "I'd like to see how you're going to pull that off."

"I will. I promise." Sebastian takes another step towards her wrapping his arms around her, and kisses her. Isabella looks at him, trying not to smile. "That's a good start."

"Yeah. You like that?"

"You know, I do."

"Alright. Now we're talking. You ready to go inside?"

"Whatever."
Sebastian places his hands on her rear end, guiding her up the stairs as they enter the house.

Later that evening, after the guest leaves their home, Isabella remains alone cleaning the kitchen. She wipes down the countertops and takes the trash out to the back. She looks around at the immaculate kitchen before heading up to the kids' room, checking on them as they sleep. As she enters her bedroom, Sebastian is lying in bed, slowly dozing off. Isabella seductively walks over to the bed, opening her blouse, exposing her bra. She takes off her blouse and kneels in the bed on top of Sebastian, kissing his neck. Sebastian awakens to her touch and is startled. He looks up at her smiling face. "Babe. Are you serious?"

"What?"

"I'm tired as hell, and you wanna do this now."

Isabella becomes annoyed, firing back at Sebastian. "Well, I couldn't do this earlier! I was in the middle of a party. Then after that, I was in the middle of cleaning up without your help."

"Come on, babe. Lower your voice."

Isabella jumps out of bed and storms into the bathroom, slamming the door behind her. Sebastian shakes his head in frustration before falling back into the bed, looking up at the ceiling. "Fuck."

Chapter 7: A Night to Remember

As father time chips away at this picturesque evening, the group of co-workers all have individually eventful evenings following the party at Isabella house. Down in Battery Park Manhattan, Kimberly and Oliver had done everything possible while attending the party to keep their hands off each other. They arrive at Oliver's building, still trying to maintain self-control. They exit the elevator on the 16th floor of the Gateway Battery Park City Apartments. They fall a few feet short of total self-control when Kimberly lustfully grabs Oliver kissing passionately. They crash through the apartment door, continuing to passionately kiss each other. Oliver closes the door behind him with his foot removing his jacket and kicks off his shoes. Kimberly removes her blouse and shoes before wrapping her arms around Oliver. Still kissing Kimberly, he removes her belt and unbuttons her pants, removing them with urgency. She pulls his shirt off over his head, exposing his abs as she kisses his chest. He grabs her hair pulling it back as he sucks on her neck. Kimberly unbuttons and removes his pants. He reaches behind her unhooking her bra, exposing her breast. She removes his underwear and gleefully looks down at his penis. "DAMN!"

Oliver looks down as well. "See what you do to me, girl. I'm hard as a rock."

"Then you know what to do."

"He spins her around, squatting to his knees, removing her panties. Her rear end is directly in front of his face. He bites her plump ass causing her to scream in delight while laughing. He sticks out his tongue, licking her from her ass to the back of her neck as his hands slide up her stomach to her breast. He kisses her neck while caressing her breast. She closes her eyes as he bends her over, entering her. They make love on the living sofa more than once for the night.

Across the bridge in Prospect Park Brooklyn at Monica's house, Monica sits on her sofa wearing a pair of shorts and a t-shirt watching TV. Behind her on the table is a cold plate of food. She clicks the remote-control channel surfing for something to watch. Her front door opens, and Kareem enters. He removes his shoes before turning to look at the food on the table behind Monica. He walks up to her leaning down, kissing her on the cheek. She looks up at him, but he doesn't make eye contact. She looks back at the TV, shaking her head. Kareem walks pass the food that was left for him entering the bedroom.

Hours later, Monica turns off the TV, walking into the kitchen, throwing out the food that was left on the table. She walks over to the bedroom door to check on Kareem. He's fast asleep on the bed wearing boxers and a tank top. Monica walks into the room, pulling the covers over him. She walks over to the other side, getting in the bed and falling asleep next to him.

That same moment across town on 23rd street and 2nd Avenue New York City. Justin is sitting on the sofa in his living room, playing a multiplayer video game on his Xbox console in front of his seventy-inch TV. He is having a great time chatting with his online friends. His apartment door opens, and Rebecca walks in. Justin turns to look up at Rebecca. "What are you doing here?"

"This is what you've been doing all night. Playing video games. It's Saturday. You're not working, and we should be doing something as a couple. I'm fucking calling you and calling you, and you don't answer your fucking phone. But I bet you jump at the fuckin chance to answer your stupid little friends online. You're so inconsiderate. I don't understand. Don't you know I love you and just wanna spend time with you? But no. You'd rather sit here in the dark playing video games."

Justin tilts his head, turning to the television. Rebecca becomes even more irate as he is no longer looking at her. "Oh no, you don't. Look at me, asshole."

Justin removed his gaming headset looking up at Rebecca. She continues to bash and complain about her disgust of him not spending enough time with her. Her mouth moves like the speed of light, but all he hears is. Blah Blah Blah Blah Blah Blah Blah!

Justin continues to listen to Rebecca complain until she runs out of breath. He shuts off the Xbox, which makes her happy. Unaware of his unhappiness, she sits next to him on the sofa, cuddling up to him. She is completely clueless to the fact that he'd rather be anywhere but there with her.

Time continues chipping away over one hundred and thirty miles south at Harrah's Casino in Atlantic City, NJ. Thomas and his father play at the craps table. They are having an unreal night. They are up $57,500 and are on the craziest winning streak. Thomas is jumping around like a maniac every time they roll the dice. The table is surrounded by onlookers excited to bet with the duo. Thomas's father is smoking a cigar, blowing smoke rings in the air as they go all in.

Heading east to a stretch of New York known as Long Island at the Old Westbury Country Club in Westbury, NY, Camille and her husband Dylan are guests of Garrett and Edith Snow, who are members of the Westbury Country Club. They attend a charity event for abused animals with a few hundred-other members and guests. Camille, who keeps her body in excellent shape, wears a tight black spaghetti strap v neck mini skirt with four-inch stiletto's. Dylan, a slim early fifty-six-foot-tall Caucasian man with dirty blonde hair, has had a few too many drinks causing Camille's hidden frustration. She watches Dylan take a sip of his alcoholic beverage, finding it tough to hide her annoyance. "I take it I'm driving home tonight?"

Not feeling particularly happy with her statement, Dylan looks over at Garrett and Edith, who look away. "No, honey. I'm feeling great. I only had a couple of drinks."

Garrett, a six-foot older gentleman in his sixties with salt and pepper receding hairline, tries to diffuse a potential argument. "Ahhh. Leave him alone. He's only had a couple. We're having a good time, right, Dylan?"

"That's right," Dylan replies as he looks over at Camille, pointing in agreement with Garrett.

"See. He gets it. We're all out here, just having a good time, honey."

Edith, a mid-sixties Caucasian woman wearing a brunette wig, leans in whispering to Garrett. "I see Roberta. I'm gonna say hi before we leave."

Garrett turns to Edith swiftly. "Wait, you wanna leave?"

Edith gestures at Dylan that she's uncomfortable. "It's getting a little late, don't you think?"

"Ok, fine. If you say so."

Camille catches on to Edith's nod at Dylan. "She's right. I think we should consider heading home soon."

Dylan laughs at Camille. "Party pooper."

Camille turns to look at Dylan like an angry parent about to pounce on a disrespectful child. Dylan realizes that he might be playing with fire dropping back in his chair, conceding defeat. "Fine, fine, fine."

Camille continues looking at Dylan, who avoids eye contact. She stands up, tapping on the table to get his attention. "I'll be right back. I'm going to get my jacket."

Dylan nods as Camille walks over to the coat check. Most of the crowd at this event are well over fifty-five. The men all turn to watch her walk across the event floor toward the coat check girl. Her dress and shoes complement her long legs and extremely tight rear end. Her muscular legs bounce with every step she takes. She can feel the wives staring at her with disgust and jealousy. She almost enjoys the hatred of the women who never talk to her. Garrett looks to see his wife talking to her friend before he turns to watch Camille walk to the coat check. With his wife's attention elsewhere, Garrett stands up, looking over at the coat check. "I'm gonna go and get Edith's coat too. I don't wanna get caught up on a line."

"Sure thing. I'll be here." Dylan replies to Garrett.

Garrett strolls over to the coat check standing directly behind Camille. "Hey, sweetheart."

Camille is unsurprised by Garrett sneaking up behind her. "Hey, Garrett."
"Did you feel all the intense peering eyes of all the jealous wife's when you walked over here?"

"Nope. I don't pay much attention to those women. It's not like any of them ever talk to me anyway. I spend my free time exercising to stay in shape, and they judge me because of it. Fuck em."

"Well, I watched all of them, and they're jealous. They were mad at the husbands for staring at you."

"Good for them."

Garrett looks down at her outfit and takes a step back. "I gotta say... you look... simply ravishing in that dress."

Camille smiles. "Do I now?"

Garrett places his hand on the small of her back, leaning forward to whisper in her ear. "If I was your husband, I would take you home and fuck your brains out."

Camille can't help but smile as she turns around in shock. "You still have that in you at your age?"

"You'd be surprised what I can do at my age."

"I'm sure I would be."

Garrett slowly moves his hands down her dress. Camille turns to view the coat check girls trying not to watch them. "I would lick you from head to toe. Dylan is the luckiest man in here."

Camille smiles from the compliment, still looking at the coat check girl. "Your hand is on my ass. Aren't you worried Edith might see you."

"I don't give a shit. When I see something I want, I go after it."

Camille turns to face Garrett. "So, you're coming after me?"

"Yeah. I don't give a shit."

The coat check girl stands at the opening, holding Camille's coat, unable to ignore their conversation. "You're playing with fire Garrett."

"Am I? Or are you kind of interested?"

"What I am is married. Even if I were interested, I don't cheat on my husband."

"You should. With me."

Camille playfully rolls her eyes, turning to the coat check girl taking her coat. She has a sense that Garrett is staring at her ass. She looks at the coat before lifting her eyes upward. "I can feel you staring at my ass Garrett."

"I bet you'd like to feel me inside your ass?"

Camille turns around, smiling. "Good night, Garrett."

"I didn't hear a no."

"You didn't hear a yes, either."

Camille walks away from Garrett as he turns to watch her walk away until she returns to her table. Garrett stops watching, turning to the coat check girl handing her his ticket. The coat check girl shakes her head side to side before turning around to retrieve his coat. Garrett smiles, turning back to Camille watching as she exits the Country Club with Dylan.

Later at the Bauman home in Massapequa, NY, Camille enters her bedroom, undressing and taking off her shoes. Dylan walks into the room behind her watching her disrobe. She removes the dress, exposing her black thong panties. Dylan seductively saunters toward Camille. "You've got the greatest ass, honey."

Camille smiles as she removes her earrings. "Do you wanna spank it?"

"Oh yeah, baby." He replies as he walks up behind her grabbing her by the hair. "Are you a bad girl?"

"I'm your bad girl, baby."

"Say I'm your bad girl Daddy."

"I'm your bad girl, daddy."

"You want me to spank you?"

"Oh yeah, daddy. I want you to spank my ass."

Dylan violently pushes Camille on their king-size bed. She lands flat on her stomach. He follows, lying next to her, slapping her rear end as hard as he can. The pain of the slap is a turn on for Camille.

"Do you like that?" Dylan says as he enjoys the pain, he inflicts on his wife.

"Uh-huh. Slap it harder, daddy."

Dylan slaps her rear end continuously until it's red. The look of pain on Camille's face is an extreme turn on for Dylan. "You've been a bad girl. You know what I'm going to do to you?"

"You gonna fuck my brains out."

"You're Damn, right. I'm gonna fuck your brains out." He says as he leans close to her ear. Dylan removes his pants and underwear. Camille removes her thong panties. She arches her back so that her rear end is elevated. She eagerly waits for Dylan to enter her. He looks down at his penis, and it is barely erect. He grabs his penis and masturbates rigorously. He is unable to see the look of expected disappointment on Camille's face as she is facing the other direction. He tries to get an erection but is unable to. He is unable to make love to his wife. Dylan becomes very frustrated. "Son of a bitch!"

"What's the matter?" Camille asks while still facing the other direction.

"Nothing, babe. Turn around and blow me."

Dylan grabs her head, forcing her to perform oral sex on his flaccid penis. Her attempts to help him get an erection have failed. She looks up at him. "Is there anything else you want me to do?" Dylan falls back into the bed in frustration." Fuck. I'm sorry."

"It's ok."

Dylan's frustration turns to anger. "FUCK!!!!"

"That's not going to help any."

"Don't be a smart-ass Cami."

"Don't take out your frustration on me. Maybe you should have held back on all the drinks."

"Oh. Here we go with the drinking! You can try to be a little sensitive, you know."

"Fine, Dylan. I'm sorry." Camille calmly stands up and heads to the bathroom. Dylan watches her perfect naked figure walk to the bathroom. He continues watching her as she brushes her teeth. Camille comes back into the room and gets a t-shirt from the dresser drawer and sits back on the bed. Dylan stands up, walking to the armoire. "You know I really didn't appreciate you insinuating like that. Saying I had too much to drink in front of Garrett and Edith."

"You're right. I don't know what I was thinking. I'm sorry for that too." She says with very little emotion.

"Now you're just trying to appease me."

"Of course, not honey. I just don't wanna argue." She replies before lying under the covers.

"I don't like your tone."

Camille continues with absolutely no emotion. "What tone is that, honey?"

Dylan aggressively points at her. "THAT! RIGHT THERE!"

"Sigh."

"And don't you huff and puff."

"How about I just go to sleep. This way, I won't say another word for you to blow completely out of proportion."

"Fuck you!"

"Good night, honey."

"Ugh. I'm going downstairs."

"Okie Dokie. Don't forget to shut the lights, honey."

Dylan angrily grabs his robe and storms downstairs in a fit of frustration. Camille remains in bed and can hear him mumbling and slamming things in the kitchen. She rolls her eyes taking a deep breath before shutting her eyes, snuggling under the covers to fall asleep.

Chapter 8: Can You Guys Just Keep It Down

A cold rainy midday at the beginning of another routine workweek in lower Manhattan. Kimberly, Thomas, and Camille sit at a table for four at Dragon Gold Chinese Restaurant about a block from their place of employment. Thomas has been keeping something from the girls that he promised to disclose at lunch. He is unable to contain his excitement as Kimberly and Camille ask questions about his adventure in Atlantic City.

"So, you're telling me that you were up over fifty thousand dollars?" Kimberly asks.

"Well, over fifty grand. I lost count. I was jumping around like an idiot. I'm thinking I could take care of some serious business with this money. My dad is standing there like he's the man. Women have all gathered around to be around Mr. Lucky. You know how much he loves that shit?"

"Your dad's a real charmer if I remember correctly," Camille adds.

"Oh. He loves the ladies. He was on a high. I think one of them grabbed his ass."

Both Kimberly and Camille burst out laughing.

"But, I'm standing there ready to cash out."

"That would be the smart thing to do," Camille interjects.

Thomas smiles, saying nothing. Camille's eyes widen as she looks Thomas in the eyes. "Don't tell me you stayed in."

Thomas sits back with a smug look on his face taking a sip of his beverage. Both women look at him, waiting for a response. Kimberly looks over at Camille then back at Thomas. "Shit. You kept playing?"

"While I had my back turned talking to this super-hot cutie. My dad yells, "LET IT RIDE." I turn around like "DAD, WHAT THE FUCK?!"

Patrons in the restaurant turn around to look at Thomas for his poor choice of words in a public area. Camille pays the patrons no mind as she chimes in. "What the fuck is right."

"Would you two stop with the cursing?" Kimberly says under her breath from embarrassment as she notices the people looking over at their table. Thomas looks around, forgetting exactly where he is. He raises his hand to acknowledge the other patrons. "Oh. Sorry. Sorry."

"So. What happened?" Camille eagerly asks.

"I was caught between a rock and a hard place. This was the most fun he's had in a long time. I didn't want to be the responsible party pooper. All he does is sit at home, tend to his garden, and watch reruns of old TV shows."

"Well, he could have a lot of fun with fifty thousand dollars," Kimberly says with conviction.

"Um. Yeah, so small detail. Half of that money would have been mine."

"How's that?" Camille asks.

"I spotted him five hundred dollars when he blew his cash on Blackjack."

"Ahh. I see."

Kimberly shakes her head, taking a drink of her water. Thomas raises his hand in the air, gesturing shaking dice. "So, then, he rolls the dice."

Kimberly and Camille stare at Thomas as he pauses for effect. Kimberly looks over at Camille, who gestures with her hands to hurry up. She looks back at Thomas, widening her eyes. "Then?!"

Thomas again gestures, throwing dice across the table. "BOOM!" He slams his hand on the table. Camille cannot believe this story. "Get the heck outta here. He won?"

Kimberly chimes in. "He won?"

"He mother fuckin WON!" Thomas yells.

"A hundred thousand dollars?" Camille asks Thomas.

Thomas shuts his eyes to remember the accurate amount. "One... Hundred thousand. . . four hundred and thirty dollars. Booyah!" Thomas throws a couple hundred dollars on the table. "Lunch is on me, today ladies."

Kimberly looks at the money on the table gleefully. "That's freakin awesome. Congratulations"

"Shit. You should take us out for drinks."

"Oh, hell no. We're getting a limo, and we're going to get fucked. . . up. We're going to paint this town red." Thomas exclaims.

"Your dad." Kimberly adds, "He must have fainted."

“That nasty old bastard had his eye on some young chick. He was trying to get her to get a room with him.”

Camille shakes her head from side to side. “What is it with older men and young women?”

“Hey. On a young woman, everything is tight. Men all ages like a woman that’s tight.”

Kimberly tilts her head, pondering Thomas’ statement. “Really?”

Thomas shuts his eyes thinking about how his last statement could have been misinterpreted. “That came out wrong.”

“I'm tight.’ Camille says calmly.

Kimberly covers her face. “TMI.”

“I think that came out wrong too,” Thomas adds while covering his face as well.

Camille laughs at making Thomas and Kimberly uncomfortable. “I mean, I've never had kids. And it's not like Dylan is hung like a horse.”

“I meant tight like firm tight skin. Tight ass. You know?”

“Oh, right. Yes. That's what I meant too. You and I are on the same page.” Camille points at Kimberly. “Polly princess over here has her head in the gutter.”
Kimberly throws a rolled-up tissue at Camille. “I know what you meant.”

“But the other tight is good too. No one ever complained about that area being too tight.”

“Especially for a little dick guy like yourself.” Camille quips.

Kimberly burst out laughing uncontrollably as Thomas stares at Camille shaking his head. Kimberly's contagious laugh spreads to Camille, who points to Thomas. Thomas reaches over the table, grabbing the money he threw down a moment ago. "You guys can pay for your own lunch." Thomas stands up, jokingly walking away from the table while Kimberly is still laughing. Camille calls out to Thomas. "Come on, buddy. I'm just kidding."

Thomas takes a few steps further as Camille calls out to Thomas a little louder than before while still laughing. "You get your ass back over here and pay for this meal, dammit!"

Thomas turns to Camille, who struggles to stop laughing as she kicks his chair out for him to sit back down. Thomas returns to the table sitting in front of Camille. "You're a funny one today, aren't ya?"

"Oh, stop it. I take all of those grandma jokes."

"I never call you, grandma. But since we're cracking jokes."

Camille points at Thomas, no longer laughing. "Say another word."

"Easy, Ms. Bauman. I'm just kidding."

Camille leans back in her chair, pointing at the table. "Now put the money back on the table and pay for my lunch, young man."

Thomas and Camille smile at each other as Kimberly finally stops laughing. "You two are off the chain."

"Yeah. We're something else, apparently," Thomas replies.

Kimberly immediately remembers that she wanted to inquire about Camille's weekend. "Oh. And speaking of grandparents."

Camille turns to look sharply at Kimberly. "Tread carefully, young lady."

"No, seriously. How was the gala on Saturday? You were surrounded by all those old people."

Thomas's face lights up as he remembers that she was at an event. "Oh yeah. All those rich old wives mad at you because you look like a Baywatch babe. I'm sure you wore something more conservative than the last time."

Camille takes a drink of her water, looking toward the back of the restaurant for the waiter. Kimberly doesn't let up. "Oh, no. You didn't?"

Camille continues drinking her water to avoid answering Kimberly. She turns forward, still drinking her water, making eye contact with Thomas. "Oh, boy. Here it comes."

"What did you wear?" Kimberly asks.

Camille finishes her water. "Ahh. That was good?"

Thomas extends his arm gesturing for Camille to hand over her cell phone. "Come on, hand it over."

Camille reluctantly reaches into her purse, retrieving her cell phone, which is locked. Thomas opens his hand, waiting for her to place the phone in his hand. Camille hands her iPhone to Thomas. Kimberly looks at Thomas click the power button, which lights up the cellphone screen. "It's password-protected, Thomas."

Camille smiles at Kimberly as Thomas unlocks the phone by entering a PIN. Thomas looks at Kimberly, giving her a quick eyebrow flash as her jaw drops. Kimberly turns to Camille. "He has access to your phone?"

"It's a long story."

"Well, excuse me," Kimberly replies.

Thomas looks through her recent pictures swiping side to side with his fingers until he finds the picture he knew he would find. “DAMMMMNNNNNN!” he shouts again, forgetting where he is. Patrons look back at their table with annoyance. Camille smiles, covering her face. Kimberly leans over to see the phone. “Lemme see?!”

Thomas stares at the photo using his fingers to widen the picture. “I’m gonna go to the bathroom with your phone. I’ll be right back.”

Camille playfully slaps his arm while laughing. “Stop it.”

Kimberly eagerly tries to see the photo. “Lemme see dammit?!”

Thomas turns the screen so Kimberly can see. Kimberly's jaw drops. “DAMMMMNNNNNN GIRL!!!!”

Camille laughs, covering her blushing face. “Oh, go on.”

“You look crazy in this dress,” Thomas says as he looks up at Camille. “I know those old broads were hating.”

“Hating. You're being far too kind. I'm sure you were called all kinds of shit.” Kimberly says.

“Yeah. I could feel their eyes burning holes of treachery through me.”

“How the hell did you sit down? Legs for days, girl.” Kimberly asks.

“And how did you keep the tata’s from popping out?” Thomas jokes.

Camille appears smug as she answers Thomas. “A lady never tells her trade secret.”

Thomas points at the photo. “I don't see a lady in the picture. This here is a hoe.”

Kimberly burst out laughing as Camille finds it hard not to laugh along. She playfully slaps Thomas's arm. "Cut it out."

Kimberly leans over to look at the photo again. "Girl. For and older chick, you fine as fuck. Damn."

"Thank you, sweetie. I really appreciate that." Camille graciously replies.

Thomas continues looking at the picture biting his bottom lip before looking at Camille. "Tonight. When I go home, I'm going to the bathroom, and I'm gonna get some KY and..."
Camille playfully punches Thomas harder than normal. "Alright. Stop it. I appreciate it but let's change the topic. I get it. I'm gorgeous."

"What did Garrett say when he saw you?" Kimberly asks.

"That he wants to fuck my brains out. Verbatim."

"Ugh. Nasty old bastard."

"Nah. He isn't nasty. He's just tired of his old car. Sure, it still runs and all, but he wants to drive a red corvette." Thomas adds.

"Like I said. Nasty." Kimberly replies. "You better watch this dude."

Camille shakes her head side to side. "Please. He's harmless."

"Keep thinking that. He's got money. He probably thinks he can do whatever he wants."

"What he thinks and what he can do are two separate things."

"But I think you kind of like the attention."

"I think you do as well," Thomas adds.

"Look. He's very handsome. And If I weren't married. Maybe."

Thomas turns to Kimberly. "Owning a yacht helps too."

Camille thinks about the yacht. "I'm not gonna lie. The boat is very nice. I've always had a fantasy about having sex on a yacht."

Thomas and Kimberly look at each other, smiling. Camille looks at them both. "What?"

Thomas turns to look at Camille. "If he gets you on that boat. It's a wrap."

Kimberly nods her head in agreement. Camille sits silently, pondering the thought of being on his boat having sex as Thomas lifts his head looking toward the kitchen. "Where's our food?"

Kimberly looks around at all the patrons eating. "We keep making so much noise. They're probably messing with it."

Thomas laughs. "Come on. Don't say that."

The waiter finally arrives from the back with a large serving tray with their food.

Kimberly taps Thomas on the arm. "Shh, shh, I think this is us." She reaches for her water taking a drink. Camille turns to look behind her at the waiter, walking toward their table with the large tray. "Good. I'm starving."

"Yeah, Ya man Garrett's gonna work up an appetite when he brings you aboard the S.S. Smash a hoe."

Kimberly burst out laughing, almost spitting out her water. She and Thomas high five each other as Camille looks at them, confused by Thomas' joke. "What does that mean?"

"I'm just messing with you. Come on. Let's eat."

The waiter places their food on the table dish by dish. Thomas reaches for the chopsticks pointing them at Camille. "Don't go digging into my shrimp again."

"Oh, shut up." Camille fires back. "You can afford to buy another one, you cheap bastard."

"Yeah, but I can't afford to wait another three hours for my food."

Camille reaches over into Thomas's plate, taking a jumbo shrimp anyway. He looks at her in disbelief as she shoves the massive prawn in her mouth. She chews on the large piece of shrimp, looking into Thomas' eyes spitefully. Thomas turns to Kimberly, reaching into his dish, taking a large piece of shrimp as well. She stuffs her mouth, looking Thomas right in the eye. She smiles at him playfully while she chews. "What?"

"You two are a real pain in the ass. You know that?"

The trio continues eating their lunch, digging into each other plates for the remainder of their lunch break. Thomas picks up the tab.

Chapter 9: We Can Do Better than Mr. Bueller

As the fall season picks up momentum going into the Thanksgiving holiday, the weather in New York City slowly dips to a cold but comfortable average of 44 degrees. New Yorkers pretty much start covering up with winter gear and hats. Pedestrians fit a uniform pattern as they travel through lower Manhattan's financial district wearing trench coats while carrying a hot cup of coffee. The pattern of pedestrians walks in uniform, traveling to their prospective building or place of work. The uniform pattern of people walking in their prospective travel route looks like ants heading up an anthill. They maintain the same pattern until they branch off as they make it to their destination.

Office Manager Trish McCoy walks through the office of The Plante Insurance group with urgency stopping in front of the conference room. She looks at her watch, which reads 8:57 am before addressing the office staff. "Excuse me, everyone. Can I have your attention?"

Benjamin walks to his desk as Trish makes her announcement. Isabella's is already sitting at her desk, listening to Trish. "Everyone. It appears that there was a water main break in the area, and it has severely affected water pressure to our building and neighboring properties. For the safety of all tenants in the building, building management has asked all tenants to vacate the building until further notice."

"Woohoo. Nice. Free day." Benjamin chants. Isabella turns to see Benjamin behind her.

"Hey. Good morning."

"Good morning,, my dear." He replies before sitting at his desk for a moment.

"Did you say free day?"

"Absolutely. You don't think I'm going home, do you?"

"Where would you go?"

Benjamin jolts his head back in shock. "Um. Is that a serious question?"

"Yes. Where would you go?"
"We're in Manhattan. The coolest city in the world. And it's early. They make movies about this city. Ferris Bueller had a day off, why can't I?"

"Ferris Bueller was filmed in Chicago, you moron," She says sarcastically.

Benjamin laughs, slowly shaking his head side to side. "They made a movie about a teenager in second rate city, and it was awesome. I'm sure an adult such as myself can have an even better time in a city like this."

Isabella compresses her lips, tilting her head side to side as she thinks about his statement. "You may have a point."

"Of course, I do. Plus, it's early. All the fun stuff won't be crowded."

Isabella locks her desk, grabbing her purse. "Well. Tell me all about it tomorrow."

Benjamin extends his hand, gesturing for her to stop. "Wait."

"What?"

"You're not gonna come with?"

"No. Are you insane?"

Benjamin looks at his watch. "Come on. It's nine o'clock. What else are you gonna do?"

"I got things I gotta do."

"Really? And how were those things supposed to get done while you were here at work?"

"I don't know, but now that I can do them, I'll take care of them today."

"Tell me three things you have to get done today?"

Isabella tilts her head, looking up at the ceiling. "Um. I gotta pick us some items at the pharmacy."

"What could be so important at the pharmacy?"

"Lady products. Mind your business."

Benjamin laughs. "Gimme a break. What else?"

Employees start to migrate to the front of the office as they continue chatting. "I dunno. Oh. I could start my Christmas shopping."

"Black Friday is in four days. You can shop then."

"If you think for a second, I'm going shopping in that mayhem. Then you really don't know me."

"I do my shopping every year on Black Friday. It's fun."

"Apparently, your definition of fun and mine greatly differ."

"This could be true, but now you can appreciate a free day as an adult, right."

"Yes."

"Then our idea of fun is just slightly skewed. But it's still relevant."

Isabella looks up at Benjamin, who is smiling back at her. "Come on. Your kids are at your mom's house anyway. No school this week."

An impish grin crawls across Isabella's face. Benjamin smiles with her, slightly nodding his head. "Whaddaya say?"

Isabella thinks before giving in. "Fine."

Benjamin fist pumps in his seat. "YES!"

"So, what do you wanna do first?"

Benjamin strokes his chin, thinking before coming up with a thought. "Twenty bucks says you haven't gone to the observation deck of the freedom tower."

"It wasn't on my list of must-do's; however, I did want to go one day."

"It's not far from here. Do you wanna go?"

"Ok. Let's do it."
"Careful how you say things to me."

Isabella Slaps his arm. "Idiot."

"I'm kidding. Relax."

"You better be." She laughs, pointing at him.

"Blah blah blah."

They head to the Freedom Tower observation deck at One World Trade Center. The elevator ride provides a virtual tour of New York City as it was constructed from the early nineteen hundreds. Once at the top, the virtual tour continues on LCD screens directly in front of them. The screen opens, and you get a spectacular 360-degree view of New York City from the one hundred and second floor. They both look at the city in amazement. Tour guides give brief tutorials of the building and its history. They both look like children at a toy store. Isabella smiles, looking out the massive plate glass window. "This is amazing."

"It's breathtaking."

Isabella looks down at the 9/11 memorial. "Did you know anyone from 9/11?"

"Yeah. An old coworker of mine had just started working there."

"That's terrible. I knew a few people that made it out thankfully."

Benjamin points out of the window, changing the subject. "Ah. Look. The statue of liberty."

"Please don't tell me you want to go there?"

"Nah. That's a sixth-grade school trip. A little boring for my taste."

They spend a little time walking around the observation deck. They look at pictures and listen to the tour guide give a history lesson about the financial district of New York City. Benjamin realizes that he hasn't eaten anything. "You hungry?"

"Actually, yeah. What did you have in mind?"

"I say we take a little trip to Little Italy after this."

"For what?"

"Izzy. Are you serious?"

"It's too early to go there."

"Yeah. That's mom talking. Let Isabella out please so we can enjoy some of this day."

Isabella laughs, shaking her head. "Ugh. you're a pain in the ass."

Benjamin abruptly stops in place, grabbing her wrist. "Wait. I've got a great idea. This will build up your appetite."

She points at Benjamin. "I swear if you say something nasty. I'm gonna knock the shit outta you."

"You don't think much of me, do you?"

"NO!" Isabella laughs.

"Whatever. Don't you think this building looks awesome from the outside."

"Benjamin. I'm not doing any daredevil shit. No ziplining or hanging from the outside of this building."

Benjamin rolls his eyes. "Sigh. You're such a stick in the mud. Let your hair down a little."

"What are you suggesting then?"

"How about I just show you. And I promise it's not that dangerous."

"Not that dangerous?!"

Benjamin smirks, tilting his head toward her. "Trust me."

"Why do I feel like I'm gonna regret this? Isabella mumbles."

"You won't."

Both finish their tour of the observation deck heading back to the main floor catching a cab to the downtown Manhattan heliport. As they pull up to the heliport, Isabella stares out the taxicab window pointing at the helicopters very seriously. "You want me to get on a helicopter?"

“Ferris Bueller ain't got shit on me."

"Yeah, no. Now you're pushing it."

"Are you getting upset?"

Isabella folds her arms. "No. I just don't think getting on a helicopter is such a good idea."

Benjamin turns towards her. "Ok. I didn't want you to get mad. I seriously just wanted to have the kind of fun that I don't normally have with a little excitement. I didn't think this was dangerous."

"I'm not a big fan of helicopters."

"I'm not a big fan of being in close-quarter, but I still manage to shoehorn my way into a crowded train and elevator every day to sit next to you, princess." He quips.

“Yeah, but helicopters are dangerous.”

“So is New York twenty-four seven. Yet here you are, every day.”

Isabella smiles, shaking her head side to side. “Come on. You know what I mean.”

"Look, I could see if I took to you open cage lion encounter at the central park zoo.”

Isabella turns to Benjamin abruptly. “Is that a real attraction?”

Benjamin chuckles. “No. I just made that up to make a point.”

“Oh. Because I was gonna say that is really dangerous and kids should never be in the zoo if that were real. What kind of parent would take their kids to something like that? I know I would never take my kids?”

Benjamin sits quietly, looking at Isabella like she’s from another planet.

“What?” She asks as he continues to stare at her.

“Do you hear yourself?”

“What? What did I say?”

“Are you always so freaking, uptight?”

“I’m not uptight.” She replies as the taxicab driver shakes his head side to side, fighting the urge to laugh. Isabella notices the cab driver shaking his head, looking back at Benjamin.

“I’m not uptight.”

Benjamin gestures, wiping sweat from his forehead. “Phew. That’s good to hear. So, then it's settled.”

“What’s settled?”

“You’re gonna get out this cab with me, and we are going to see New York City and all its Majesty from a helicopter.”

Isabella sits quietly, staring at the heliport. The cab driver turns to look back at them.

"Sir. You are aware that your fare is still running, right?"

"I do." He replies to the cab driver before looking over at Isabelle, who continues to stare at the heliport. Benjamin shakes his head side to side, turning to the cab driver. "Can you take us to Mulberry street, please."

The driver places the car in the drive, about to drive off when Isabella taps on the cab drivers' seat. "Wait. We'll get off here."

"What? Why?" Benjamin asks.

"I've decided to go on the helicopter tour."

"Are you sure? I'm not forcing you. It's ok if you don't want t--"

Isabella interrupts. "I actually want to. Let's go."

"Are you sure?" He asks, placing his hand on her shoulder.

"Very."

"Okay." He says before he pays the cab driver and they both exit walking toward the heliport. "Care to tell me why the change of heart?"

"I dunno. I guess I'm just tired of being a stick in the mud. My friends from my last job used to say the same thing."

"Really?"

"Yeah. Even my kids have more fun playing with their father. When he plays with their dolls, he makes it fun. I try to organize the dollhouse and make the dolls talk like adults at work, and... you know what?"

"What's up?"

"I'll spare you those lovely details. I'm gonna try to relax a little today. Just a little."

Hey. I'll take what I can get."

"Yeah. I bet."

They take the helicopter tour around New York City. Isabella sits beside Benjamin, grabbing hold of his arm for most of the tour. They fly around the freedom tower, the 9/11 memorial, Liberty Island, The Empire State Building, and many other New York City scenic landmarks. Isabella finds it hard to hide her enjoyment. After the tour comes to an end, they walk arm and arm, catching a taxi to their next destination.

Later they arrive at Benito One Italian restaurant on Mulberry Street. The day is still early, so the restaurant only caters to a handful of patrons. They have the place to themselves. They enjoy a wonderful lunch, spending most of the time laughing rather than eating.

After their lunch, they take a taxi over to Chelsea Piers on the west side of Manhattan to bowl a few games at the bowling alley. It's still fairly early, so many of the lanes are unoccupied. Disco music echoes through the establishment to set a mood that only a handful of patrons can enjoy. Isabella sits and enters their names into the computer while Benjamin laces up his bowling shoes. She places his name first. "Why did you place my name first?"

"It was an accident. I just typed it first. Does that mean you go first?"

"Yeah. But, It's ok. Normally I would have let you go first."

"I'm sorry. Do you want me to change it?"

"No. It's ok."

"Do you know how to play?"

"I've been known to hold my own. I'll take it easy on you. I promise."

"Ok, thanks."

Benjamin walks up to the lane lining up to bowl. He walks then trots to the line releasing the ball. The ball goes straight down the middle of the lane hitting the middle pin, consequently knocking down all the pins

Benjamin spins around, pointing at Isabella. "STRIKE!"

"Wow. That was really good. Is that what you're supposed to do?"

Benjamin squints his eyes, looking at Isabella like she's speaking a foreign language. "Are you serious right now?"

"Yeah. Why? What?"

"Nothing at all. Your turn?"

"Can you show me how this is done?"

"Sure. Come on."

Isabella stands at the line holding the ball awkwardly. Benjamin stands right behind her. He places both hands on her hip. She bends over a little forcing her rear end into him. He looks down at her rear end in her tight dress slacks. He shakes it off, focusing on her bowling. He whispers what she must do next and backs off. She tosses the ball down the lane with a flick of her wrist. The ball heads right towards the gutter. She turns around dancing to the song on the loudspeaker before the ball turns back into the middle lane. She can hear the ball make contact with the pins.

"Strike!" She hysterically laughs.

"Son of a bitch." He laughs as he watches Isabella continue to dance.

She turns, pointing at Benjamin. "Thought it was going to be easy, huh?"

"I just taught you everything in one shot. I'm awesome."

"You are awesome, but you didn't teach me a thing."

Benjamin stands up to bowl, shaking his head, laughing. Before he bowls, Isabella walks beside him dancing to distract him. She bumps her hip into his. His next attempt is a gutter ball. She pinches her nose, gesturing drowning as he stands in place, looking at her. She falls back into her seat, hysterical laughing, pointing at him. "You're such a loser." She says as he stands in place motionless, staring at her. He smiles and attempts to bowl again. She runs behind him, grabbing his hips the same way he grabbed her hips, blowing into his ear. His eyes widen as he moves toward the lane, releasing that ball. He only knocks over three pins. "SHIT!" He yells.

Isabella dances back toward her seat, laughing. His frustration doesn't last long as he watches her dance from behind. She turns around, laughing, catching him watching her. Even though she is trying not to be uptight, she realizes that she's cutting loose a little and is having fun. She continues dancing, backing up toward the chair, and sits down, continuing to smile. They continue to stare at each other as she points at him. "You're such a sucker. This is going to be too easy."

"You're something else. You know that."

They continue to play bowl, and after two games, they decide to call it quits. They gather their belongings and exit the bowling alley. They stand outside, looking around as Isabella looks at her watch. "I think we've had enough fun for one day, don't you think?"

"You're done already?" Benjamin asks.

"Yeah. You haven't had enough."

"I'm just getting started."

"You gotta be kidding me. It's 2:30."

"So. Haven't you had fun today?"

"Yes. A lot of fun. Thank you."

"So why stop the fun train?" He says, mocking the moonwalk.

Isabella looks around, shaking her head, laughing. "I kinda feel like we're pushing our luck."

"How so?"

Isabella looks at him like he's an idiot.

"What's that look for?"

"Look. I'm not gonna lie. I'm having a blast. I haven't laughed this hard in a while. But we're both married and..."

"What the fuck. Did I miss the visit to the hotel room? Because if I did, I'd love to see those pictures."

"You know what I mean."

"No. I don't. Just like you, I'm having a blast. It's still early, and I want to have a little more fun. Come on, Cameron. Don't be a dweeb. We still got the Ferrari for another three hours."

Isabella takes a deep breath looking around as she contemplates what to do. She looks back at Benjamin and reluctantly answers. "I can't believe I'm gonna say this."

"Say it!"

"What else did you have in mind?"

"YES! That's my girl. Have you ever seen the Tom and Jerry episode titled, Mice Follies?"

Isabella squints her eyes, thinking about his question. "What?"

Moments later, they arrive at the Wollman Skating Rink in Central Park. Benjamin stands at the observation area, pointing at the rink. "Ta-da!"

"Are you aware that we have to work tomorrow?"

"I've got unused sick days."

"My legs are going to be in pain for a week."

"I've seen your legs. I'm sure they can take a few pirouettes."

Isabella looks over sarcastically at Benjamin. "You would think that."

"Are you in?"

"Do you even know how to skate?" She asks.

"I tried it when I was eleven. I'm sure I'll get the hang of it."

"Disaster. I see disaster."

Benjamin flashes his eyebrows, pulling her arm to follow him. "Vamanos muchacha."

They walk down to the rink where they rent ice skates. Isabella steps onto the ice and appears a little rusty. She releases that handrail and begins to skate. She looks back for Benjamin, who is taking baby steps while holding onto the handrails. He stumbles and falls. Isabella laughs and keeps skating until she gets back around to him. "Hey. Are you sure you wanna do this?"

"Oh yeah. I'm good. Don't you worry about me."

"Isabella skates off but doesn't see Benjamin stand up and skate toward her flawlessly. He effortlessly passes her, waving as he passes. Isabella is shocked. "Oh shit."

Appearing smug, Benjamin spins around skating backward while talking to her. "Ahhhh. Didn't know a brotha could skate, huh? I can run a hustle too now, girl."

"Son of a bitch." She says as she smiles in amazement. Isabella extends her right hand to Benjamin. He takes her hand with his left, and they skate around the rink flawlessly and effortlessly. For the moment, there is no one on the ice beside them. She breaks away from Benjamin and does a few ice-skating turns and spins, meeting up with him again. They attract a small crowd of clapping spectators. Feeling confident from the crowd support, he attempts to pick her up over his head. The move throws Isabella for a loop as she panics when he gets her up in the air. "What are you doing? NO!"

As he picks her up, she fights being lifted off the ice, causing him to lose his balance. The unintentional shift in body weight causes them to fall on the ice. She turns around to see if he is ok.

"Are you ok?"

Benjamin experiences extreme pain as he holds his hand. "My hand."

Isabella crawls over to Benjamin to check his hand. "Lemme see?"

He slowly extends his arm. As Isabella takes his hand, he can feel a throbbing pain in his hand. "Oh, man. I think I broke something."

Isabella opens her eyes wide when she sees his finger-pointing in the opposite direction. "Shit. You're gonna need a doctor."

"That bad, huh."

"I knew we were pushing it too far."

People start to gather around as one particular skater cuts through the crowd of people.

"Are you ok, sir?" The skater asks.

"I think so," Benjamin replies.

"I'm an E.R. doctor. Can I see your hand?"

Benjamin extends his hand, allowing the doctor to take a closer look. The doctor can see the pinky is pointed in the opposite direction. "I think it's just dislocated. I should be able to pop it back into place."

"Are you sure?" Isabella squeamishly asks the doctor.

"Oh yeah. I see this all the time."

"Hey. If you can fix it, that would be great." Benjamin states to the doctor.

"It's gonna hurt like hell, though."

"I'll take my chances, doc."

The doctor snaps Benjamin's finger back into place, causing Benjamin to scream. The doctor looks again at his finger, gesturing that it all looks ok. "Yep. All good now."

"Thanks, doc."

"My pleasure. You may want to put ice on it to keep the swelling down."

"Will do. Thanks again, doc."

"Are you ok?" Isabella asks.

Benjamin stands up with the assistance of the doctor. "Yeah. I'm great."

Everyone claps and cheers as Benjamin stands up, skating away with Isabella. She skates beside Benjamin, looking at him. He looks at her as they return to the skate rental window. "You really are an idiot."

"I'm so sorry. I got caught up in the moment and was trying to impress you."

"Can we just go? Please?"

Benjamin hangs his head from embarrassment. "Fine."

They remain quiet as they lace up their shoes and exit the skating facility. Moments
later, they sit on stairs at the corner of a crowded 58th street and 5th Avenue eating hot dogs. Benjamin looks over at Isabella, who is enjoying her hot dog, not looking at him. "Ya know... It's still kinda early."

"Shut the hell up!"

Chapter 10: We Should Have Just Gone To a Bar

Every major sport has its typical traditions all over the world. Trekking across states with family and friends to see your team fight to the end during a playoff run is one of the bigger, more severe traditions that can lead to absolute bliss or heartache. Sitting outside of a sporting arena cooking on a grill while throwing a ball around with a few buddies and strangers is one of the more common wish list sporting traditions of all time. For those who work white or blue collared jobs that are unable to travel to see their teams play at an arena, there's the local bar. This chilly Monday night sparks an old tradition that only includes a few small ingredients for it to be a success. A close friend, beer, food, and a girl free bachelor pad.

Week eleven of the NFL season has the Dallas Cowboys playing host to the New York Giants. Justin and Oliver look up at the numbers on the elevator as they ascend to the eleventh floor of Justin's apartment building in the Lenox Hill section of Manhattan. Justin steps off the elevator, reaching into his pocket to retrieve his apartment keys. Justin extends his hands to grab the doorknob when he hears music coming from inside his apartment. He turns to look at Oliver, who looks back at Justin, shrugging his shoulders. "Don't look at me. I'm out here with you."

Justice turns the key entering his apartment, looking into the kitchen at his girlfriend, Rebecca. She turns towards them, both smiling as she cooks a meal over the stove. "Oh. Hey Oliver. Hi baby."

Oliver's expression is one of confusion as he looks at Justin before looking back at Rebecca. "Um. Hey."

"What are you doing here?" Justin asks her.

"That's how you greet me?"

"Yeah! Especially when you're not supposed to be here."

"Well... I thought I would surprise you and make dinner for us.

"I told you I'm having a friend over for the game tonight."

"What game?"

"Giants-Cowboys. I even marked it on the calendar in your apartment."

"Can't you catch that some other time?"

"ARE FUCKING INSANE?!"

"WHAT?! Don't they play all the time?!

Justin takes a deep breath while making a fist. Rebecca showing up unannounced on a game night seems to be the straw that breaks Justin's back. "Fuck this! I can't with you anymore. Get out!"

"EXCUSE ME!"

Justin points at the door. "GET THE FUCK OUT!"

Oliver covers his face, mumbling under his breath. "Ah, shit. Here we go."

Rebecca looks directly looks into Justin's eyes. "NO! I'm not going anywhere!"

“I don't think you get it. It's over. This relationship is fucking over. I’m done with you. Gimme the fuckin keys and get the fuck out!

Oliver steps back in disbelief, trying to say nothing. Rebecca storms into the kitchen, grabbing a pot tossing it at Justin, who moves out of the way. "FUCK YOU!"

"What the fuck!” Justin yells as the food falls all over the floor. "Stop that shit!"

Rebecca tosses another pot of green peas at Justin. He moves out of the way. "You mother fucker! I hate you!"

"Yeah, whatever! Just get the fuck out!"

Oliver realizes that the evening is most likely shot. "Um. I’m just gonna leave."

"No. Stay right there!" Justin yells at Oliver.

Rebecca walks down the hall to the bathroom. Justin walks behind her. "Where the hell do you think you going?"

"I'm taking all of my stuff, asshole!"

"NO. I SAID, GET OUT! I’LL MAIL YOUR STUFF TO YOU!"

Oliver holds a bag of Chinese food, looking up at the ceiling, talking to himself. "Why didn't I do this at my house?"

Justin turns to Oliver. "You were right, man. I should have ended this a long time ago."

Rebecca storms out of the bathroom with the plunger hitting Justin in the head, knocking him to the floor. "Should have dumped me a long time ago?"

Oliver witnesses her hit Justin. "What the fuck is the matter with you?"

Rebecca turns to address Oliver. "You think he should have dumped me?!"

Oliver raises his hands for her to stop. "No. I didn't say that."

Rebecca points the plunger at him. "Then what did you say?"

Justin stands up, rushing Rebecca, who fights back vigorously. "Now, I'm going to throw you out!"

Oliver opens the door, so Justin can throw Rebecca out. "There you go."
LET GO OF ME! LET GO, YOU ASSHOLE!!! HELP!!!! HELP!!!! HE'S HURTING ME!!!! OUCH!!

Everyone on the eleventh floor hears Rebecca's commotion. Oliver listens to Rebecca screaming and looks up to the ceiling. "For fuck sake. Let her go before—"

"Yo. Let her go!" A nearby tenant says from the hallway. Rebecca hears the voice of the male tenant and continues yelling and starts to cry. "Sir. Please help me. He's hurting me!"

Oliver tries to diffuse the situation turning to address the male tenant. "Sir. It's not how it looks."

The male tenant walks toward Justin, pointing at him. "Shut the fuck up! Let her go... I'm not saying it again!"
"Sir. Step back and mind your business, please." Oliver interjects.

"What the fuck did you say to me bitch?"

A female tenant from the other side of the hallway yells from her apartment at another tenant who is sticking their head out of her apartment. "I think he's trying to rape that woman! call 9-1-1."

"NO!" Justin screams. "I'm just breaking up with her. Don't call the police."

Oliver and the male tenant get into an altercation shoving each other, not throwing any real punches. Other tenants come to the aid of Rebecca, banding together to hold Justin down until the police arrive. It takes about three people to hold Justin down. Rebecca stands behind the tenants, making eye contact with Justin smirking as the tenant holds him down, further fueling his rage. He tries his best to get up, but Rebecca begs them to hold him down. Once the police arrive, all four are taken to the police station for further questioning

About an hour later, at the police station, Justin, Oliver, and the tenant sit together while the police take a statement from Rebecca. Oliver sits with his head in his hands. "This is such bullshit."

"I'm sorry, man. I really am."

"It's all good," Oliver replies before turning to the tenant. "And you. You don't even fucking belong here. But you had to stick your nose where it didn't belong."

“Hey. I heard a lady screaming. I had help."

“So, you fight me instead of the guy holding the woman down. Now you're down here. Great help you were"

Tenant shrugs his shoulders. "What can I tell you?”

“Well, here's what I can tell you. The cops have another black man in custody when he should be home relaxing. Idiot."

"Fuck you." The tenant replies.

“Right back at you.”

Justin stands up and starts pacing. "This is insane. I'm missing the damn game.”

All three-sit waiting to be questioned by an officer. Oliver can hear the football game in the background of the police precinct. An officer walks by drinking a cup of coffee. Oliver reaches over to get her attention. He speaks softly to the detective. "Excuse me, officer?"

"It's Detective Valdez." She replies.

"Sorry, Detective. Hi. Can you please tell me the score of the game? Please?"

Detective Valdez looks at the three men one by one. Then looks at the T.V. that the three men are unable to view.

"14 to 10 Dallas."

"Thank you, Detective."
Detective Valdez takes a step before turning to the men. "What are you guys in here for? Is this some type of bar fight over the game?"

Oliver takes a deep breath pointing at Justin and himself before talking. "He and I just got off of work. We were going to his house to see the game. When we got there, his girlfriend was in the house uninvited. They got into an argument because he wanted to watch the game. They both started yelling. He told her to get out, and she lost it. You can check his ID; he lives at the house. She hit him over the head with a plunger, and then he physically tried throwing her out. That's when captain courageous over here came out of his house and punched me in the face."

"Is anyone pressing charges."

"Detective. All I want is my key back." Justin says to the detective.

The tenant raises his hands. "I just want to go home, detective."

Detective Valdez points toward Rebecca. "And what is she saying?"

"She's probably saying that I assaulted her. Which isn't true."
"Sigh. If she says you assaulted her, we're going to have to take a statement from the three of you. And you're sure no one wants to press charges?" Detective Valdez asks all three.

Oliver points at the tenant. "I won't be pressing charges against this idiot. I just want to get outta here."

"Chances are you may be here for a while. I'll talk to the officers who made the arrest. But if she says you assaulted her. Chances are you might be here for a while."
Justin hangs his head, shutting his eyes. "I really should have dumped that psycho a long time ago."

Oliver places his hand on Justin's shoulder. "That's life, man. You live and learn."

Everyone remains at the precinct for a few hours waiting to talk to the arresting officer. They remain in the precinct overnight until the desk sergeant walks up to Oliver at around 3 am tapping on the shoulder. They have a brief conversation before everyone is released.

Chapter 11: That Was So Worth it

Day to day and week to week routines are exactly that. Routines filled with processes people complete in uniform on a daily basis. Nine to fivers across the world follow the same patterns of sleep time, meals and break, trips to the restroom as well as travel patterns. Asking someone who follows a pattern around their workweek what they did on a Tuesday three weeks ago will turn up a result of an individual not remembering. Tuesday, on the week of Thanksgiving, at Plante Insurance Group, Isabella Maldonado sits at a table alone in the office break room. She takes a bite of her sandwich while looking at her e-reader. She lifts her head at the sound of Benjamin's voice approaching. Isabella looks at her watch, which read 12:17 pm. Benjamin, who has just arrived at work, enters the break room, followed by fellow employees Jacob and Xavier. Jacob squeezed through the door looking at Benjamin's bandage covered hand. He makes a lewd gesture towards Benjamin's hand. "That looks, painful man. I guess no more shaking dice for you, buddy."

"Usually, people use the index finger." Xavier chimes in as Benjamin walks over to the coffee machine.

"Oh, no. Your wife asked me to use my pinky since it closely resembles your dick."

Isabella spits out all of her drink on the break room table, bursting out laughing. Xavier looks over at Isabella, laughing before turning back to Benjamin. "Why do you have to go there?"

"Because you made it that easy." Benjamin turns around, moving Xavier out of his way. "Excuse me, boys."

Benjamin walks over to Isabella's table as Xavier watches him walk away. "He's such an asshole."

Jacob fights laughter, pointing at Xavier. "Burn." Both Jacob and Xavier exit the break room leaving Benjamin and Isabella alone. "You're out of control. You know that?" Isabella says to Benjamin. He smiles, looking at the wet table before walking to the utility closet, grabbing sanitizing wipes, handing it to Isabella. "He walked right into that. He's such an idiot."

Isabella takes the wipes from Benjamin. "Thank you."

Benjamin looks around the small break room, observing if anyone can hear him. "How are you?"

"I'm good." She says with a smile on her face. "Tired. How are you?"

Benjamin holds up his injured hand while pointing at the chair next to her, requesting permission to sit. "Great if you couldn't tell. May I?"

"You're really going to ask me that? Just sit down."

Benjamin leans in speaking a little lower. "No, seriously. How are you? You fell on your ass."

"I'm good. I landed on your hand, so it wasn't that bad."

"Right. Thank you for that, by the way."

Isabella smirks. "What did the doctor say?"

"Wear this splint for a few weeks. Ice it from time to time. Blah blah blah. The usual."

They sit quietly for a moment, searching for something more to say to one another.

"Look. I know by the end of our day I kind of gave you a little bit of a hard time."

Benjamin waves her off. "Don't worry abo--"

"Let me finish." She interrupts.

"Ok."

"When I got home, the house was empty. I paced around a bit, but I really had nothing to do. So, I took a bath." She points at him as he opens his mouth to say something slick. "Shut up."

Benjamin closes his mouth, sitting back in his chair, simply smiling.

"While I was in the bath. I thought about you."

Benjamin again opens his mouth to say something. Isabella's eyes widen as she raises her hand, pointing her finger at him. "I swear if you say anything nasty."
Benjamin gestures, buttoning his lips. "I won't say a word."

"Anyway, I thought about you. We've worked together for a few months, and it kinda meant something to me that you wanted to share a day like that with me. One, I really appreciate that. Two, I just wanted to say thank you. I couldn't figure out why my face was hurting. But It was because I hadn't laughed that hard in a long time. I had such an enjoyable day with you."

Benjamin smiles and doesn't say a word. Isabella's eyes move side to side, waiting for a response. He leans forward, looking in her eyes. "Soooo. Where were your hands while you were thinking about me? Particularly your fingers?"

“You know what? I can't with you. Your mind is always in the gutter."

Benjamin laughs, falling back into his chair. "I'm kidding. I am kidding. Relax."

"You're an ass."

"I’m sorry. But listen, seriously. I genuinely like you. I like you more than most people, especially when you loosen up. I truly enjoy your company here at work. You have a great sense of humor, and outside of work, you don't take things too seriously. Plus, you make me laugh. The workday isn't so boring when you’re at your desk. I was always curious about what you’d be like outside of work, and now I know. No liquor required.”

Isabella smiles at the compliment as Benjamin continues. "I consider you a friend."

"Awwww."

"And if I ever lift you up like that again. And you feel like you're going to fall."

Isabella's smile fades. "I’m warning you."

"Try to aim for my face."

Benjamin stands up and quickly trots out of the cafeteria, laughing before Isabella could react. Isabella crumples up the disinfectant wipes throwing it at him as he exits the breakroom.

"Idiot."

Chapter 12: I'm Only Going To Say This Once

It's cold, but it's not fully winter yet. But still, New York City in December is pretty cold. Saturday evening at the AMC Loew Lincoln Square in New York City, Monica, Kimberly, Oliver, and Thomas exit the theater, followed by several other patrons. As they exit the theater, they bundle up, putting on their hats, gloves, and scarves to combat the frigid night. The group walks gleefully satisfied with the movie they just finished watching.

"How did I let you guys convince me to watch Honeymoon in the hood part 2?" Thomas asks everyone.

Kimberly reach's out, placing her hand across his chest. "Hold up. You didn't like it?"

"No. I didn't."

"You trippin. That shit was crazy funny." Monica interjects.

"I thought it was hilarious. What's the matter with you?" Oliver asks.

"I thought it was trash. But hey. What do I know?" Thomas addresses everyone.

"Not much, apparently," Monica adds sarcastically.

Kimberly looks over at Monica. "I thought it was cute, the way she told him she was pregnant."
"Right. I thought he was gonna wild out. But he said."

Monica and Kimberly say the lines from the movie together. "That's all I really ever wanted, baby."

Thomas rolls his eyes, listening to Monica and Kimberly.

"That was so sweet. I loved him." Kimberly adds as she looks over to Monica. "See, that's a real man."

"Yeah. Working in a hardware store struggling to make ends meet. Then they have a kid on the way living in an apartment that needs massive repairs.... "In the hood." Sounds like a stupid man to me." Thomas fires back at them both.

Monica looks at Thomas. "You're such a hater."

Kimberly adds. "Well. He's entitled to his opinion. Even if it's stupid."

Monica laughs as Kimberly grabs Oliver's arm. She gets as close as she can to Oliver for warmth. "It's cold as hell tonight."

"What do you guys wanna do next?" Monica asks the group.

Oliver and Kimberly look at each other. "I think we're gonna just head home."

"Are you serious?" Monica replies.

"Yeah. It's cold, and I'm getting tired."

"Are you heading out to Brooklyn or you staying at Ollie's crib?"

"She's staying with me," Oliver answers Monica.

"Damn. It's like that?"

"Like what?"

"I gotta go home on the train by myself?"

Thomas stops walking. "Really? You knew I drove in. I'll take you home."

Monica crushes Thomas with a massive hug. "See. That's my dude right there. That's what's up."

Thomas rolls his eyes, shaking his head. "Yeah. It's all good. I'll drive out of my way to Brooklyn then back home to Whitestone. Yeah. It's no problem." He says with a sarcastic tone.

Monica pulls away from Thomas. "Why you gotta be so extra?"

Thomas shakes his head playfully, grabbing Monica's arm, pulling her in the opposite direction. "Come on. I'll catch you guys later."

Oliver stops Thomas from leaving. "Hey, Thomas. One second."

"What's up?"

"I didn't get to thank you earlier. But thanks for whatever it is that you did a few weeks ago with Justin and his girl."

"Oh. That was no problem, man. I just made a call to the desk Sergeant."

"Well, thanks, man. I really appreciate it."

"Anytime. Tell your buddy to stay away from those headcases, man."

"I have been. He may have finally learned his lesson, though."

Oliver extends his hand to Thomas. They shake hands before Thomas and Monica head in the opposite direction. "Alright, guys. See you later. See you Monday, Kimmy."

They say their goodbyes and walk away from each other. Monica and Thomas walk toward 69th street, turning into the block, which looks like a beautiful picturesque Thomas Kinkead painting. Every house is covered from ground to roof with Christmas lights and holiday decorations. The holiday lights illuminate brighter than the streetlamps. Monica grabs hold of Thomas' arm. "You don't really want to go home just yet, right?"

"Well, the later I stay out, the later I get home."

"Come on. Stop bitchin. Wanna shoot some pool?"

Thomas ponders her request. Monica playfully tugs at his arm. "Come ooon. I see you thinking about it."

"Fine. But we're playing for money."

"You better empty your wallet, bruh. You know the Asian in me sees those pool cues like chopsticks. We know how to play some pool."

"This ain't mahjong. I will whip your ass."

Thomas reaches into his coat pocket for his key fob to disarm his car. Monica walks over to the passenger side as his cell phone rings. He pulls the phone out of his other pocket, looking at the screen. The caller ID reads Phoebe. "SHIT!

"What?!"

Thomas looks up at Monica, pointing at the phone. "It's Phoebe.'

"That fine bitch from work?"

Thomas disapproves of Monica using bitch as a term of endearment. He rolls his eyes, pointing at the phone. "I'm gonna take this call. Get in the car and be quiet."

"Come on, really?"

Thomas points at the car." GET IN THE CAR!"

"Ok. Jeez."

Thomas clears his throat before taking the call. "Hello."

"Hey. Hi. How are you?"

"Good. I'm really good. How are you doing?

"I'm good. Just sitting around my house."

"So, what are you doing?"

"Nothing. I just got home from Miami, and I saw that you had called me, so I figured I would call you back."

Monica looks through the window, watching Thomas smile. "That was nice of you. Thanks for returning my call. Did you have fun in Miami?"

"Yeah. It was my friend's bachelorette party."

"That's cool. It sounds like you had a good time." Thomas replies as a taxicab drives by, hitting a pothole in the middle of the street.

"I did have a good time. . . Where are you? It sounds like you're outside on the street."

Monica exits the car and whispers. "Gimme the keys."

Thomas, fearing that Phoebe will hear another woman's voice, flashes his hand for Monica to go away. He focuses back on the conversation. "Yeah. I'm in Manhattan about to meet up with some friends."

"Oh, ok. Then I won't keep you. I just wanted to return your call, so you didn't think I was ignoring you."

Monica whispers. "Gimme the keys. It's cold."

Thomas violently reaches in his pockets and tosses the keys at Monica, flipping her the bird. He goes back to speaking with Phoebe. "It's no problem. I was just happy to see it was you calling."

"Aww. Well, call me tomorrow if you want."

"I will."

Thomas can see Monica through the windshield, making lewd gestures poking her index finger through her fist as he listens to Phoebe.

"Ok. Then I'll talk to you tomorrow. Good night."

"Goodnight."

"Oh. And be careful."

"Thank you. Will do. Good night."

Thomas ends the call and enters the car slamming the door turning to Monica. She turns to him, laughing mocking smooching sounds. "I love you, Phoebe. Mwa, mwa mwa."

"What was that, four minutes? You couldn't just sit in the car for four fucking minutes?"

"It's cold, and you got heated seats."

"You're such a pain in the ass. Your car has heated seats, too, you know."

Monica laughs, paying no mind to his frustration of her. "So, what. You guys got a date?"

"Shut up!"

Monica burst out laughing, looking over at Thomas. "Mr. Sensitive."

They drive across town to East River Billiards, where they get settled in for a game of pool. The location dimly lit like most pool halls, a light over each of the several tables throughout the business. For the holidays, the pool hall is sparingly covered with holiday lights and decorations. Holiday music echoes through the poolhall. Thomas walks up to the table handing Monica one of two beers he's carrying. She takes a swig before she breaks, knocking in two balls while Thomas takes a seat on the side, watching her break.

"Since it's just you and me here."

Monica looks around the pool hall at all the patrons turning back to Thomas sarcastically. "These people around us don't count?"

"I gotta talk to you about something that's been bothering me lately, and I didn't want to talk around our friends."

"Can it wait until I'm done with this shot?"

"Fine."

Thomas drinks his beer, waiting until it's his turn. Monica misses a shot walking to the side, grabbing her beer. "Ok. So, what's bothering you, Papa smurf?

"Kareem putting his hands on you."

Monica's jovial expression changes. "You wait until we're out having a good time to bring that shit up?"

"Oh. So, there's a good time to talk about this?"

"Tommy. Change the subject."

"No. I'm not changing the subject. I saw the cover-up on your shirt and around your neck."

"So, I put on too much makeup, and now you think he's choking me or something?"

"If I'm wrong. Show me your neck right now?

"Pervert. I'm not showing you shit." She points at the table. "It's your turn."

Thomas walks up to the table to play while Monica drinks her beer. He leans over to hit the ball, looking up at Monica. "You suddenly wear those sheer scarfs at work to cover your neck. You didn't think I would notice?"

"I wear them because they're pretty."

"Yeah. Pretty stupid looking."

"Now you're insulting my fashion sense. Really?"

"No. Just your thought process."

"My thought process now is thinking I should have just gone home rather than spend
time getting a lecture."

"Then I would have had this talk with you in the car. Remember, I was going to drive you home?"

"I would have taken the train."

Thomas knocks in three balls before it's Monica's turn. Monica walks past him bumping him out of her way. He leans on a chair, watching her. "At the risk of beating a dead horse. I'm just saying you don't need to be with a guy who puts his hands on you. You should know your self-worth."

"Look. We're good now. We had a talk, and he promised that he is no longer going to do that."

"Do what? Stop hitting on you for the holidays? How sweet."

"Whatever."

Thomas walks around the table toward Monica. "He's a fucking punk bitch."
Monica looks away as she chalks her cue. "Can we change the subject?"

"Sure. But not before I say this."

Monica looks up at Thomas, who has gotten within inches of her face as he speaks with authority through his teeth. "If he lays another hand on you..... I'm gonna FUCK him up."

Both stare at each other for a moment as Thomas brings a smile to his face. "Your turn."

Monica shakes her head. "Why are you being so smug?"
Thomas continues to smile, looking in her eyes. "What are you talking about? We're here to play pool."

"I don't feel like playing anymore."

"Why?"

Monica throws the pool cue on the pool table, grabbing her coat from the coat rack, walking toward the exit.

"Where are you going?"

"Home."

"Are you serious?"

"Yep. Goodnight."

"Monica. Monica!"

Monica exits the pool hall walking down the stairs. Thomas follows her, leaving his coat behind. Thomas catches up to her, tugging at her arm. "What the fuck? You can't just take the train home this late. Lemme take you home."

"You should have thought of that before you opened your big fuckin mouth."

Thomas grabs her arm. "Come on. Cut it out."

"Let go of me, Thomas."

Thomas releases her arm as she walks away. She takes a few steps before Thomas yells out to her. "You're willing to walk away from me. But not from someone who physically hurts you?!"

Monica stops walking and turns around, charging at Thomas, pointing in his face. "FUCK YOU! How dare you talk about my shit out here in the street."

"You're just mad because the truth hurts. You know I'm right. I'm here, your friend. The friend that means you no harm. The friend who is upset that you're someone's punching bag."
"SHUT UP! SHUT THE FUCK UP!" She continues pointing in his face.

"The friend who wants to help you. The friend that actually can help you."

"SHUT UP, SHUT UP, SHUT UP!!!!" Monica punches Thomas as hard as she can in the chest.

Thomas takes the punches. "What the hell is the matter with you?"

Monica continues to punch him. "You're an asshole!"

Thomas and Monica stand in front of each other as Monica catches her breath. Thomas rubs his arms for warmth. He looks at

Monica, who is looking away from him. He feels conflicted as he watches her fighting tears. He leans close to her face. "I'll own up to the fact that I may have ruined your night, but it wasn't unintentional. If you want to go home, that's fine. But I can't let you go home angry by yourself. Come back upstairs, lemme get my jacket and I will take you home. You are not obligated to say a word to me.

"Fine, because I don't have shit to say to you. Just take me home and don't say another fucking word to me."

Monica pushes Thomas out of her way, walking back toward the pool hall as Thomas follows behind. They go upstairs so that Thomas can retrieve his jacket and settle up with the cashier before they exit, and he drives her home.

Chapter 13: You're an Old Dog, But This Is Not A New Trick

Massapequa NY is a nice town nestled near the south shores of Nassau County, New York. Homes in this town are moderately more comfortable than houses just west headed into Queens. Residents have the added comfort of spreading their wings, so to speak as compared to homeowners in Brooklyn and Queens. At a strip mall in the heart of the town of Massapequa, NY, Camille strolls through an aisle of the Massapequa Spirits liquor store. The store is crowded with patrons purchasing liquor. Camille is shopping alone, pushing a small cart through one of the center aisles. She strolls through the store, picking up different items for a Holiday party that kicks off at her home within the next hour.

Garrett enters the store noticing her standing in the aisle with her back turned to him. Garrett looks at his reflection through a glass to make sure his hair is in place. He licks his hand, slicking his thinning hair backward. He unzips his leather jacket and loosens his scarf as he walks toward her noticing her short leather jacket, mini skirt, and high leather boots. He stares at her legs, shutting his eyes, imagining them wrapped around him. He takes a deep breath before sneaking up behind her grabbing Camille by the waist. "Hey, sweetheart."

A startled Camille whips around to see Garrett behind her. "What the–Oh, hey, Garrett. You scared the shit outta me."

“How ya doing, doll face?

Camille smiles at his cute, corny statement. “I'm good. It's nice to see you.”

“It's always good to see you. What are you doing in here?’”
“I’m having a little get together at my place for some co-workers. I'm picking up a few extra bottles of wine.”

“Sounds like a blast. Why wasn't I invited?”

“Apparently, you weren't listening when I just said I was having some coworkers over. The operable word being ‘Coworkers.’”

“Yeah. You did say that–my mistake. I was looking at you in those boots. Marone a mi. I couldn't concentrate.”

“I could be wearing flip flops and a granny coat, and you would still say that.”

“Yeah. Because you’d be gorgeous in it, but you already know that?”

“It's nice to know when it comes to me, you always have on your love goggles.”
“These aren't love goggles, baby.”

“Whatever they are, it's always sweet and appreciated?”

“When are you gonna let me take you out?”

Camille shy’s away, looking at the bottles of wine she holds in her hand. “Garrett. Come on.”

“No, seriously. I’m gonna be honest with you. I like you. I know you're married. You know I'm married. But I’m in a dead relationship.”

Camille places the wine bottle back on the shelf and slowly continues down the aisle. "So, why do I see you two together all the time?"

"For appearances. You only see us out at social events. When was the last time you can recall seeing us together around town or out to dinner?"

Camille thinks for a moment before Garrett answers for her. "Never. But come this spring, we're calling it quits."

Camille turns to Garrett. "Are you serious?"

"Very. It's been a long time coming. Whatever spark we had years ago is completely gone."

"I'm so sorry to hear that."

"I'm not. I'm not happy, and I want out. She's not happy. We just grew apart. These things happen."

"It sucks when it does. But you have a point."

"I watch you and Dylan. You two look like you're stuck in neutral. You never look him in the eye anymore. It's like you've fallen out of love with him too."

"So, you're a psychologist now?"

"No. I'm just – "

"Trying to get into my pants by any means necessary." She abruptly interrupts him.

"Cami. I'm gonna be totally honest with you. I've wanted you from the first time I laid eyes on you. You're so hot; you don't even belong here on the Island. I picture you as one of those hot pin-up girl types in a David Lee Roth video. There's no woman hotter than you on the island. So, me trying to get in your pants. Yes. That's true, but I'm not trying to dissect your marriage to do so. I'm just telling you that I don't think you're happy. And I would love to be the guy to take on that challenge. That's all."

A small grin comes across Camille's face. "Fine. I shouldn't have bitten your head off."

"It's ok. I don't mind if you wanna take out your aggression on me. If you do, you can take it out on me in the sack."

Camille turns away bashfully. "Is that all you think about?"

"When I think of you, especially in this cold weather, I think you using your inner thighs as earmuffs."

Camille cracks up laughing. The sight of Camille laughing that hard is an even bigger turn-on for Garrett. "You'd like that, right?"

"You've dialed up the perverted charm to ten today. Huh?"

"It's on ten all the time for you, baby."

Camille looks Garrett in the eyes as can see a sliver of sincerity. "You are something else."

"Come on, sweetheart. Let me take you out once in the Vette? We can go down to the Jersey Shore. Let me spoil you for a few days."

"And what do you suppose I tell my husband?"

"Tell him you got a business trip. You don't even have to pack. I'll buy you whatever you need. It's not like you'll need any clothes. I'll get us the nicest hotel room overlooking the ocean. We can order up room service and everything."

Camille slowly continues walking up the aisle. She thinks about his proposal but is far from comfortable cheating on her husband. "I don't know, Garrett."

Garrett walks faster to get in front of her blocking her path. "What's there to know about? Come on, baby. At least think about it. Please?"

The thought of being desired as much as Garrett is pushing is tempting her to her core. "I'm not making any promises."

"At this point in time, I'll take what I can get."

"You might get nothing."

"Yeah, but I might get it all." Garrett leans in to kiss her. Camille turns her face allowing him to kiss her cheek.

"Come on, Garrett, we're out in public."
"I don't give a shit." He keeps his face close to her kissing her more than once on the cheek. "Merry Christmas, sweetheart."

Camille turns to Garrett only inches away from his face. "Merry Christmas."

Garrett pulls away, walking to the front of the store. He turns to look at her as she turns to look back at him. He smiles, continuing to walk backward, watching her before exiting the store allowing Camille to finish her shopping.

Chapter 14: We're Not Home Alone

Mechanical deer's and spiral Christmas trees cover the massive front lawn of the Bauman's massive four-bedroom residence. Each of the downstairs windows is decorated with Christmas lights and garlands. The roofline is wrapped from end to end with beautiful white lights mirroring most of the homes in the neighborhood. The holiday lights add to a bright glow in the neighborhood. Camille Bauman drives up to her home, where she sees a few cars are already parked outside. Plenty of her guests have arrived earlier than the invitation indicated. Dylan runs outside to help Camille with the bags of wine. "Hey, honey."

Camille exits her car looking at the cars parked alongside her property. "Hey."

"What took you so long?"

"I ran into a friend at the store. I'm sorry."

"Oh, no. Please don't worry about it. It's just that some of your coworkers arrived a little early."

"I'm used to people always trying to be fashionably late. What's the term for arriving early?" Camille stops talking to look at Dylan's sweater. "What are you wearing?"

A very jovial Dylan smiles, standing erect, pulling at the sweater so that Camille can see it. He's wearing a mock neck red sweater that reads HUBBY. "It came in the mail today. I wanted to surprise you. You like it? I got one for you too. It says wifey."

Camille hides her disgust, letting out an uncomfortable laugh. "You got one for me too, huh?"

Dylan laughs from excitement. "Yep. It's cute, isn't it? Hubby and Wifey."

"It's something. Let's get these inside." She hands him a bag of wine and champagne.

"The caterers have everything already set up. It looks great."
I can't wait to see it."

They both enter the house through the side entrance walking into the kitchen. The culmination of holiday music, the smell of the pine tree, and a decorated house make for a wonderful hallmark moment. Isabella, Sebastian, Thomas, Kimberly Oliver, and other friends and coworkers stand around talking. They all cheer at the arrival of Camille. Camille's face lights up at the sight of everyone in her home. Her party, from the start, is a massive success. She walks out to greet her friends. "Hi, guys!"

"There she is.' Thomas yells, pointing at her.

"Hey, girl!" Kimberly yells.

Isabella turns to see Camille, who she hasn't seen in months. She runs up to Camille, screaming as they embrace each other. "It's so good to see you!"

Camille pulls away to look at Isabella. "You look great. I miss you so much."

"I miss you too," Isabella replies as she spins Camille around, checking out her attire and body. "Still keeping that ass tight, I see."

"One hundred crunches and five miles a day."

“You never looked better.”

“Awww. Thank you.”

Kimberly stops in place, pulling her hair out of the way to look down at Camille’s boots. “Bitch, no way. Are those Stuart Weitzman's?”

Camille mocks walking a fashion show runway. “You know your boots.”

“No. I know those boots. You’re ballin!” Kimberly playfully replies.

Camille laughs as she points toward the kitchen. “Have you guys had anything to eat yet?”

Thomas eats crackers and cheese answers with a full mouth. “Oh Yeah. Dylan’s been keeping us filled with food. Don't you worry.”

“Good,” Camille replies, turning to Dylan laughing. “Thanks, Honey!”

“Anything for you, honey.”

Kimberly watches Dylan and Camille, enjoying fabricated marital bliss. “You guys are so cute.”

“Thanks,” Camille replies.

Dylan quickly heads to the bedroom returning with the matching sweater he purchased for Camille expressing immense delight. “Loooook, what I got!”

Camille turns around and fights the urge to retch. She gathers herself, looking up at the happy eyes of her husband, who she wants so desperately to punch in the face at this moment. “Oh.”

Kimberly adds fuel to Camille fire. "OH, MY GOODNESS! THAT IS SO CUTE!"

Everyone from the party hears Kimberly yell. They turn to see what's the commotion. Isabella chimes in. "oh no. That is too cute."

The statements from Kimberly and Isabella only give Dylan the approval he was hoping for from their guest, not knowing how ugly Camille thinks the sweater is. Dylan smiles from ear to ear. "See. They all think it's cute,"

Camille looks around at the smiling guest then back at the sweater putting on the fakest smile only she can put on. "It's nice, honey."

Dylan continues to smile. "Why don't you put it on?"

Camille looks around and notices Thomas standing behind all the guests, hysterically laughing before turning away. He hopes Camille doesn't see him as he holds his stomach, trying to keep food from falling out of his mouth. Camille takes a deep breath, taking the sweater from Dylan. "Sure. Sure thing."
As Camille walks away, she hears Kimberly. "That's going to be so cute. Hubby and wifey."

"Yeah. We should get one." Oliver says. Only ours should read his and hers or something like that."

Kimberly turns to him with a smug smile. "Or soon to be?"

Oliver laughs. "Or that. Yeah."

Isabella walks across the living room over to Thomas by the fireplace. "So, when are we going to meet your new girlfriend?"

"What makes you think I have a new girlfriend?"

"Oh, please stop it. I've heard all about Phoebe. The thick Latina with the juicy lips. I hear everything."

"You girls talk too much. Who told you? Kim?"

"Yep. You're not keeping her a secret, are you?"

"No. Not at all. It's a work in progress."

"Good luck with that. . . Oh!"

Thomas's eyes widen. "What?"

"I also heard that we're all going out for a night on the town in a limo." She playfully dances in place.

"Yes. My crew from North Mutual are going for that night on the town. You quit, remember?"

"What?! Shit. I'm coming whether you like it or not."

"Nah. It's gonna be on a school night. You gotta take care of the kids, remember."

"Babe, he's right. You can't be hanging out all hours of the night." Sabastian says as he leans over listening to their conversation.

Isabella abruptly turns to Sebastian. "Diga otra cosa te doy cocotazo."

Thomas fights laughter as Sebastian smiles, shaking his head. "Seriously?"

Thomas leans closer to Sebastian. "I take it she desperately needs a night out."

"Apparently."

"Don't think you guys are going out without me," Isabella says with absolution.

Thomas continues with the charade. "No, seriously. You can't come."

Isabella starts to believe Thomas and turns around pouting. "Don't be like that. I miss you guys."

"So, hang out with them on your dime."

"Are you seriously going to exclude me?"

Thomas chuckles but senses that her feelings are getting hurt. "Nah... You can come. I was just messing with you."

"Because I heard you're getting a limo and everything."

"Yep. I pick the venue. I pick the night."

"It doesn't matter to me. As long as I get to hang out with my girls."

Camille returns from the bathroom wearing the red Wifey Christmas sweater. Everyone lets out a collective cheer of approval. Dylan stands next to her as some of the guests take photographs of the moment. Camille can see Thomas behind everyone fighting laughter as he covers his face. Oliver whispers to Kimberly. "That shit is tacky."

"No, it's not. It's cute." She replies as Isabella walks over to chime in. "That is so cute."

Ding dong, the doorbell rings. Camille is quick to pull away, walking over to the door to greet her next guest. Monica stands outside with a gift-wrapped bottle. Camille's face lights up at the sight of Monica. "Hey. Merry Christmas."

"Merry Christmas," Monica replies as she hands the bottle to Camille.

"You didn't have to bring anything."

"Nah, boo. It's all good. I remember you saying how much you liked a good Riesling, so I brought you a good one."

Camille is genuinely touched by the thoughtful gesture. "Thank you so much. That was so thoughtful."

"No problem," Monica replies as she looks at Camille's sweater. "That sweater is ugly as fuck, though."

Camille laughs, leaning forward, whispering to Monica. "For the first time EVER, I agree with you."

Monica laughs with Camille. "Then, take that shit off."

"I can't. I'm stuck with it for the night. I'll tell you all about it at work."

Camille shuts the door taking Monica's coat. Monica walks over to Isabella, greeting her and the rest of her coworkers. Camille returns from placing Monica's coat in the bedroom, walking over to Thomas, who makes eye contact with her. He smiles, trying to look away as Camille approaches with her arms folded. "What's so damn funny?"

Thomas continues laughing. "You just got bullied into wearing that hideous sweater. The look on your face was classic."

"You noticed that?"

"Yep. Oddly, no one else did."

"I'm so mad at him right now."

"Whatever. It's Christmas. He just wanted to do something cute."

"I went out and spent time putting together my outfit, and he just bullied me into wearing this shit."

"I say count your losses and call it a day. The party is turning out to be good. Everyone is having a fantastic time. We're all drinking and socializing. Shit. I'd say your party is a huge success."

"Yeah, you could say that."

"You need to relax. Don't let it ruin your night."

"Good luck to that."

Monica sees Thomas over by the fireplace talking to Camille. She walks through several of the party guests until she reaches Thomas. "So, Thomas. You just gonna hide back here."

"Who's hiding?"

"You. You saw me come through the door, and you couldn't come say hi to me?"

"Oh, so you've decided to talk to me now?"

Camille's face lights up from thought as she stands next to Monica and Thomas. "I'll spill something on this hideous thing." She mumbles under her breath, looking down at the sweater before she walks off, leaving them to talk.

"I never wasn't talking to you. I'm not allowed to be upset?" Monica asks Thomas.

"You're allowed to do whatever you want."

"Well, I did."

"Did what?"

"I did whatever I wanted. I got you something."

Monica reaches into her bag to retrieve a small gift-wrapped box handing it to Thomas. Thomas looks at the gift wrap package for a moment. "Why did you do that?"

"Really? You know why?"

Thomas holds the gift looking at her. He extends his arms. "Come here."

Monica walks toward Thomas as he wraps his arms around her kissing her on the cheek, lifting her off the floor. "Merry Christmas."

"Merry Christmas, Tommy."

On the other side of the living room, Isabella leans over to Kimberly, whispering in her ear. "I swear, I think those two are fucking."

"That's is the strangest friendship on the planet. One minute they hate each other, the next minute they're best friends."

"I got something for you too," Thomas says to Monica.

"Are you serious?"

Thomas pulls a small box out of his pocket. "Yep. Here you go."

Back on the other side of the living room, Oliver says to Kimberly and Isabella. "You think that's an engagement ring."

"It better not be," Isabella replies. "He's old enough to be her father."

"It's just a gift. Trust me when I tell you, Monica is like a daughter to him. If not that, then more like a bratty little sister."

Isabelle turns to Kimberly. "Come on. Let's be real. Have you seen the body on Monica?

Kimberly nods, raising her eyebrows. "Yes. She's got the goods."

"There's no way Thomas can miss an ass like that. No black man on the planet can miss an ass like that. Rumor has it that Monica's mother had to have a c section because her ass was so fat."

Kimberly chuckles, covering her mouth with one hand pushing Isabelle's arm. Oliver smiles, shaking his head side to side.

"Ass is so big that she turns all of her panties into thongs. Even the granny period panties. She takes two steps, and they just wedge up there."

Oliver chuckles while Kimberly continues to cover her face fighting the urge to burst out laughing, waving her other hand at Isabella to stop.

"Ass so big that even J-Lo be like, "' Damn girl. You got a fat ass."'

Kimberly can no longer hold the laughter as she burst out hysterical laughing. A few of Camille's guests turn to see Kimberly hysterical, laughing with Isabella and Oliver laughing alongside her.

"Stop it." Kimberly pleads with Isabelle. "I get it." She says as she slowly calms down.

"And let's not forget those breasts."

"Alright, alright, alright. Enough. That's still my girl."

"All I'm saying is no red-blooded man can look away from her body."

"Well, apparently, he can, and he does. She's a pain in the ass, but he loves her and is very protective of her."

"I don't get it," Isabella says, shaking her head side to side.

I don't either, but he trusts her." She says as she turns to Isabella lowering her voice. "Did you know Monica is the only person he talks to about his son?"

"Are you serious?"

"Yeah. If I bring up anything with his son, he changes the subject and gets moody."

"Why would you bring that up?"

"He's my friend. I just want him to know I'm always here."

"If any of my kids died like that, I don't know if I could go on. I mean, that guy tried to kill Thomas, and the bullet struck his son." She says, closing her eyes, taking a deep breath, shaking her head side to side.

"I know. It's tragic. His wife just couldn't take and left him."

"She's a coward."

"I don't know. I hear no marriage is ever really the same after the death of a child."

"Fuck that. You need support. Who are you supposed to lean on?"

Kimberly looks at Isabella and points toward Thomas and Monica. "Your friends."

Isabella says nothing as she acknowledges Kimberly's statement.

"From what I hear from Monica, He even takes her with him to the cemetery."

Isabella's eyes widen as Kimberly does the same nodding her head. "Yep. But don't you ever repeat that. She wasn't supposed to tell me that. It slipped one day, and she freaked out, making me promise that I wouldn't say anything. Oh no. And I just said something."

Isabella looks Kimberly in her eyes. "No. I won't say a word. I promise."

"Ok. Thank you."

"What ever happened to the man that killed Thomas' son?"

"Girl, they found him and two members of his crew in the Harlem River."

"Are you serious?" Isabelle asks as Kimberly nod her head. They both react, turning around as quickly as Camille yells in horror from the Kitchen. "OH SHIT!!!!"

Everyone turns to see what the commotion is as Dylan yells. "Oh, no." Unable to see anything, Kimberly looks side to side to see what's going on. "What happened?"

"Shit. I just spilled red wine all over my sweater. I'm gonna have to soak it to get the stain out."

Kimberly let's out a distressing sound of disappointment. "Oh, noooooo. That's terrible."

"Quick, go to the laundry room and take it off. I'll soak it so that we can get the stain out." Dylan exclaims.

"I'm so sorry, sweetie," Camille replies to Dylan.

"No. It's ok. I'll get it all cleaned up before Christmas."

As Camille walks to the laundry room, she makes eye contact with Thomas, who is quietly laughing with Monica at the mishap. She smirks and keeps walking to the back of her house as the guests all remain in the living room, mingling and enjoying the festive house party. Moments later, Camille returns in her original blouse and maneuvers through her guest mingling and making sure they have enough to eat and drink. She stands at the opening of her living room, watching everyone enjoy themselves. Camille's Christmas party is a massive success.

Chapter 15: The Most Wonderful Time of The Year?

Christmas Eve

Shady Storms Nursing Home has put together a makeshift theater where family members have put together a play for the nursing home residents. Kimberly sits next to her mother, enjoying the show along with the other attendees. The stage is set up like a living room with fake windows. Fake snowflakes fall outside the fake windows. On stage, Oliver is sitting on a sofa reading a book next to a fake fireplace wearing a robe and pajama hat. Justin climbed through the window as the ghost of Christmas past. Justin missteps climbing into the window and falls onto the stage. The makeshift wall and window fall exposing the stagehand tossing the fake snow behind the wall. Oliver covers his face in embarrassment as the audience erupts with laughter. Kimberly looks over at her mother, who laughs just as hard as the other residents. This visit has proven to be a very good visit for Kimberly and her mother.

The twins happily sit beside the gift-filled Christmas tree in their holiday-decorated living room. Sebastian has agreed that everyone can open one gift each. The girls eagerly wait for Sebastian to hand them a gift. Isabella returns from the kitchen sitting next to the girls. One of the girls picks up a small gift marked to Izzy from secret Santa handing it to their mother. Everyone opens one gift. Isabella rips open her gift and turns it around. "Ferris Bueller's day off." She smiles, shaking her head side to side.

Monica sits on her sofa watching television next to Kareem, who has fallen asleep, resting his feet on Monica's lap. She softly removes his feet getting up from the sofa. She walks to her bedroom to retrieve her cell phone. She unlocks the phone to make a phone call

Thomas sits around his kitchen table alone. He takes a drink from a stainless-steel flask, placing it on the table. The flask is engraved "Merry Christmas Homie. Love Monica." Thomas opens his wallet, removing a picture of himself with a little boy with their faces together, looking at the camera laughing. He flips the picture over to see the writing which reads "Elijah and dad at Rye Playland." A tattoo on his arm reads Elijah with dates marking ten years. Thomas looks over at his ringing cell phone to see Monica's name appears on the caller ID screen. He picks up the phone, smiling gradually before the smile fades. He places the phone back on the table, letting the phone ring until the voicemail activates.

Monica ends the call sending a text message *[What up, Playa! Don't forget the condoms when you see ya girl. Peace. Merry Christmas.]* She places the phone down on the night table and returns to the living room where sits next to Kareem to finish watching A Christmas story.

Camille and Dylan attend a Christmas Eve gala at the Country club. Dylan socializes with a few of the male members, leaving Camille standing alone in a red sweetheart tight fitting formal evening gown with a plunging neckline, drinking a glass of white wine. Her hairstyle looks like a 1940's pin-up model. Her bracelets, earrings, and necklace are covered in diamonds. She slowly turns to her left making eye contact with Garrett, who is staring at her. He lifts his left hand, revealing a mistletoe. She smiles from ear to ear, gesturing for him to put it down. He lowers it and walks toward her, standing in front of her, slowly looking her up and down. He wishes her a Merry Christmas before kissing her on the cheek.

Chapter 16: A Plan Starts Coming Together

It's been several months since Oliver and Justin have submitted their financial project to the heads on AUA Japan America in Tokyo, Japan. The owners have put the plan in motion but have been keeping the results close to the chest, leaving Oliver and Justin in the dark. Franklin McDaniel, a senior director of the AUA Japan America office in San Francisco, has scheduled a video chat with Oliver and Justin to give them an update on the status of their budget plan. Oliver sits in the conference room, watching the monitor connect to the San Francisco office. Franklin appears on the screen relaxed, tossing a baseball repeatedly up in the air. Franklin turns to the look at Oliver. "Hey, buddy. How are you?"

"I'm good, man. Just waiting for Justin to join us."

"How's the weather in New York?"

"It's about forty-six degrees right now. How about you guys?"

"It's about seventy-seven."

"The joys of living out west."

"You can say that again. I love the weather out here. The winters back in Chicago were brutal. I'm good with never seeing snow again."

"I heard about those winters in Chicago. Brutal."

Franklin smiles, shaking his head side to side. "You have no idea. I know you guys get your fair share of snowstorms, but you haven't experienced a snowstorm in a big city until you've experienced a Chicago snowstorm."

"Yeah. I'll stick to my New York snow any day."

Franklin moves his eyes over to a document on his desk before looking back into the camera. "Anyway. The reason for this brief meeting. Mr. Yamamoto and Higashi sent me the specs of your budgetary model."

"You already got your hands on that?"

"Yes, Sir."

"I'm nervous to ask, but what are your thoughts?"

"Kid. I don't know how you put all this together, but it works. It really works. My team alone has already seen a thirty percent profit margin. The Tokyo team in Japan has seen a three hundred percent increase through all our entities.

Oliver's eyes widen from the data results. "Get the heck outta here."

"I kid you not, young man. Good work. Expect a call or a visit from the big boys very soon."

"Wow... I'm just... Wow." Oliver laughs, unable to talk.

"All I can say is thank you."

"Why are you thanking me?"

"Are you kidding me? You made my team's job a lot easier. I no longer have to justify our budget, thanks to you."

"Well, since you put it like that, you're very welcome."

"I know the VP of marketing and development are keeping this close to the chest, so I thought you should know. When you make it out here, I gotta take you boys out for a beer or something."

"I may come out for an Angels' game with my girlfriend when they play the Yankees."

"That would be awesome, man. I would love to finally meet you face to face. Just give me a heads up, so I can mark my calendar."

"Will do Franklin. Talk to you soon. And thank you so much for that update."

"Anytime, Oliver. I'll talk to you later."

The transmission ends as the AUA Japan America logo appears on the screen. Oliver stares at the screen smiling from ear to ear with the good news. Justin enters the conference room tossing has a steno pad on the table next to Oliver. "Phew. Looks like I didn't miss anything."

Oliver turns to Justin. "Are you kidding me? You're late."

Justin looks at the screen then at Oliver. "What are you talking about?"

"The call. It just happened. The meeting is over, and you missed it."

Justin sits back in the chair, covering his face. "SHIT!"

Oliver smiles, reaching over to pull Justin's hands away from his face. "Justin. Don't worry about it. I spoke to Franklin, and I have some really good news.

Justin looks at Oliver smiling from ear to ear. He squints his eyes leaning in towards Oliver. “What’s the good news?”

“You and I are about to get some much-earned recognition.”

Chapter 17: What Was I Supposed To Do Again?

A stormy late Saturday afternoon, Isabella is returning home, carrying a few shopping bags from her local neighborhood pharmacy. The kids are off from school next week, and the family is headed to Orlando for a week. While walking home, Isabella remembers something. "OH SHIT! Shit, shit, shit, shit, shit!"

She reaches for her cell phone and calls Benjamin. Isabella stands in the rain listening as the phone rings a few times. Finally, Benjamin answers. "Hello."

"Hi. I'm so so sorry to bother you on your day off."

"It's no problem. I figured it must be important. You never call my cell phone."

I know, and yes. It is important. And again. I am sorry to bother you."

"I accept your apology. So, what's up?"

"The meeting this Monday."

"Yeah."

"The U.S.A. Car rental renewal meeting."

"Uh-huh."

"The meeting I'm supposed to be a part of but can't because of spring break."

"Oh. You mean the important meeting where the clients are flying in to meet you, and you can't be there. Yes. I know the meeting."

"I put together a fifty-two-page packet for the customer, underwriting, and risk management team along with a PowerPoint presentation."

"Yes, I remember. I helped you with that presentation."

"Yeah. I emailed the presentation to Mr. Plante. I printed the documentation, but I left them on my desk. They have not been bound. They need a clear cover in the front with the black backing. I have all the material on my desk."

"Shit. It sounds like a massive problem."

Isabella's body language drop as she takes a deep breath. "All of our office assistants were all in a meeting and were unable to get to it. I forgot to put in a request for someone else to do it."

"What are you gonna do?"

"I have a huge favor to asks."

"Of who, me?"

Isabella bites her lip, wishing she had another option. "Yes."

"Ok, what?"

"Sigh. I need you to go into the office... and put them together for me."

"Are you serious?"

Isabella shuts her eyes, covering her face knowing she's asking a lot. "I know. I know what I'm asking is big. But I'm fucked if those pamphlets are not ready for that meeting on Monday."

"Ugh."

"I know. I'm sorry to asks. Look. I will make it up to you when I come back."

"Yeah, right.?

"No, seriously. Lunch for a week is on me?"

"You gotta do better than that. Who wants to go into work on a Saturday? It's pouring
out."

Isabella understands that she is asking a lot of a person on a rainy Saturday for something that was her responsibility. She slowly starts to walk back to her house. "I know. I don't know what I was thinking. I was desperate, and you were the only person I could think of that I trust. I know you're probably with your family and... I'm sorry."

The phone is filled with silence as she continues to walk towards the house. "So that's it. You gonna just give up?" Benjamin asks.

"It's my mess. I'm sorry I even called."

"Jeez. You're such a quitter."

Isabella looks defeated as she walks to the front of her house. "I gotta go. I'll see you when I get back."

"Ok. Enjoy your trip. But wait. Before you hang up."

"What?"

"Ask me where I am right now?"

"You have really odd timing."

"No, seriously, ask me where I am right now?"

"Sigh. Where are you right now, Benjamin?"

"I'm sitting at your desk."

"What? What do you mean?"

"I saw that you didn't get that done. So I took the kids to their friend's house, got my oil
changed then came in to get this done."

Isabella stands outside in amazement. She lifts her head, looking up in the raining sky when she asks. "Are you serious?"

"Yep. I'm looking at a picture of you and your family at a Nets game.

Isabella continues listening, standing in the rain, speechless.
"Hey, you still there?" He asks, waiting for a response.

"You are fucking amazing."

"This, I know." Benjamin laughs

"Thank you so much. You're a great friend."

"Well, I try. Oh, and I will be collecting on those lunches."

"I'd be more than happy to buy you lunch."

"Um no. Lunches. Plural. Not lunch."

Isabella playfully smiles. "Yes. Lunches."

“Ok, good. Now go be with your family and enjoy the trip. I wanna wrap this up."

"Yes, Sir. Thank you, Benjamin."

"You’re welcome."

Isabella ends the call staring at the phone, smiling, shaking her head before she trots upstairs, entering her home.

Chapter 18: Wine Does Apparently Get Better with Age.

That evening at the home of Camille and Dylan Bauman in Massapequa, NY, the rain has become increasingly heavy. Dylan is packed and ready to go away on a business trip with two coworkers who wait outside in their car. Camille kneels on a chair, looking out the window. "They're here, honey."

Dylan runs down the stairs. "Ok. Lemme just grab my shoes."

Camille points beyond the kitchen. "I put them in the mudroom."
"Thanks, sweetie."

Dylan runs to the mudroom putting on the shoes before grabbing his raincoat. Camille is at the front door waiting for him with his luggage. He trots over to the front door, kissing her and taking the luggage. "Thanks, babe. I'll be back on Thursday."

"Ok. Have a safe trip."

"Love you."

"Love you too."

Dylan exits their home walking down to the car while Camille watches from the open door. He gets in the car and drives off, waving to Camille, who waves back. The car drives up the road passing a Black Maserati parked in the street. Camille closes and locks the front door walking to the kitchen where she opens the refrigerator. She removes a bottle of wine and reaches into the cupboard for a wine glass when she hears a knock at the door. She places everything down on the countertop and walks to the front door. "Dodo. He must have forgotten something."

Camille opens the front door to Garrett, standing in front of her. The shock of Garrett standing in front of her standing in the rain leaves Camille speechless. She opens her mouth to gasp as Garrett takes two steps into the house, closing the door behind him. He picks her up, kissing her passionately. Camille's attempt to resist fades immediately as she wraps her arms and legs around Garrett. He carries her to the living room and places her on the sofa, where they continue to embrace each other while passionately kissing. He lays her back onto the sofa removing her shorts and tank top while he removes his shirt. Still kissing Garrett, she moves her hands down to unbuckle his pants. They continue kissing before making love.

Chapter 19: So, You Guys Really Like Me.

A year passes, and we find ourselves in the middle of May at North Mutual Insurance Company. Kimberly and Oliver's relationship has grown to a full-blown stage five love connection. Their love for each other seems to grow more and more every day. They are constantly on the phone together. Weekend trips have become a biweekly ritual. When together, Oliver never walks anywhere without holding Kimberly's hand. Oliver can't get enough of her stolen kisses as she feels the same. To say that they are a match made in heaven is an understatement.

Kimberly sits at her desk, reading emails while on her office phone talking to Oliver. She looks around to see if anyone is watching her chat gleefully on the phone. "I know, baby. I can't believe it's been a year already."

"Time flies when you're having this much fun."

"It has been fun, hasn't it? I can't wait to see you tonight."

"I'm already doing sit-ups getting ready for you tonight, girl."

"Nasty." Kimberly laughs.

"Yeah. After that, I'm gonna do some Jumping jacks. It's going down tonight, girl. I'm not taking you out to dinner or anything. We're heading right to the bedroom."

"Okay, good. I'm gonna do some crunches after this call to get ready myself." She plays along when she sees Camille walking towards her desk with a look of intensity on her face. "Let me call you back."

"Alright."

Camille stands at the door, making eye contact with Kimberly. "Hey. We need you in the conference room right now."

"Why? What's going on? And who's we?

Camille turns around, walking away toward the conference. Kimberly stands up and walks toward the conference room, passing Monica's desk. "Do you know what's going on in the conference room?"

"You trippin if you think anybody tells me anything," Monica replies.

"Kimberly continues to the conference room as she walks past Thomas's desk. Thomas is on the phone but makes eye contact with Kim covering the receiver, whispering. "What's up?"

"Conference room. I have to go there."

"What for?"

Kimberly shrugs her shoulders and continues to the conference room. She enters the conference room where Harry Goldfarb and Ronald Parella are sitting with Camille at the very end of the conference room table. Harry Goldfarb smiles, waving Kimberly in. "Kimberly. Come in. Come in. Grab a seat."

"Yes, sir." She replies as she looks over at Camille, who remains poker-faced. She looks back at Mr. Goldfarb.

"Kimberly. I'm gonna cut right to the chase and tell you that we love your work and dedication. Saying that you are an asset to our organization is an understatement."

Kimberly smiles, remaining poised as she looks over at Camille, who is now smiling. "Thank you, sir,"

"We've had an organizational change, which I'm sure you're aware of."

"Yes. O'Connor has taken an indefinite leave of absence." Kimberly replies.

"Correct. Ronald and I have been talking about moving you up to the position of manager for some time now."

Kimberly takes a deep breath, fighting excitement. "Thank you. It's what I've been striving for."

Harry looks over to Ronald. "But with O'Connor stepping down, we have a hole that needs to be filled."

"We think that you would be the best candidate to fill that spot," Ronald interjects as he takes over.

"Please don't take it that since O'Connor stepped down that now, we're recognizing you. That's not the case. We just realized that you would be a better fit for a regional manager."

"I'm, I'm speechless, sir."

"Speechless or not, you're going to have to tell us whether you want this position or not," Harry replies.

"I can tell you right now that I would be more than happy to accept this new position."

"Obviously, there will be a pay increase, company phone, corporate card. All of that stuff that's trivial right now. But yes, those are perks."

"I am ready for this endeavor, and I'd like to thank you both for this opportunity."

Harry smiles, looking at Kimberly. "No. Thank you. If we had two more with your work ethic, we'd never have to come in."

"Congratulations," Camille adds.

Kimberly takes a deep breath. "Thank you. Thank you so much."

"See my secretary in the morning. She'll let you know which office you will be occupying."

"Ok. Will do. And again, thank you so much for having faith in me."

Kimberly stands up, calmly exiting the conference room, and walks to Thomas's office. Thomas sits quietly, watching a surveillance video from a property damage claim on his computer screen. He looks up at Kimberly. "Hey."

Kimberly shuts the door behind her and sits down, covering her face with both hands.
Her eyes fill with tears. "I'm at a loss for words."

"What happened? Why are you crying?"

"These are tears of Joy. I've just been promoted to regional manager."

"Oh. Yeah, I heard about that. Congratulations."
Thomas stands up, walking over to Kimberly, hugging her. Monica can see their interaction from her desk. Kimberly pulls away. "You knew?"

"I'm SIU. I pretty much know everything."

Monica opens the door to Thomas's office. "I saw yall hugging through the glass. What happened?"

Kimberly turns to Monica. "You're so nosey."

"I know. So, what happened?"

Kimberly points to herself. "There is a new regional manager in the office."

"Really! Are you serious?"

"Oh Yeah, baby."

"So. You know we're gonna have to celebrate, right."

Thomas smiles at Kimberly. "I know it's been a long time coming, but I'm still planning our limo escapade. No time like the present."

Monica is startled by a vibrating notification coming from her cell phone. She reaches into her bra to grab her cell phone. She smiles while reading a text message. "Oh shit." Kimberly and Thomas look at each other as Monica starts to blush. She replies to the message stuffing the phone back in her bra, turning back to Kimberly. "Ok. Sorry about that. What were you saying?"

Thomas points at Monica's breast about to inquire about the nature of her text message when he decides not to and continues with the night out. "I'm still in the planning stage of our night out. Details to follow."

"Yeah, you're taking forever with this. Hopefully, Kimberly's promotion will light a fire under your ass."

Kimberly points at Monica, looking at Thomas. "She might be on to something, Thomas. Start planning. I can't have you paying for parties once I become your boss. You know... nepotism and all."

"Thomas shakes his head in agreement. "I'll get right on it, boss."

Kimberly stands up to exit his office. She stops and thinks about Thomas's statement. She looks back at him, pointing. "Boss. I like that. Especially coming from you. You can call me that from now on."

"Sure. Get out of my office, boss."

Kimberly's smile fades. "See. Now you're on my bad side. Three strikes, young man."

Thomas smiles, rolling his eyes. "Whatever, Kimmy."

Kimberly guides Monica out the door. "And you. I'm gonna need you to get my coffee in the morning."

"Bitch, you buggin." Monica fires back

Kimberly stops in place, staring at Monica. "Oh no, you didn't."

Monica jovially turns around, quickly hugging Kimberly. "I'm just playing, girl."

Kimberly gives Monica the side-eye as Monica continues to playfully hug Kimberly. "Girl, trust me. I'll get you whatever you want. You want a coffee with Boston Kreme, right?"

Kimberly laughs. "See. That's why you're my girl. And yes, Boston Kreme would be great in the Morning with sprinkles."

"Sprinkles? They don't put sprinkles on Boston Kreme Donuts."

"Then, you better get down to the supermarket, pick up some sprinkles, and put it on the donut for me if you wanna keep this job."

"Oh, so it's like that now?"

"You're damn right. Get back to work." Kimberly replies, playfully smacking Monica's rear end.

Thomas shakes his head, watching the exchange between Monica and Kimberly. As they get completely out of view, Thomas switches the screen to the website for the Full Mune Night club. Full Mune Club is a nightclub where the men and women wait staff dress with very little clothing. He books a reservation for a private VIP room for his group of coworkers. On the second screen is a website for a limousine company. Thomas adds his credit card, securing a super stretch Lincoln Navigator. Next, he composes an invite email titled "A night to remember" to Camille, Kimberly, Jessica, and Monica."

Chapter 20: Two Birds. One Stone. Different Result.

Two days later, Oliver and Justin sit an office away from each other on the 36th floor at AUA Japan America. Their building is located on the Avenue of the Americas in midtown Manhattan. Oliver looks over a file while Justin tosses crumpled paper on a toy basketball hoop hanging over his trash can. Their boss Mr. Hamilton rushes into Justin's office, startling Justin. "Hey, I was just working on. . ."

"Justin." Mr. Hamilton Interrupts Justin mid-sentence.

"Yes, sir."

"Please tell me you have a blazer and a tie somewhere in this office."

"I do. It's been sitting in my --"

"Good. Put it on." Mr. Hamilton demands with a sense of urgency.

"Why?"

"Dammit, just put it on. Mr. Yamamoto and Mr. Higashi are on their way here now."

Justin waste no time as he makes a mad dash to his closet, grabbing his suit. "Shit."

Mr. Hamilton walks over to Oliver's office, storming in. "Hey, Oliver."

"Mr. Hamilton. How are y – "

"Do you have a suit?" Mr. Hamilton interrupts again with urgency.

"Yeah, I have a whole – "
"Do you have the suit here in the office?

"Yeah. I do."

"Good. Put it on. Mr. Yamamoto and Mr. Higashi are on their way here now."
"Ah, shit."

Oliver and Justin shut the doors to their offices, putting on their suits. They sit in their office watching through the glass as Mr. Yamamoto and Mr. Higashi are escorted through the office with an entourage. Mr. Hamilton breaks away from the entourage and asks Oliver and Justin to meet in the Mount Fuji conference room. Oliver reaches for his cell phone, sending a text to Kimberly. *[I think this is it. The heads of the company have come to meet with Justin and I. Wish me, luck babe.]* Oliver and Justin walk into the conference room, sitting on the large marble top table. Mr. Yamamoto and Mr. Higashi sit at the other end of the conference room table, very serious. Oliver looks at both of them and finds it difficult to gauge if this is going to be a good meeting or not. A petite young Japanese woman in a tan business suit sits beside Mr. Yamamoto and Mr. Higashi. "Mr. Yamamoto and Mr. Higashi are very happy to be here and meet the two of you."

"We are happy to meet you both as well," Oliver replies.

"Yeah. The pleasure is all ours." Justin adds.

Mr. Higashi says something in Japanese as the young woman listens to translate. She turns toward Justin and Oliver. "Mr. Higashi says that your budgetary model far exceeds the original projections. Your projections estimated that our income would increase three times the previous year when, in fact, it has increased over seven times last year's income revenue."

Another young Japanese woman walks over to Oliver and Justin, handing them a monthly breakdown of the monthly income financial report for the Japanese market. Oliver and Justin look over the figures before looking at each other in shock and smile. Oliver turns to Mr. Yamamoto and Mr. Higashi. "Honestly, we had hoped for this outcome, but we had to project the cost of material and overhead. Franklin McDaniel of our San Francisco office gave us the figures for the U.S. market. But this is our first time seeing the Japanese profit margin. I think it safe to say; we're pretty shocked."

"The numbers don't lie." The Japanese woman replies.

"We spent a few months working on every contingency before we presented the draft to you all," Oliver says, addressing both men.

The Japanese woman interprets back to Mr. Higashi, who says something to her in Japanese. She translates back to Oliver and Justin. "Mr. Higashi thanks you."

"You're welcome, sir," Oliver replies.

Mr. Yamamoto says a lot in Japanese while smiling. Oliver and Justin carefully observe his body language before looking at each other, smiling. Justin playfully kicks Oliver under the table as the Japanese woman turns to Oliver and Justin. "Mr. Yamamoto and Mr. Higashi would like to know if you are married."

Oliver looks across the table with a look of confusion. He answers. "No. We're not married."

"Do you have children?"

Justin laughs looking back at the Japanese woman. "We definitely don't have any children."

“Mr. Yamamoto and Mr. Higashi would like you both to come and work at our headquarters in Tokyo. You would be in charge of the entire division.”

“Yes,” Justin replies without hesitation. Oliver processes the information but is unable to answer as he forces an uncomfortable laugh. “Wait. Um.”

The Japanese woman begins to give bullet points. “If you are concerned about your salary, you shouldn't be. There will be a substantial salary increase. We will furnish you with an apartment at the company's expense. Any travel to and from the United States to take care of personal matters will be handled by the company directly.

Justin leans in whispering to Oliver. “Just say yes.”

Oliver thinks for a second before sitting up in his chair. “Wait. So, how long would we have to work in Japan.”

“Indefinitely. Also, if you own property such as a home, we will purchase that from you and sell it so that you don't have to worry about those details.”

A shocked Oliver doesn't answer as Justin leans in to whisper again. “Dude. What’s the problem?”

The Japanese woman leaves very little time for Oliver to think. “This is an offer that they are seeking an answer for right now. Once we leave here, our next stop will be to our Chicago office to speak with members of our acquisitions team before we head home tomorrow evening.”

Oliver’s mind races as he thinks about Kimberly. He thinks about the long hours he put in trying to make this day a reality. He looks over at Justin, who is having a tough time processing why he hasn’t answered yet. He takes a deep breath. “Yes. I accept.”

The Japanese woman speaks Japanese to Mr. Yamamoto and Mr. Higashi. They both smile, shaking their heads in approval before they reply to her in Japanese. She turns back to Oliver and Justin, smiling. "Mr. Yamamoto and Mr. Higashi express their gratitude and welcome you to our team in Japan. Mr. Akagi will remain behind and provide you with paperwork for you to complete to make this transition as easy as possible."

Mr. Yamamoto and Mr. Higashi walk over to Oliver and Justin, shaking their hands. Justin gleefully shakes their hand, even throwing in a hug for good measure. Oliver turns around, slowly walking back to his office. Once in the office, he walks to the window staring at the New York City skyline. Shortly thereafter, Justin follows Oliver to his office, opening the door. "Dude. How awesome is this?"

"How the fuck am I going to tell Kimberly? I just made a decision that completely ends our relationship."

"Oh, come on. You can ask her to come along. She'd be a fool not to come. You both love each other. No way you guys break up for this. You did the right thing. Plus, we'll be making a truckload of money and not paying any rent. All that hard work paid off."

Oliver falls back into his office chair, continuing to look out the window. Justin can only think of the opportunity and not how Oliver is feeling. "Buddy. Come on. Did our hard work bear fruit? Yes! This is far better than what we imagined. We worked our asses off, and it paid off. We're heading up the entire division."

"I can't talk right now. Can you just go and close the door?

"You're throwing me out of your office?"

"No. I just need a moment to process what just happened. It's not you, man. I agree. We did a phenomenal job with this project, but in one brief moment, I just ended my relationship."

"How do you know that? What if she considers a long-distance relationship?

"St. Louis is long distance. This is halfway across the globe."

"You never know, man."

Oliver stands up and walks out of the office. "I gotta get outta here.

"Wait. Where ya going?"

Oliver grabs his sport coat from the coat rack and exits the office.

Later that evening. Kimberly sits curled up in the corner of the sofa in her living room, checking emails on her smartphone. She looks up for a moment to view the TV for today's birthdays on access Hollywood. On the kitchen table, there is a large bag filled with Chinese food from a recent delivery. Kimberly waits for Oliver to stop by, so they can have dinner together and watch her favorite reality show, The Voice. The doorbell rings, and Kimberly eagerly trots over to the door to let Oliver in. She opens the door and smiles, opening her arms, embracing him with a massive hug. Oliver hugs her back. She kisses him lovingly on the lips.

"Hey, babe."

"Hey, Kim."

Kimberly pulls him into the apartment. "Soo. You gonna tell me about your meeting?"

"Yeah."

"So, what happened?"

They both walk to the living room. She sits in the middle of the sofa, and he remains standing. Oliver takes a deep breath. "Well." He pauses as he struggles to find the right way to tell her about his day.

"Babe. Why don't you sit down?"

"I'm good right now."

Kimberly half-smiles squinting her eyes as her women's intuition kicks in, sensing something is mildly off about Oliver. "Is everything ok?"

"Uhhh." He starts pacing.

Kimberly ignores her gut, thinking that something out of the ordinary must have happened, and he's just thinking of a great way to tell her the story. She playfully smiles, grabbing his hand. "Just tell me. Whatever it is, it can't be that bad."

"All the work I put into this project."

"Yeah."

"It paid off tenfold."

Kimberly's face lights up. "Baby, that's great!"

"You are looking at the new Director of offshore manufacturing."

Kimberly's jaw drops. "Are you fucking kidding me?"

"No. I got the promotion on the spot."

Kimberly rushes him leaping into his arms. "I AM SO PROUD OF YOU!"

"Thanks, baby."

Kimberly smothers him with kisses to his face as she remains in his arms. "That's phenomenal news. What were you so worried about?"

"The position's in Tokyo."

Kimberly stops kissing him, pulling her face away. "As in Japan?"

"Yeah. Tokyo, Japan."

"Pacific Ocean Japan?"

"Yes. That Japan"

Kimberly slowly drops her legs to the floor. "What are you going to do?"

Oliver doesn't answer.

"Oliver. Are you thinking about taking it?"

"I start in two weeks."

"TWO WEEKS?!"

Oliver looks into her eyes. "Yeah. I had no choice, baby."

Kimberly stands quietly in shock with her mouth open, continuing to look in his eyes.

"One minute, they were praising me. The next, they were pretty much demanding that we start in two weeks. They had already planned this. They have everything ready for me to start."

"How long do you have to do this?"

"Indefinitely."

Kimberly sits on the sofa, keeping eye contact with Oliver. "And what about us?"

"I had to make a split decision and –"

"And you chose that job over us?"

"No. No no no no no..."

"Yes. Yes, you did."

"I thought that you might want to come to live with me."

"I'M NOT MOVING TO JAPAN! WHAT ABOUT MY MOTHER?!"

Oliver's eyes bolt left to right, thinking while mumbling. "Shit."

"You didn't think about that, did you? Plus, I just made regional manager. I busted my ass to get that position."

"I know, baby. I know."

"You don't know shit. I love you, and I thought we were in this for the long haul. I don't want to sound presumptuous, but that was what I was hoping for."

"Babe. You know I love you."

"Not more than this job, apparently."

"I love you more than words can describe."

"Oh, please. Words? Actions just spoke much louder."

"I just wanted us to figure this out. I'm not ending our relationship."

"You ended us when you agreed to go to Japan."

"Baby. I had to make a decision right then and there. I couldn't say no."

"But, you could say no to us, though."

"Kimmy. I'm begging you to try to be rational and just think with me."

"I am thinking rationally. And the thought of you going four thousand miles away... I can't even talk right now."

"It's over six thousand miles."

Kimberly leans her head to the side, looking up at Oliver with discontent. "Now is not the time to correct me." She takes a deep breath stroking her face with her hands. "I can't even cry right now. I'm just so upset."

Oliver sits next to Kimberly, which strikes a nerve. "No! You didn't want to sit down when you came in. Don't sit next to me now. Get up."

"Kimmy. Come on."

"Get up!"

Oliver complies, standing up in front of her.

"Baby. Please don't be like this. I can fly back here, and you can come to see me."

Kimberly's body language drops as she exhales. She appears defeated, and he can see the effect this is taking on her. She shakes her head, looking away from him.

"Oliver... This is not like our weekend trips. Flying down to Florida can get a bit overbearing if you do it too often. We've flown to San Francisco and San Diego, and when I got back, it was enough. Japan is a whole other beast."

"I'm sure we can think of something."

Tears flow down Kimberly's face as she drops her head into her hands. "Oh, Oliver."

Watching Kimberly cry feels like a knife being pushed through his heart. His eyes fill with tears. "Kimberly. Please let's just think about this. I'm sure you and I can come up with something."

"I'm doing my best to see this through your eyes. But I gotta say, When I look at me through your eyes, I see love. I can feel it. You taking this job doesn't feel like you love me. That may sound selfish and fucked up, but it's how I feel. If the tables were turned... I would have said no. And I know that might make me stupid, but I felt like we were going somewhere. I guess I was wrong."

"I don't have to take the job, baby."

"You should have done that already. I don't want you resenting me later."

"I wouldn't resent you."

Kimberly looks up at Oliver. "Yeah. You would. Do me a favor and just go."

"What?"

"Go. Get out. Go home."

"Are you seriously throwing me out?"

Kimberly stands up, walking to the door. "Yeah."
Oliver stands in front of Kimberly, blocking her. "Baby. I love you so much. You know that, right?"

"I do. I honestly know that you love me. But still, I need you to go."

"Baby. Don't do th–"

"Please. Just go. Just fucking go."

"I can't go."

"I wish you would have said that to your bosses."

"Baby... Please don't do this to us."
Kimberly opens the door, guiding him out. "I didn't do this to us. You did this to us."
"Kimmy."

"Good night."

Kimberly closes the door in Oliver's face. He stands outside of her door for a few minutes leaning his head against the door. Inside, Kimberly cries as she leans her back on the door. She gathers herself for a moment to walk over to the TV, turning it off. She walks through the apartment, shutting off the lights before walking into her bedroom. Kimberly calmly lays on the bed, getting under the covers. She reaches for the lamp on the night table shutting off the lights. She cries herself to sleep alone in the dark.

Chapter 21: Going Through The Motions

There are a handful of days that people in relationships dread. The day their significant other dies is, by far, one of the worst fears to experience in a normal loving relationship. The other is the days following a breakup. If you have no real life, you can luckily suffer alone. Lock yourself in the house eating ice cream listening to sad breakup songs. You can ignore the phone, stay in bed all day, cry alone in ways you never want anyone to witness, or hurt yourself. Kimberly is extremely emotional at this moment, but thankfully she is very levelheaded. But levelheaded or not, she is fighting her urge to just fall apart.

Early Friday morning at North Mutual Insurance Group, Monica sits at her desk talking on the telephone. Kimberly swiftly walks through the office towards her office, wearing sunglasses. Monica continues her conversing on the phone while watching Kimberly walk to her office. "Ok. So, you're sure? Tonight? Ok. I'll see you then. Bye"

Monica ends her call, locks her PC, and trots over to Kimberly's new office. She taps on the door popping her head into the office. "What up, Boss? You ready for tomorrow. Limo ride to the city like ballers yo!"

Kimberly stares at her computer screen, not saying anything to Monica. Monica takes a step into the office. "Kimmy?"

Kimberly still stares blankly at the screen. She appears to be daydreaming as Monica enters the office, tapping on the desk. "YO!"

Kimberly jumps, looking up at Monica. "What?"

"You trippin or something?"

"Why? What? What are you talking about??"

"I'm standing right here, and you're locked on the screen." Monica looks at the screen with nothing on it. "Are you ok?"

"Sorry. I'm just not... feeling well."

"Are you sick with the hustle or something? Cause tomorrow it's gonna be poppin, girl!"
"Yes," she replies while turning to the computer screen. She turns on the computer and continues staring at the screen. Monica leans in to see what she's looking at. "Yo. What's up with you today?"

"I'm really not myself today."

"What's the matter?"

Kimberly looks up at Monica, staring into her eyes for a brief moment. She contemplates regurgitating the events of her evening with Oliver. "I think I'm getting my period or something."

"Nah. Can't be. We're in sync. We had it two weeks ago."

"Or something."

"What's something?"

"I'm crampy and moody. I just figured it might be that. I don't know. I'm just off today."

"Ok. Well, you did see the email from Thomas, right? We're going out tomorrow."

Kimberly's attention drifts as her cell phone vibrates from a call. She digs through her purse, searching for her phone. "If I still feel like this, I may not go."

"Oh, yes, you will go. He's been planning this for a while. And he wants to celebrate your promotion. You have to go."

Kimberly continues digging through her purse. "I-I-I don't know. We'll see." She retrieves her cell phone from her purse, looking at the screen. The caller ID reads Oliver. She swipes the screen sending the call to voicemail.

"Are you sure you're ok?" Monica asks.

Kimberly still appears distracted as she looks away from Monica. "Yeah. I'm fine. I wanna just get through the day and go home. I just need some rest, I guess. I dunno."

Monica finds her behavior unusual but can't figure out what's wrong with Kimberly.

"You're acting straaaannnge right now. I'm gonna go back to my desk. If you need me for anything. Just call me."

Monica turns around to walk out of the office.

"Ok. Oh, and close the door behind you. Please?"

"Yes, Boss."

Monica walks out of her office, passing Camille as she heads to Kimberly's office. "Is she in there?"

"Yeah, but she's acting a little. . . " Monica gestures that she's crazy

"Hmmm. Let me go check on her."

"Good luck with that."

Camille walks up to Kimberly's office, looking through the glass. Kimberly holds her desk phone to her ear. Camille gestures that she will come by later. As Camille walks away, Kimberly places the handset down, hanging up the phone. She sits at her desk with her head in her hands.

Lunchtime that Friday afternoon before Memorial Day weekend. Benjamin and Isabella take a walk during their lunch break, heading toward Battery Park on a beautiful clear sunny day. Park-goers listen to a Big band jazz group dressed in 1940's apparel. The band plays the instrumental for *Boogie Woogie bugle boy from Company B* as several choreographed dancers put on a show for the crowd. Benjamin and Isabella stand to the side, enjoying the show. Benjamin looks down at Isabella's shoes as she taps her feet, moving to the music. He looks up at her face and smiles. She shakes her head side to side. "Whatever you're thinking of doing, don't!"

Benjamin grabs her hand, and spontaneously pulls her in with the other dancers. "Come on."

"Mother fucker. NO!"

Benjamin keeps pulling her while grabbing her other hand from her face. "It'll be fun."

"I don't know how to dance to this."

"Yeah, right. You're Latin. Just follow my lead."
Isabella gets out of her comfort zone and dances with Benjamin. She tries to follow along with his dance steps but is unaware of 1940's swing dancing. She smirks, looking at Benjamin. "I swear to – Payback is gonna a bitch."

"Just dance with me. It'll be fun."

Her reluctance turns to a good time. Benjamin spins her around, mocking what the other dances are doing until they look like they are apart of the show. Isabella catches on quickly, having a great time.

The song ends, and the onlookers applaud the band, the dancers along with Benjamin and Isabella. An embarrassed Isabella covers her face. Benjamin takes a bow and points to Isabella. "MY LOVELY PARTNER! ISABELLA!"

"Shut up."

Benjamin laughs hysterically as they walk away from the crowd. "Yo. That was awesome." Yells Monica, who stands in front of Isabella and Benjamin with Thomas.

"Yeah. I didn't know you could dance like that." Thomas adds.

Isabella stands shocked and speechless. She gathers herself from shock. "Uh. Oh. Hi guys. W-w-what are you doing here?"

"I didn't know she could do that either," Benjamin adds.

Thomas and Monica look at Benjamin then back at Isabella.

"Oh. This is my coworker Benjamin."

Benjamin extends his hands to Thomas and Monica. Thomas smirks, extending his hand to Benjamin. "Hey, man. I'm Thomas. And this is Monica. We're old co-workers of Izzy."

Monica jovially extends her left-hand shaking Benjamins' hand next. She tilts his hand, exposing his wedding ring, raising her eyebrow. "Hi. Wow. That's a nice wedding ring."

Thomas shakes his head, laughing as Monica looks over at Isabella.

"Really?" Isabella replies, staring at Monica seriously.

Benjamin looks at his ring. "You know. The way the gold glistens of my skin really brings out the gold. You're right. I mean... look at it."

Thomas burst out laughing, finding Benjamin's sarcasm right up his alley. "I don't know, man. There's something very distinguishing about a man in a wedding band in the spring."

"Thomas, Benjamin, and Monica laugh like old friends as Isabella continues to stare at Monica with rage. She looks over at Thomas seriously as Thomas gestures for her to lighten up slightly, shaking his head side to side. "What are you guys doing here?" Isabella asks

"Watching you pop that ass, girl." Monica quips.

Isabella smiles, wagging her finger side to side. "There was no popping."

"Well, you didn't see that ass from where we were standing. Right, Thomas?" Monica elbows Thomas.

"BA-BLAM!!" Thomas playfully replies as he imitates Isabella's movements from moments ago.
Isabella and Benjamin bust out, laughing together with Thomas and Monica for a brief moment.

Thomas interrupts their laughter. "So, Izzy."

"Yeah. What's up?"

"You did get my email about tomorrow, right? Because I didn't get a response."

"Oh Yeah. No rules Saturday."

"Ok, good. We start at Seven tomorrow. I'll text you with more details tomorrow."

"Ok, cool. This is going to be so much fun."

"Hell yeah. wait until you see the limo."

"I can't wait."

"Great. Well, we gotta go pick up lunch."

"Yeah. These bitches hear that we're going to Dragon Gold, and they all start with that bullshit. 'Can you buy me a wonton soup? Can you buy me a number six with no onions?' I know, I'm half Asian, but I'm not the fucking delivery girl." Monica adds.

"Well, next time, don't yell across the office. 'Thomas. Do you want Dragon gold?'"

"Yeah. I said, 'THOMAS.' I didn't say, 'hey, everyone.' I'm so sick of that shit."

Isabella laughs at Monica. "It's the same shit across corporate America."

"That's why I just walk out of the office. I don't say shit." Thomas points at Monica.

Monica rolls her eyes. "You're just shady."

"No. It's called living and learning. Something you never do."

"Whatever."

"Anyway, I've gotta take baby here to get a bottle. Benjamin. Nice meeting you, man."

"Same here. Nice meeting you both."

Isabella hugs Thomas and Monica. "See you guys tomorrow."

Thomas and Monica walk off when Monica turns around. "And bring a change of shoes."

"Will do. Bye, guys."

Isabella and Benjamin walk in the other direction as Monica and Thomas head to Dragon Gold.

"Your ex-coworkers seem really cool."

Isabella's smile fades. "I'm gonna slap the shit outta her tomorrow."

"Whoa. What the hell?"

"She had a lot of nerve pointing out your wedding ring like that. It's like she was implying something."

"Yeah, that my ring was nice. What's the matter with you?"

"Stop being funny for once, Ben."

"Why would I do that?"

"Because I need you to be serious for a second."

"I'm at lunch. I refuse to be serious. You can do that by yourself."

"Sometimes, you get on my nerves," Isabella says as she turns around, walking away from Benjamin. Benjamin remains at the park to listen to the band play more music as Isabella walks about fifty feet before she stops walking to turns around looking for Benjamin. As the band plays music, Benjamin is imitating the dance from a famous TV show where the character dances to Tom Jones. She observes him dancing, fighting the urge to smile. As she continues to watch, she finds it hard not to laugh. She laughs and walks back to him, tapping him on the shoulder. "Really?"

"What?"

"You look like a fool."

"I figure you could stay serious for both of us. I would just stay out here and enjoy myself."

"What's that supposed to mean?"

Benjamin stops dancing. "You take yourself so seriously all the time. I've known you for a year now. And it sometimes seems like you haven't learned anything from me."

"Are you trying to say I'm not fun?

"Not at all. When we hang out, you're loads of fun. Why do you think I like hanging out with you? My oldest is like you. Always serious about everything. Takes everything so seriously. So, I have to be silly all the time to make her relax."

"Maybe she's driven. And she's focused on –"

"She's nine, Izzy. Gimme a break. Nine-year-olds should be playing and having fun."

"Fine. You might have a point."

"Every time I do something stupid, you're so serious until the end result makes you laugh. I have a one hundred percent success rate. You need to go with the flow."

Isabella listens carefully while he talks.

"Right now, you're thinking. I can see it in your eyes. Just stop. Your little friend with the wedding ring comment. Who cares? It was funny. Your other friend made fun of it, and it's over."

"I just don't like what she may have been implying."

"What could she imply? We haven't done anything wrong. If people see a man and woman laughing, it's a sin. I haven't done shit wrong."

"Ok, so did you ever tell your wife that you spent the whole day with me."

"Fuck no. Are you insane?

Isabella burst out laughing hysterically.

"That would be suicide. But still. We haven't done anything."

"But then you're being a hypocrite."

"Nope. I'm airing on the side of caution. Very big difference."

Isabella smiles while looking at Benjamin. "You're so full of shit."

"I know." Benjamin laughs as they both start to walk back toward the office.

"So, what would your wife say if she found out you hang out with me as much as you do."

"I don't know. And I don't want to know. That's how I find the time to relax. I don't think about that shit. I especially don't tell her I dislocated my finger on a coworker's ass."

"Point taken."
"Oh, and again. Thanks for that."

"You don't always have to thank me for that."

"Speak for yourself."

They walk one city block before coming across a hot dog stand. "Would you like a hot dog?" Isabella asks.

"I most certainly would."

"It's on me."

"Damn right it is." He replies while looking at his watch.

"You in a rush?"

“Nope. Just gotta make sure one of the office assistants are available to print a few spreadsheets for a proposal on Monday. Who would I call to come in on a Saturday for me."

Isabella looks back at Benjamin sarcastically. "Don't be an ass.”

"Oh, and this does not constitute a lunch."

"I'm aware. You want me to spend real money. Such a gentleman."

"That's right. I'll pull out the seat for you, princess."

"You know. Since we're collecting on debts, don't forget March Madness. I had more points than you did. So... You've got some planning to do."

"I get my lunches first. Then you can get your... your whatever." He laughs.

"No. I cash in when I cash in. You don't get lunch first."

"Whatever you say, Izzy."

"See. You're learning." She playfully blows a kiss.

Chapter 22: A Perfect Mess

Isabella, Kimberly, Camille, Monica, and Thomas ride in the back of a stretched Cadillac Escalade limousine through Manhattan. The Limo bar is stacked with a mixture of different liquors—the limo's interior lights cycle through purple, blue, yellow, green, and orange. Everyone is having an amazing time except for Kimberly, who struggles to enjoy herself. The group pulls up to a prominent upscale club on the east side of Manhattan. They exit the limousine-like superstars walking right into the club, where they are directed to the VIP section overlooking the club's dancefloor. Monica enters first wearing a purple blouse, mini skirt, and thigh-high leather boots. She grabs a bottle of Moet, popping the top, raising it over her head, screaming. The girls all raise their glasses to be filled as Monica complies, making a mess with the bottle of champagne.

A shirtless muscular waiter wearing black shiny bikini briefs and a bow tie enters with a large tray of finger foods. The girls love it and get up to dance around him. Monica grabs his ass and kisses his chest. A waitress only wearing a thong and a bra top arrives with more finger foods for the group to nibble on. Monica breaks away from the male dancer to dance with the waitress while still holding the bottle of champagne. The waitress welcomes her playful advances placing the tray on the velour sofa to dance with Monica briefly. The group drinks, dances, and laughs for a good portion of the evening. After a few hours of cutting loose, the group sits around the sofa telling stories. Kimberly sits fairly quiet as Monica starts a story. "Yo. I gotta tell you guys something totally crazy that happened to me."

Isabella stops drinking to look at Monica. "What's up?"

"Last night... Was fucking crazy."

"What happened?" Camille asks.

"My ex came to see me."

"Who, Avondre`?" Kimberly Inquires.

"Yeah. He's been calling me all week. Telling me how much he misses me and shit. Kimmy, you know me. I love me some Avondre`?"

An inebriated Camille rolls her eyes at the start of the story.
"So, dude is working me with the charm and shit. He's telling me how when he sees me, he's gonna make me cum harder than I ever came before. I was like Heeeey." Monica dances playfully in place on her seat.

Camille's interest peaks as the story is getting somewhere.

"So, we agree to meet up at my place."

"Wait. What about Kareem?" Kimberly asks with a hint of annoyance.

"Lemme finish, girl, damn," Monica replies as she goes back to the story. "So, I'm at work thinking, how am I gonna get Kareem to leave the house?"

"With the promise he made, you better get Kareem out of that house quick," Camille says after taking another drink.

Thomas shakes his head side to side. "You guys are all fucked up. Finish the story."

Isabella ignores Thomas, gesturing at Monica to continue with the story. "Yeah. Tell the story."

"So, I call Kareem and tell him that when I get home from work, I'm expecting my parents to come by. He doesn't get along with my parents, so I knew he wouldn't stay."

"Did he stay?" Isabella asks.

"Nope. But when I get home, he was out, and he even cleaned up the house for me."

"He's such a gentleman," Thomas adds.

"He is," Monica replies to Thomas as she gives him the side-eye before continuing the story. "So, when I get home, I jump in the shower. I wash every part of my body. I wash my ass like three times."

Isabella burst out laughing. "T.M.I."

"Then I put on some sexy ass shorts and a tank top. Put on my push up bra. Titties were smashed together like this." She cups her breast squeezing them together.

"Work it, girl!" Camille yells as Isabella laughs along.
"The bell rings, and I opened the door... ."

Isabella hangs on every word like she's watching a novella on TV. "And?"

"This mother fucker was looking FINE! Pair of Jeans with some buttas and a muscle shirt. He was tall, extra dark, and fine like a mother fucka. I was feeling this dude."
Isabella turns around, waving at the waitress. "I'm gonna need another drink."

"So, I let him in. This nigga pushes me into the house and closes the door. He grabs me and picks me up, carrying me to the bedroom. He pulls my hair back and starts sucking on my neck."

"See. Now, this shit just got good." Camille leans forward, listening with intensity.

"He throws me on the bed and rips off my shorts. He kisses me right below my belly button. Then he teases me, going up to my tits. I take off my shirt, and he's sucking on my tits."

Isabella and Camille can't get enough of this story. Kimberly listens reluctantly as she turns to look at Thomas shaking his head.

"I look down, and his dick looks like the tube on a roll of paper towel. I told him to put it in. He said, 'Nah. Ima eat that pussy, girl.'"

"DAAAAMN!" Isabella yells.

"And he did, girl. I came so hard that I almost passed the fuck out."

"NOW WE'RE TALKING!" Camille yells.

"Yo. Then he spun me around on all fours and put it in. It felt like it just kept going and going."

Camille and Isabella laugh, high fiving each other. They don't notice the look of disgust on Kimberly's face.

"He fucked the hell outta me. He kept saying, 'WHO'S PUSSY IS THIS?' I was so busy screaming that I didn't answer him. He pulled out and pulled me by the hair, whispering in my ear, 'I asked you, who's fucking pussy is this?' I said, 'Your's, baby.' He let me go and said, 'You better remember that.' He went back in and fuck the shit out of me. I mean, he pounded that ass. I came so hard that I was crying."

Camille and Isabella can't get enough. They continue listening, not paying attention to Thomas or Kimberly, who both continue to shake their heads.

"So, we're lying in bed, and his dick is still hard as fuck. I can't breathe because of the beatdown my pussy just got."

"That was one hell of a beatdown," Isabella says while continuing to laugh.

"This dude opens my legs and goes in for seconds. I'm like, my nigga. Take a break. Again, he's like 'Bitch. This pussy is mine tonight. I'm gonna punish that ass. You want this punishment, right?'"

"I know your ass was like 'Yes Daddy.'" Camille replies.

"I took that shit like a champ. He put my knee over my head and went to fucking work, yo."

"I'm so fucking wet right now," Camille interjects while laughing with Isabella.

"Oh, it gets better. He nutted before, so this time he's going in. straight five minutes of fuckin. Bam, bam, bam, bam, bam. I'm thinking like dude, cum already. Beads of sweat are dripping off his body. I can't take much more of this shit."

"Damn." Camille and Isabella say together.

"After like twenty minutes, he finally cums."

"Shit!" Isabella says with disbelief.

"So finally, were done, and we head to the shower. This dude is still all over me. He's behind me in the shower, kissing my ass, rubbing on my thighs. That shit was so sexy."

"I bet. I would have blown him for putting in all that work." Camille says.

Monica points at Camille. "I was about to girl. The second I turned around, he picked me up."

"Oh, no. Not again." Isabella adds.

"He fucked me right there in the shower again. He pinned me up against the shower wall. I raised my hands to hold on to the wall while he was sucking on my neck. I came so hard again that I couldn't stand up. I just collapsed in the shower."

"You're making this shit up!" Thomas exclaims.

"Hell no. Mandigo was in the mother fuckin house."

Camille shakes her head in disbelief. "This guy's like the terminator."

"Yeah. Going from planet to planet smashing chicks." Thomas adds.

Camille looks back at Thomas and burst out laughing before turning back to Monica. "Did you call it a night after that?"

"He carried me to the bed, and he spooned me."

"Awww." Isabella gushes at the romantic sentiment.

"That shit lasted all of two minutes. I could feel his dick. He was still hard."

"No way. No fucking way!" Camille yells, pointing at Monica.

"Yes, way. He put it in again, from behind. He didn't miss a beat. He went in again. I mean, this dude must be on some kinda drug because he nutted a whole load again."

"You're bullshittin," Thomas says, waving her off.

"Tommy. I can't make this shit up. I had to put my pussy in witness protection because this dude tried to murder that shit."

Isabella, Camille, and Thomas hysterically burst out laughing! Kimberly continues to remain quiet.

"Yo. This nigga came to work. I haven't been fucked like that ever in my life."

Camille raises her hand to get Monica's attention. "Can I just interject for a second?"

"What's up?"

"Why do you use that word so much?"

"What, fuck?"

"No smart ass. The N-word?"

"What? Nigga? I dunno."

"See. You say it like nothing. Thomas and Kimberly are right there. I feel like you're being rude?"

"Cause they know what's up. Why you trippin? I just tell you the craziest sex story, and you gotta bring this shit up. They don't care."

"Is this true, Thomas?" Camille ask.

"Ugh. Look. Monica is mixed with all kinds of ethnicities. You see her as mixed. I see a black woman. She's ratchet as hell. All of her friends are like her. She just looks Asian, but again, she's black. I know when we're at work, she turns it off. So, I don't give a shit."

"What if I said it?"

"Try it and see what happens." Playfully balling his fist, laughing.

Camille chuckles. "Yeah. Let's not and say I didn't."

Thomas strolls over to Camille, still laughing as he hugs her. "You're good. You know how much we love you."

"You're so sweet." Camille replies."

"I know. Let's just drop this topic."

Camille nods in approval. "I can take a hint."

"I swear, grandma. You know how to kill the mood. Damn." Monica states.

"Don't you feel bad about Kareem?" Kimberly interrupts.

"Hell no."

"He cleans up your house for you, so you could fuck someone else."

"Why are you trippin? You don't even like him."

"It just seems foul."

"I'm not worried about it. Shit, you shouldn't either. These things happen. Right, Izzy?

"Izzy, what? What the fuck was that?" Isabella says with a hint of annoyance.

"You out there dancing with that fine ass brother yesterday."

"Don't play yourself. Just finish your trifling ass story. Don't try to throw shade."

"Boo. For real. I'm just playing. No disrespect."

"Well, you think you're the only one with shit going on?" Camille interrupts as her
liquor gives her momentary clarity as she tries to unburden herself.

"Ahhh Shit. What you got?" Monica asks.

"You guys know that guy Garrett."

Thomas and Kimberly look at each other. "That old dude from the country club?" Isabella ask.

Camille shuts her eyes in annoyance. "You guys are relentless with that old crap. YES, HIM!"

"What about him?" Thomas asks.

"We made love."

Monica's mouth drops from shock. "WHAT?!"

Camille half-smiles as a tear streams down the side of her face as she feels guilt. "Yeah."

Thomas leans in. "Are you serious?"

"Yeah. He just kept coming at me. And I gotta tell you. I really like the attention. He makes me feel sexy. I don't feel old. He talks to me... in a certain way that no man has ever talked to me before. Dylan's drinking has gotten out of control, and it's affecting his manhood."

"What? He can't get it up?" Thomas asks.

"Nope. He really tries hard. But over the past few years, it's gotten progressively worse. I try to give him oral, and nothing works."

The look on Monica's face is pure disgust. "Eww. T.M.I."

Camille ignores Monica and continues. "Then, when he doesn't get hard, he gets verbally abusive. I just have to ignore him."

Isabella extends her hand, placing it on Camille's lap. "I'm sorry. I had no idea. Dylan is so sweet. I can't see him being abusive."

"It's ok. I didn't tell anyone. But it's not that bad. At least he doesn't hit me like my ex did."

Monica stands motionless at the news of Camille ever being physically abused.

"I know there's levels of abuse. But abuse is abuse," Thomas says while looking directly at Monica, who shys away.

"So, when Garrett would come on to me. I loved it. I secretly dressed sexy just to get his attention. I had no intention of ever sleeping with him. But it just happened."

"What happened?" Isabella asks.

"He came over when Dylan left for a business trip. I opened the door, and he rushed in, lifting me off my feet. It wasn't as animated and Monica's story, but it was wonderful. He was gentle and rough and sexy. He made love to me on my sofa."

"Please tell me this happened after the party because I sat on that sofa?" Monica abruptly adds.
Camille turns to looks over at Monica with a look of extreme disgust. Isabella can see that Camille may have reached a boiling point as she quickly asks a follow-up question. "What's going on now? Are you still seeing him?"

"I see him every chance I get. I take half days from work to meet him at hotels. I tell Dylan I'm going into work on a Saturday, but I go to see him. I lied and said I went on a business trip to spend a weekend with him."

"Wow."

"Wow is right," Thomas replies to Isabella.

"The worst part is, I have fallen completely in love with him."

"What?" Isabella asks.

"Yes. And at the same time, I have fallen completely out of love with Dylan. I don't even want him to touch me. I do everything to avoid physical contact with him."

"I can't believe what I'm hearing. I'm shocked." Isabella says in disbelief.
Kimberly exhales and while Mumbling under her breath. "I have fucked up friends."

Thomas looks at Kimberly and back at the girls. No one else hears her statement

"Yo. That's fucked up." Monica says, pointing at Camille.

"Excuse me?" Camille asks.

"How can you do that to Dylan?"

"Monica. Sometimes these things do just happen. When you get older –"

"Don't give me that older shit. You just said my story made you wet. So, don't come at me with when I get older shit. Dylan is the nicest dude I know. He treats you like a fucking princess, and this is how you do him."

"You don't know what the fuck you're talking about. You see a facade, and now you want to pass judgment. You fuck a dude the second your boyfriend leaves the house."
"You did the same shit. You call it making love. But you cheated on your husband, you dummy. You stood before a priest and committed yourself to him forever. I can't respect what you did."

"I don't need your respect. I'm telling you about something I'm going through, and the first thing you do is judge." She rants as she looks around the lounge at Isabella, Thomas, and Kimberly. "This is why I hate when you guys bring this bitch anywhere."

"Fuck you, grandma. Only dick you could get was some old bastard with his old wrinkled balls."

Camille lunges at Monica swinging her right hand, slapping her on the arm. "I fucking warned you about that grandma shit."

Isabella and Thomas stand up to break them up as Camille continues to slap Monica. Monica protects herself, placing her hands over her face. "This bitch is crazy."

Thomas restrains Camille as Isabella stands in front of Monica. "Monica, this time you went too far."

"No, I didn't. That bitch is fucking grimy. Who cheats on their fucking husband? I know I'm not shit for what I did, but Kareem is not my fucking husband."

"Kareem is a piece of shit. And that makes you an asshole for staying with him."

Camille fires back at Monica.

"Ok. Relax. We've all got a lot of liquor in our system, and now we're just acting stupid." Thomas says, trying to deescalate.

Still, no one pays any mind to Kimberly, who does nothing to help diffuse this feud.

"Oliver broke up with me."
Everyone remains silent for a moment turning to Kimberly. Monica turns to Kimberly. "What?"

"Oliver broke up with me on Thursday." Kimberly starts to cry.

Monica and Isabella walk toward Kimberly to console her. Thomas releases Camille, who walks over to Kimberly. "I wasn't going to say anything, but this night has just turned to shit."

"Why didn't you tell me?" Monica asks.

"You should have called me. I would have come over right away." Isabella adds.

"What the hell happened?"

"He's moving to Japan. He chose a job over me." She drops her head into her hands, covering her face. "I'm sorry."

"Why are you sorry?" Isabella asks.

"I'm crying. I don't want to cry."

"Sweetie. It's ok. Do you want to talk about it?" Camille sits beside her, placing her arms around her.

"No. I'm just so heartbroken. My heart is torn in two. I don't want to lose him."

Thomas stands a few feet behind her. "So. He's just packing up and moving?"

"To Japan. Yes."

"Kimmy. I'm so sorry. I've seen you two over the last year. I know you two love each other with every ounce of your hearts. No way this was easy for him. I can't see it." Thomas adds.

"I think that's why I feel so sick. I can feel that he loves me. Just thinking about it now makes me want to throw up."

Isabella struggles to believe that Oliver would hurt Kimberly. "Thomas is right. He lives for you. Have you guys talked?"

Kimberly struggles to talk. "I told him to leave shortly after he told me. We haven't spoken since then."

"You need to take the time to talk to him."

Kimberly starts dry heaving. "I gotta go to the bathroom," Kimberly says as she slowly stands up.

"Come on; I'll take you," Isabella says while standing up to take her to the restroom before pointing at Monica and Camille. "Thomas, watch these two please?"

"Isabella and Kimberly exit the VIP lounge to go to the restroom. Isabella takes Kimberly by the hand, guiding her to the restroom. Camille still being bothered by

Monica's presence, addresses her directly. "Well. At least they're not married. By your logic, everything should be a.o.k."

"Don't think I won't slap the shit outta you. You just sucker-punched me, bitch! I won't forget that."

"Yeah, but you forget everything else."

"What? What did you say?"

"You heard me, Everlast."

"What the fuck does that mean?"

"It means you're too stupid to know when you've been insulted."

"Bitch, I know what the fuck you meant. You're calling me a punching bag."

Monica grabs a bottle of wine and charges Camille. Thomas jumps up, grabbing Monica's hand, stopping her from striking Camille, who seems completely unafraid.

"Calm down! What the fuck is the matter with you?" Thomas yells at Monica as she struggles to pull away. "Let go of my hand, Thomas!"

Camille removes her high heels tossing them to the side. "Yeah, Thomas, let her go. Let her go so I can show her a proper grandma ass whipping."

"JUST STOP! BOTH OF YOU! DAMMIT!"

Monica struggles to get away from Thomas as he has a firm grip on her. She pulls and pulls, yelling obscenities toward Camille, who stand in front of her looking into a rage-filled Monica. She looks up at Thomas, who holds Monica back. She starts to feel a sickness in the pit of her stomach. She no longer wants anything to do with this night, Monica or any of her so-called friends. "I'm done."

Thomas forces Monica to sit on the lounge sofa turning to Camille. "What?"

"I'm fucking done. I'm going home. I thought you were my friends."

"We are your friends."

"We ain't friends bitch. Bye Grandma. I don't even know Thomas invited your stupid ass."

Thomas walks over to Camille, trying to deescalate the situation. "No. Come on. I think we all had way too much alcohol, and it's fucked with our judgment."

"I've got a buzz going for sure. But I'm not staying here. I'm going home. Tell Kimberly I will call her in the morning. I just can't stay here."

Thomas places his hand on Camille's shoulder. "Let me at least walk you down to get a cab."

"No. I just want out. Goodnight."

Camille picks up her shoes and grabs her purse exiting the club. She stands alone on the sidewalk before she hails a taxicab.

Thomas drops his head. "Sigh. What a fucking mess."

"Stupid ass bitch."

Thomas slowly turns to Monica, looking right at her. "What's the matter with you?"

"What's the matter with me? Look, dad. I can't respect when a married woman or married man cheats on their significant other. There's no excuse. Have you seen how Dylan treats her? Shit. If he was my husband, I'd rub his fucking feet. Dude makes crazy money, buys her all the finest shit. Takes her away to exotic places, and I'm supposed to sympathize because his dick doesn't work. My dude. Viagra."

"Sometimes, all that stuff you think is important in a relationship isn't."

"So, you're saying you condone that shit."

"No. But she's my friend. She knows what she did was wrong. But she needed our ear tonight. And now she's sitting in a cab by herself feeling judged."

"You reap what you sow."

"Yeah... Well, those who live in glass houses."

"You should know," Monica replies looking Thomas in the eye.

Thomas points in her face. "You got a fucking mouth tonight, don't you?"

Monica says nothing, turning her back on Thomas to look out the VIP lounge window onto the dance floor. The dance floor is packed with people dancing and having a good time. She stands up, walking past Thomas exiting the lounge. Thomas stands along in the lounge, looking around the now empty VIP lounge. He turns to look out the lounge window taking a deep breath. "What a mess."

The waiter enters the lounge and can see the mild mess caused by the ruckus. "Is everything ok, sir?"

Thomas turns to the waiter looking at the mess, shaking his head side to side. "Not at all."

Downstairs In the ladies' room, Kimberly is in the stall dry heaving while Isabella stands beside her holding her hair and rubbing her back. "I think you should come home with me tonight."

"I just want to sleep. I've been numb for the past few days." Kimberly replies, struggling as she gags.

"Um. I think you should definitely come home with me tonight. I can't imagine how you must feel right now. I'd be crying every day."

"That's just it. I haven't cried once. I think I was in shock."

"You probably are in shock. . . Has he called you?"

"He's been calling me every minute. I haven't answered any of the calls." She says as she begins to dry-heave again.

"Oh, boy."

Kimberly stands upright, taking a deep breath. "This just sucks."

"Yeah. It does. Do you want to head home?"

"No. Thomas put so much effort into this night. I don't wanna ruin it."

"The night has already been ruined. I'm sure Camille would like to kill Monica right now."

"I want to at least apologize to Thomas."

"Then let's go back to the VIP lounge. Hopefully, everyone has cooled off."

"I hope so. I'd really hate to ruin this night. I don't want him to be mad at me."

"Girl, please. When have you known Thomas to get upset with you?"

"I know what you're saying. I just feel bad."

"If there's anyone we should be upset with, it's Monica."

They make their way back to the VIP lounge. Upon entering, they notice Thomas sitting alone on a circular chair looking at his cell phone. Isabella looks at Kimberly before looking at Thomas.

"Hey, Thomas."

Thomas stands up and walks over to Kimberly. "Hey. You ok?"

"I'll be fine." She nods. "Where is everyone?"

"Cami left. She was pissed, to say the least."

"Not at us, right?" Isabella asks.
"I think she's mad in general, but I'd gander to say most of her frustration is with Monica."

"I don't get her sometimes."

Kimberly reaches for Thomas' shoulder. "Thomas. I'm so sorry for ruining your night. We were all looking forward to it."

"Don't be sorry. It's not your fault." He replies as he hugs Kimberly. "Had I known you were going through that, I would have canceled our plans."

"That's why I didn't say anything. I didn't want to ruin your plans."

"It's water under the bridge now. Do you guys want to go home?"

"I'm gonna take her home with me," Isabella says to Thomas.

"Ok. I'll tell the limo driver to come pick us up."

"No. We'll take a cab. You stay here and finish off your night."

“That's crazy. I have a limo paid for until the morning.”

"We just figured you two can stay here. We'll just head out. Monica might be a little hot under the collar, and maybe it would be best if we went our separate ways for the night. Plus, I know Monica, she's going to need a babysitter tonight."

"Are you sure?"

"Yes. I promise we will make this up to you."

"It's not necessary for you to say that."

"Yes, it is."

Thomas smiles at Isabella's sentiment. "Whatever. Let me at least walk you guys out."

Thomas walks the girls out, hailing a cab. Kimberly and Isabella enter the cab and head across town to Isabella's house on Central Park West.

Kimberly sits at the island in Isabella's kitchen, drinking a cup of coffee, staring into the cup. Isabella stands across the counter, watching Kimberly. Kimberly takes a deep breath looking up at Isabella. "This coffee isn't really helping. I'm beat."

"I can imagine. You look wasted.”

"I am so drained. I don't have the energy to lift my arms."

Isabella reaches across the counter, grabbing Kimberly's cup. "The guest room is all ready for you. Just go in there and sleep. If it gets late tomorrow, don't feel bad. Just try to get some rest."

Isabella walks around the counter and hugs Kimberly as she stands up. "Thank you so much. I really appreciate this."

"No problem, girl. I'm happy to do it."

Isabella escorts Kimberly into the guest room, where it takes only moments for Kimberly to fall asleep once under the covers. Isabella walks upstairs, checking on the kids before entering her bedroom. Sebastian lays across the bed, watching T.V. smiling at Isabella. She greets him, kissing him on the lips.

Sebastian keeps his eyes glued to the television. "Hey, babe. Did you have fun tonight?"

"It was amazing right up until."

"Wow," Sebastian answers before Isabella finishes her sentence.

Isabella unzips her dress continuing her story. "It went straight to shit. Did you know that Oliver is moving to Japan?"

"Nah."

"Yeah. He and Kim are probably going to break up."

"Wow."

Isabella turns to Sebastian, who is fixated on the TV. "Are you even listening to me?"

Sebastian points to the TV. "Come on. You see, I'm watching TV, and you want to have a conversation."

Isabella stands in place in her underwear, giving Sebastian a death stare, mumbling.
"This is why people cheat."

"I'm sorry. What was that?"

"Nothing. Enjoy your show, honey." She replies before walking to the bathroom, closing the door behind her. Sebastian watches her walk away. "Don't be like that. I was just in the middle of an interesting program. You're not even supposed to be home this early."

Sebastian listens for Isabella to respond. He only hears the sound of running water shaking his head, "Sigh. And now you're mad?"

He looks back at the television. "Great."

Chapter 23: Monday Morning Between Friends

After the Saturday night that was supposed to be the greatest night ever that turned into a complete disaster, Thomas, Kimberly Camille, and Monica start a new work week. Camille, Kimberly, and Thomas sit in their individual offices. Kimberly still tucks herself away behind a shut office door; Camille takes a call from a client while Thomas is going through a small folder viewing claim damage pictures. Monica walks in and marches to her desk, saying nothing to anyone. Phoebe walks through the office, entering Thomas' office. "Hey, you." She says, startling Thomas.

"Oh, hey. Come in. Sit down."

Phoebe enters, sitting down in front of Thomas. "How was your weekend?"

"In a word. Strange." He says while laughing.

"What happened?"

"Just. . . egh. Nothing. How was your weekend?"

"It was quiet. I went to my girlfriend's house, and we ordered a movie. Honeymoon in the hood 2."

"I don't know how you sat through that?"

"Two hours of my life that I can't get back. It was awful."

"I saw that crap in the theater. It was trash."

Phoebe laughs. "Calling it crap is being kind."

"You're right. I just didn't want to curse in front of a lady."

"You're so sweet."

"I am." He replies as he laughs.

"Do you want to have lunch with me one day this week?"

"Absolutely. Maybe we can go twice."

"If you're lucky."

"You're here in my office. I'm already feeling lucky."

"You should feel lucky." Phoebe flirtatiously replies.

"I'll be sure to count my blessings."

They smile at each other for a moment before Phoebe leans over his desk, briefly touching his hand. "Anyway. I just came by to say hello. I gotta get back to work. I'll see you later?"

"I'd much rather you stay here and see me right now."

Phoebe stands up, walking out of his office. Thomas watches her every move as she looks back at him smiling. As she gets out of view, he makes eye contact with Monica, who is making another lewd gesture with her hands laughing. Thomas' smile fades as he shakes his head. Thomas stands up and walks over to Monica's desk. "Good morning."

"What's up, lover boy?"

"At some point today, are you going to go talk to Camille?"

"For what?"

"What do you mean for what?"

"I don't have shit to say to her."

"We're all friends. You can't judge your friend on an indiscretion."

"Look. You know what I've been through. I've seen first hand how cheating can ruin a family. My mom cheated on my dad constantly. She treated him like shit. He's a good man, and he didn't deserve that. He pretty much raised the five of us on his own while she was out whoring."

"I know all of this. But she isn't your mother."

"I know I do some wild shit. But I'm telling you, Thomas. Once I get married, If I find out my husband cheats on me, he's dead. Till death do us part."

"You're being ridiculous."

Monica stands up to walk to the kitchen. "This conversation's wack. I need some coffee."

"Wait. Did you talk to Kimberly at all this weekend?" Thomas reaches for her arm to stop her.

"Ahhh." She reacts to Thomas touching her left arm as Monica nurses it.

"What happened to your arm?"

Monica realizes that Thomas is going to badger her. "Sigh. Look. It's over. He hit me again on Saturday. I threw him out. I took my keys and everything."

Thomas quickly pulls up her shirt sleeve and can see a bruise. His eyes widen as he looks up at Monica. "Really?"

Monica, fearing embarrassment, yanks her arm away, pulling her sleeve down as she looks around the office. "We had a big fight when I got in late on Saturday. He hit me. I said enough is enough and threw him out. Okay. So, drop it. He's gone."

Thomas stands quietly, looking at Monica. She looks around to make sure that no one can see their interaction. She turns back to Thomas as he continues to stare at her. "What?"

Thomas calmly shakes his head side to side. "Nothing. Nothing at all."

"So. I'm gonna go and get some coffee now. Is that ok?" She turns around, walking away from Thomas, who stands motionless as she walks off. Thomas walks back to his office and looks in on Kimberly, who has just taken a call. Kimberly picks up the handset, answering. "North Mutual Insurance. Kimberly speaking."

"Baby. I'm begging you. Please don't hang up. Please." Oliver begs on the other end of the line

"What do you want, Oliver?"

"Baby, I love you, and I'm so sorry."

"You said all that already." She hangs up the phone.

Uptown Oliver sits at his desk as Kimberly hangs up. "Hello! Hello! Fuck."

Justin, hearing Oliver's conversation, walks into his office. "Kim?"

"Yes, Kim. Who else would it be?" Appearing highly annoyed.

"Relax, man. I just –"

"What do you want?"

"Nothing, man. I just feel helpless."

"Well, that's better than how I feel. But you coming in here every second to ask me a stupid question like, "Is that Kim" is pissing me off. If you don't come in here and ask me that every second. I'd appreciate that."

"Ok. I just –"

"Just go to your office."

Justin does an about-face walking back to his office sitting at his desk

Chapter 24: Taken For Granted

Monday evening at the Maldonado resident on the upper west side, Isabella and her family are having dinner around the table. The twins, Grace, and Hope have finished their meals and are doing impressions. Isabella enjoys watching the girls joke around. Sebastian is looking at his phone while he eats his dinner. The girls point to their mother to do an impression. "Ok, ok. Who's this. 'Yo no se, yo no se,'" she says, mocking the person she imitates by raising both of her hands.

Grace laughs, pointing at Isabella. "That's Abuela?"

"Wait. I have one. Who is this?" Hope interrupts. She Imitates someone looking at a phone very seriously.

Grace points to her father. "Papi."

"Yeah. He's always on the phone." Hope says of her father.

Isabella laughs, looking over at Sebastian. "You hear that?"

Sebastian doesn't answer as he continues to stare into the phone.

"Sebastian." She calls out to him.

He continues looking at the phone. "What?"

"Your daughter hit the nail on the head with her impersonation of you."

"That's nice."

"You missed it. You should put the phone down."

"I know." He says while not paying attention to Isabella."

Isabella sits motionless, looking at Sebastian. Both kids turn to look at Isabella. She smiles as she turns her attention to the children. Sebastian's phone rings from a call. He stands up, walking away from the table. "Hey, man. What's up?"

Isabella realizes that the children are watching her reaction. She continues to smile. "Ok, girls. Pick up your plates and bring them to the kitchen."

"What about daddy's plate?" Grace asks her mother.

"He can pick up his own plate. He's a big boy."

Isabella walks to the kitchen carrying her plate along with an empty wine glass. The girls place their plates in the sink before heading upstairs to their bedroom. Isabella reaches into her purse to get her cell phone. She looks up to see that Sebastian is sitting on the loveseat, talking on his cell phone. She places a call to Camille, who sits on the sofa next to Dylan in their living room. "Hello."

"Hi, Camille. How are you?"

"I'm doing well. Just sitting here having a glass of wine with Dylan."

"I haven't spoken to you since Saturday, and I wanted to just check on you."

"You didn't have to. I'm fine. Really."

"Well, at the club, I took Kim to the ladies' room and didn't see you when I came back to the VIP room. You said a lot, and we all never got to let you finish."

"You didn't want me to continue that now, right?"

"Absolutely not. But I just wanted to say to you. I didn't judge you, and I don't judge you. I heard everything you said. I think I understand what you are going through."

Camille looks over at Dylan, who watches the television. She swiftly stands up from the sofa walking to the kitchen. "Thank you for saying that."

"You're welcome. I should have called you yesterday, but Kim was here all day, and I was talking with her until I took her home."

"I understand. But what you said is greatly appreciated. I wanted to tell someone. It's been a burden on me, and I haven't told anyone until Saturday night."

"I know you're with Dylan right now, so you can't really talk, but If you need me. Just call."

"I will. Thank you."

"You're welcome. . . Did you see Kimberly at all today?"

"Yeah. I stopped by her office. She was in no mood to talk about Oliver."

"Yeah. I feel sick to my stomach for her."

"Her situation sucks."

"She really needs to talk to him, or she will regret it."

"She's a smart cookie. She'll come to her senses."

"I hope so."

"Anyway. I'm going to enjoy this chardonnay with my husband."

"Alright. I'll talk to you soon."

"Yes, you will. We'll talk soon."

"Good night."

"Good night."

"Isabella ends the call as Sebastian ends his call and heads upstairs.

"Excuse me." Isabella stops him from going upstairs.

"What's up?"

"You left your dish on the table, and it's your turn to wash the dishes."

"You couldn't just put it in the sink for me?"

"No. I couldn't." She smiles.

Sebastian slowly walks to the table, picking up his plate, taking it to the kitchen sink. Isabella playfully walks behind him.
"You know how sexy it is when you wash the dishes."

"Whatever."

Isabella walks up to him, hugging him from behind as he turns on the faucet. "My sexy man, washing dishes, getting all wet."

Sebastian is in no mood for Isabella's playful side. "What are you talking about?"

Isabella whispers in his ear. "Just play along."

"Sigh. Play along with what?"

"I'm the boss at a restaurant, and all of my employees have gone home for the night. It's just me and the dishwasher. The sexy Latin dishwasher with abs of steel. You know what happens when the boss is horny."

"What happens?"

Isabella grabs his penis from behind.

"The boss takes what she wants. And tonight, the boss wants to give you a blow job."

"Come on, Izzy. The kids are still awake."

"So. Once I'm down there, they can't see anything with the counter blocking me. All you have to do is warn me. Plus, if they open their door, we'll hear the squeak of their door."

"Nah. It's not a good idea."

"Come on! You love it when we role-play."

"Not tonight, babe."

"Are you serious? You're gonna turn down a blow job?"

"I'm not in the mood right now."

"I'm willing to give you head to make some kinda contact with you, and you're
seriously not in the mood? I seriously don't know what's with you lately."
"What do you mean, what's wrong with me lately? I'm fine."

"Keep telling yourself that. I'm not gonna beg you for sex, though."

"I never said you had to."

Isabella mocks him using an annoying version of a dopey man's voice. "*I never said you had to. I never said you had to.* Gimme a break. I'm going upstairs."

"It's always something with you."

Isabella takes three steps up the staircase when she hears the last thing Sebastian says. "What the fuck is that supposed to mean?"

Sebastian continues washing the dishes. "What it sounds like. You always complaining about some shit; how your job is filled with idiots who can't make deadlines. It was the same complaint at your last job—shit with your friends, shit with the train ride home. Then you come home and have these passive-aggressive attitudes with me over dumb shit. You never hear me complain about the same shit twice."

Isabella's face turns beet red as she walks back toward the kitchen. "Ooohhh. So, when I come home, and I vent to you about work, that's dumb shit?!"

"Yep."

"You're such a selfish prick. You're my husband and supposed to be my best friend. Who the fuck else would I talk to or want to talk to for that matter? When you're losing money or lose a contract, I sit up all night and help you with shit that looks dumb to me but makes sense to you. Because that's my fucking job as your wife. When you have to fire someone from a job, and it bothers you. Who the fuck listens to that shit? ME! All I have to fucking do is understand you and listen. But when I need it, It's dumb shit."

"See. You always take shit too far. I'm talking about the stuff you repeat all the time."

"Ooooh, go fuck yourself. You get on my nerves. How dare you say I complain about dumb shit."

"Look. Sometimes I just don't wanna hear about the shit you talk about. Especially when it comes to your friends or your job."

"Fine. You won't hear that shit anymore."

"Wait. All I'm saying is –"
"You've said all you're saying and all I'm willing to listen to. Goodnight."

Isabella turns around and walks upstairs.

Sebastian rolls his eyes, calling Isabella. "Come back here! Izzy wait! Izzy!"

Isabella head upstairs fuming but restrains herself from slamming the bedroom door. She undresses, tossing her clothes on the bed before heading to the bathroom, closing the door behind her.

Chapter 25: Following Up

Late evening in the Queensbridge section of New York City, Kareem walks up Fortieth Avenue carrying a large duffle bag in his right hand. He can sense that someone is walking behind him. He turns around to see a few people on the sidewalk; however, one particular pedestrian stands out wearing a long sleeve shirt, tan cargo pants, and Zoo York baseball hat. Kareem continues to walk toward Twenty-third Street. He crosses the street, turning around again only to see the man appearing closer. Kareem places the bag over his left shoulder as it rests on his right hip. He begins to walk faster toward Twenty-second Street, where he turns down that street. Twenty-second Street is much less crowded.

Kareem trots down the street about fifty feet turning around to see if the man is still following him. After a few seconds, the man turns the corner and stops. It's dark out, and Kareem cannot see his face. Fear comes over Kareem as he starts to walk backward. The man remains still at the end of the block while looking at Kareem walk backward. The man starts to run fast towards Kareem, which causes Kareem to panic as his eyes widen from panic. He turns around to run as fast as he can in the other direction when he is stopped by a fist directly to his face from a second man he didn't know was walking behind him in the other direction. He falls to the ground hitting the pavement.

"Sup bitch?" The second man says while standing over Kareem. The first man arrives, standing over Kareem, who is unable to see their faces. It's dark, and they are wearing face shields pulled up to their eyes.

"What the fuck, yo?!" Kareem yells at his attackers. "I ain't got no money!"

"Pick his ass up." The first man says to the other. The second man lifts Kareem to his feet as Kareem attempts to scream. "HELP!"

The first man punches Kareem in the face. "Shut the fuck up."

They drag him down a dark industrial alley tossing him to the floor. The second man stands behind him while the first man faces him.

"What the fuck yall want?" Kareem asks.

Neither man says anything. Kareem can see the first man making a fist with both hands. The first man squats down to Kareem. Kareem struggles to see the man's face.
"What, man? What the fuck do you want?" Kareem asks.

The first man backhands Kareem's face getting within an inch of his face. "You like beating on women, don't you?"

"Is that what this is about? Fuck that bitch."

The first man becomes enraged, grabbing Kareem by his neck, lifting him off the ground.
"What did you call her?"

"Ugh." Kareem struggles for air.

"Say it again, you piece of shit!" The man says while choking Kareem before throwing
Kareem to the floor. He then lunges at him, punching him in the face several times. The second man lifts Kareem up to face the first man. Kareem is crying and begs them to stop. "I'm sorry."

The first man uppercuts Kareem's stomach causing him to lurch forward. He grabs him by his dreadlocks, pulling his head up. "If you ever come near her or any other woman again. I'm gonna remove your fingers and your toes and feed them to you. Do you understand me?"

Kareem shakes his head yes, which aggregates Kareem's attacker. "Say it, mother fucker."

"I understand." He says while struggling to breathe."

The second man drops Kareem before they both disappear into the dark alley leaving Kareem lying on the ground.

Chapter 26: I'm Not Saying We're Good

Time heals all wounds in most cases. Anger today turns into frustration tomorrow. So, even though your first reaction is usually the correct one, it would be best to keep your emotions in check. You will always need time to process your emotions because, more often than none, you do more harm than good from a gut reaction.

On a warm breezy early Saturday evening, the sun begins its descent, appearing to fall into New Jersey across the Hudson River. Oliver walks home to his battery park home, returning from the store. He looks over to the west catching the glow of orange cascade across the sky. As he arrives at his building, he turns his head and can see Kimberly standing out front. He smiles and walks faster to get to her. He grabs her and hugs her. She has minimal reaction to seeing him as he pulls away, looking at her face. "Hey, babe."

"Hello, Oliver."

"I miss you so much. This has been the worst week."

"Oliver."

"Yes."

"I gotta ask you this question."

"What?"

"Did you think about me at all when they made this offer for the job?"

"You were the first thing I thought about. I didn't answer them right away because I knew It would kill us. Justin didn't even break a sweat. He said yes immediately."

"Wow."

"Then, I thought. If I say yes, I'm sure I can think of something. Something that would either keep me here or bring you with me. Kimberly, I swear. You were the only thing on my mind the entire time."

“I feel like I’ve been split in two. I love you so much, and I’m bitter with you. I’ve been sitting at home thinking and putting myself in your shoes. What would I do? And The logical side of me takes your side. You have a career, and the work you do brought you an opportunity of a lifetime.”

"Yes. But –"

"Let me finish, please."

"Ok. I'm sorry." Oliver replies.

"But the girlfriend side of me is completely heartbroken. I don't want you to leave." She says, looking away from Oliver.

"Kimmy. Nothing is etched in stone. Just let me work this out. I will do everything possible to keep us together. I’m begging you to trust me and let me do what I gotta do."

Kimberly looks up at Oliver, saying nothing.

"Say something, please?" Oliver begs Kimberly.

"You do what you have to."

"I promise I will. Come upstairs so we can talk, babe. I miss you."

"I miss you too. But I'm going home."

"Why? Please stay."

"It hurts too much, and I feel drained just coming here."

"I can't let you go home."

"Oliver. I'm going home. Don't waste your breath, trying to get me to stay here. I didn't waste mine when you said you were leaving for Japan. I'll talk to you later." She walks away from Oliver.

"Can you at least call me when you get home?"

"I'll text you."

"Fine. I'll take that."

"You don't have a choice. Kinda like me." Kimberly walks over to her car, avoiding eye contact. She enters her car, driving off as Oliver stands on the sidewalk, watching her car drive away.

Chapter 27: I'm Not Going To Be Ignored

Beautiful picturesque sunny Sunday afternoon at Matt's Marina in Seaford, NY. Camille drives into the fairly crowded parking lot pulling into an available parking space. She walks aggressively down the pier toward Garrett's Yacht. Garrett sits in the aft portion of his yacht, smoking a cigar talking on his mobile phone. Camille storms down the boat slip up to the yacht. "You son of a bitch!"

Garrett looks down at Camille, standing outside of the yacht. "Ah, shit. Artie, I'll have to call you back." He says to his friends before ending his call

"What the fuck is your problem?" Camille yells from the boat slip.

"Sweetheart. You gotta relax." Garrett says while looking around at people who can hear Camille yelling.

"Don't sweetheart me. I've been calling you for two weeks, and you have yet to return any of my calls. What the fuck is your problem?!"

"Would you lower your voice?"

"Why haven't you returned any of my calls?"

"I've been busy with work. You know how it is."

"No, Garrett. I don't know how it is. Tell me. Why don't you explain it to me?"

"Look. Camille. We're two adults. We had fun, and you know. . ."

"Stop talking to me like an idiot Garrett. What the fuck does any of that mean?"

"We had a good time."

"Yes. I know. You said you loved me."

"I mean, Camille. You and I said a lot of shit when things got hot and heavy. It's not like either one of us is going to leave our spouses."

"YOU SAID YOU WERE LEAVING YOUR WIFE!!!!!"

.

"I know, but we're working things out. We're married thirty-seven years. I can't just leave her for a piece of ass."

As Garrett lets those words fly out of his mouth, he realizes from the look on her face that he should have chosen his words a little bit more carefully.

"PIECE OF ASS! PIECE OF ASS! DID YOU JUST CALL ME A PIECE OF ASS?!?!"

"I didn't mean it like that."

"Permission to come aboard, captain?!!" Camille says sarcastically as she climbs aboard his yacht.

Garrett calmly watches Camille come aboard. "Camille. You gotta cut this shit out. You're making a fool of yourself."

Camille rushes Garrett slapping the cigar out of his hand. "I made a fool of myself when I slept with you."

"Why are you doing this?" Garrett says as he continues to look around as everyone witnesses Camille's meltdown.

"Because you're an asshole."
Camille swings her right hand, punching him in the face.

Garrett holds his nose. "You bitch. What's the matter with you?"

"I have all of your fucking text messages. "You're my little sweet cheeks. You're my little sweetheart." You're so full of shit Garrett. Don't think for a second that I'm not going to show your wife."

Garrett points in Camille's face. "If you go near my wife, I'll kill you. Mark my words."

Camille is unphased by his threat. She swiftly kicks him in the groin.
"You don't have the balls, asshole. Literally."

Garrett falls to the floor in pain, holding his groin while other boaters watch.
"Get the fuck off of my boat bitch."

Camille salutes. "Aye aye, captain. There's a blue corvette outside waiting for me."
Camille jumps off the boat speed walking towards Garretts Blue Corvette Stingray.
Garrett covers his eye with one hand and nursing his scrotum with the other. "Stay the fuck away from my car."

Camille opens the trunk of her SUV and removes one of Dylan's golf clubs. She goes to work on Garrett's new Corvette Stingray: Denting the hood, the door, and tail lights while smashing all the windows. She catches her breath then gets in her car, driving off. As she travels down the road, she feels a sense of exuberance. She feels great, but that feeling is short-lived as she starts to feel a heavy emotion. She thinks about how much of a fool Garrett made of her. She allowed him to wear her down when she knew that an affair would be such a terrible idea. Now she's filled with regret. She pulls into a

Home Depot parking lot and cries hysterically while talking to herself. I'm such an idiot. I'm so stupid. I'm a walking cliche`." She drops her head forward on the steering wheel as she cries uncontrollably.

Chapter 28: Why Do I Even Bother?

Thomas and Monica sit outside on a gorgeous warm summer afternoon, eating a slice of pizza during their lunch hour. Oddly they sit next to each other, not saying much. Monica turns to look at Thomas. "So, don't get mad."

Thomas takes a bite of his pizza. "Uh-huh."

"I spoke with Kareem."

Thomas's posture drops, making no eye contact with Monica. "When?"

"Over the weekend."

"Why are you talking to that asshole?"

"I was just checking on him. I wanted to see if he was ok."

"WHY?!"

"I can't just walk away from him like that. That's my boo. I still love him."

"I just lost my fucking appetite."

"Why are you being so fucking dramatic right now?"

Thomas continues to sit, not saying a word.

"Anyway, he got jumped. They beat him up really bad. He didn't really want to talk about it."

Thomas wraps up his pizza, remaining quiet as he stares into the street.

"You gonna just sit there and not say anything?"

"No. I'm going to let you enjoy your lunch by yourself." Thomas stands up, walking away.

Monica walks behind him, grabbing his arm, stopping him from leaving.
"Stop being a little bitch."

"Get off me." Thomas pulls his hand away. Monica sees the bruise on his knuckles. She grabs his hand, pulling it closer to her face. "GASP! Yo. Was it you?"

Thomas pulls away, continuing to walk as Monica runs in front of him, placing her hand on his chest. "It was you. Why did you do that?"

"What did I say would happen if he touched you again?"

"I don't give a fuck what you said. You should mind your business."

"You know what. I should have because you are too stupid to stop this from happening to you. You break up with him, then throw him out. Then you want to call him to see my baby's ok. How am I friends with such an idiot?"

"Fuck you! I never told you to stick your fucking nose in my business. How are you gonna go around New York fuckin people up? You can't fuckin save everybody. I'm not your fucking kid that you can just take matters into your hands and fix shit. Stop trying to protect everybody."

"Don't mention my kid

"I said I'm not your kid asshole. I never mentioned your kid. Is that what this is about? Your kid?"

Thomas points in her face. "Monica. . . Choose your words very carefully."

"I'll say what the fuck I wanna say. Stop fucking trying to protect me. I don't fucking need your help. I'm good on my own."

"Fine. Stay the fuck away from me then. Don't call me anymore. Don't talk to me anymore. Run back to that piece of shit."

"No. You don't talk to me anymore. I don't fucking need you. I never asked you for your help. Not once. And you take it upon yourself to go beat up my boyfriend."

Thomas looks in her eyes with disappointment. "You're pathetic. Move." He moves her out of his path.
"Fuck you!"

"Fuck you!"

Thomas leaves her outside, walking to the office alone. Monica remains on the sidewalk, watching Thomas walk away. She sits back down, finishing her pizza. Thomas enters NMIC, walking past Camille's office. He stops and takes a step backward, peeking into her office. Camille is standing at the window of her office, looking out over the city. Thomas pokes his head in. "You ok?"

Camille turns to look at Thomas.
"No."

He enters her office. "What's the matter?"

"I'm an idiot."

Thomas senses she's in a dark place and attempts humor. "You've been known to do some stupid shit in the time I've known you, but nothing that would constitute you calling yourself an idiot."

Camille turns around to look at Thomas. "Your words are so enlightening."

"I know. But really. Why are you calling yourself an idiot?"

"I had an affair with Garrett, as you know."

"Right."

Monica walks into the office, making eye contact with Thomas through Camille's office glass wall. Thomas takes a step back, closing the door to Camille's office.

"I ended up falling in love with him."

Thomas takes a deep breath shaking his head.

"I have everything I think I could need in life and, yet I was willing to throw it away. I've pretty much ruined my marriage."

"Does Dylan know about you and Garrett?"

"No. But in the same token, I have fallen completely out of love with Dylan. I don't want him to even touch me anymore. I felt like I was cheating on Garrett. How twisted is that?"

"Wow. Ok, so, did something happen that's making you think you're an idiot more now than before."

"Yeah. I lost my cool."

"How so?"

"I confronted him on his boat yesterday. I punched him, kicked him in the balls, and completely Taylor Swift'd his car."

Thomas thinks. "Taylor Swift?"

"Yeah. The video where she wrecked the guys' car."

Thomas shakes his head no. "Can't say I've seen it."

"Well, it was a beautiful car. She just went berserk and destroyed it."

"Ahh, shit."

"He pretty much told me I didn't mean anything to him. My marriage is destroyed, and I have egg all over my face. At this point, I don't know if I can even stay with married to Dylan."

"Don't go doing anything hasty. You should really think about your next move. You still love Dylan, right?"

"No. I don't. And that's the honest truth."

"Let me rephrase. I know you may not be in love with him, but do you still love him or have love for him."

"I care for him, but I think any love I had for him is gone. This affair just let me know that it's possible that I may have never loved him. We just looked good on paper."

"That's. . . Wow. . . Ok. . ."

"He's not a dummy. He's gotta know something is off."

"That's possible. But before you do anything rash. Please take time for yourself and think."

"I dunno, Thomas. I'm just over it all." Camille catches a glimpse of Thomas's bruised hand. "What happened there?"

Thomas looks at his hand for a moment. "Let just call it stupidity."

"Yeah. It's been that kind of weekend. I'm waiting for the police to come to my house at any moment to arrest me for what I did to this asshole's car. Not to mention the assault on him."

"Do you need me to make a call?"

"No. I'll deal with this mess myself. I don't want you exhausting favors with your old police buddies."

"Are you sure? I know people. No need to step in front of a firing squad if you don't have to."

"It's ok. I actually have some leverage to keep myself safe."

"That a girl."

"I have learned a few things from you. Even at my age."

"Then, I have served my purpose."

Camille's desk phone rings. She picks up the handset.

"Camille speaking....Yeah. Tell him I'm on my way."

"That's my cue."

Camille hangs up the phone. "Thanks for coming in here and talking to me."

"No problem," Thomas replies as he opens her office door

"Oh. By the way. How are things with Phoebe?"

"Seriously. You want me to squeeze all of that into the four seconds it will take you to walk from behind that desk and walk away?"

Camille laughs. "You're right. I'm sorry."

"Yeah. You better be." Thomas walks to his office while Camille walks toward the conference room. Both ignore Monica, who is sitting at her desk directly in front of them.

Chapter 29: Right Out of a Movie

Today has some significance for Kimberly Richardson. For the first time in over a week, she is fast asleep in the bedroom of her Brooklyn apartment. She has been struggling to get a decent night's sleep since Oliver gave her the news of his new job in Japan. Her blissful state of sleep comes to an abrupt end as she opens one eye to the sound of her doorbell. The doorbell keeps ringing. She gets up and walks to the door.

"Who is it?"

"It's me, Playa!" Monica replies from the other side of the door.

Kimberly opens the door, letting Monica rush in. "What are you doing here so early?"

"I had an epiphany this week. I've been thinking and thinking and thinking. I know you've been really bummed at work, and the last two weeks have probably been the worst, right?"

"How could you tell? I've been doing such a great job of masking my feelings." She adds with a hint of sarcasm.

"Haha, funny. But seriously. I've seen a lot of heartbreak over the years. I know a lot of people who don't belong together for whatever reason or the other. But, when you met Oliver, it was different. I love watching you two together. I've never had a man treat me the way he treats you. Have you ever had a man treat you the way he does?" Monica places her hand on Kimberly's back, directing Kimberly to her bedroom.

"Sigh. No. Not really."

Monica opens the bedroom closet. "Right. Whenever we all go out, I spent most of that time watching you. I want what you have. I want a man that comes up behind me and kisses me for no reason or hugs me just because he can. Someone who smiles when I walk into a room."

"Monica. I agree with you. But..." Kimberly realizes that Monica is going through her closet. "Wait. What are you doing?"

Monica laughs, realizing that she didn't tell Kimberly why she was at her house this early in the morning. "Oh. Right. Here I am just going through your shit. You're probably like, 'what the hell is she doing?'"

"Yes. What the hell are you doing?"

"His flight is leaving today, right?"

"Yes."

"So, yeah. We're going to the airport."

Kimberly looks at Monica, expressing no emotion. "I am **not** going to the airport."

"If he came to the door right now and told you he's not going. Would you take him back?"

"I dunno."

"Stop bullshittin me and be serious. If he came to the door right now. This second and said he's not going to Japan. Would you take him back? Keep it real."

"Yes. I would take him back."

"See. I don't think you hate him. I think you still love him. I get that you're hurt, but you can't let the last year go to waste. That's a year of love. You guys are like a deck of fifty-two cards that all have their individual values. Fifty-two cards that belong together. If one card is removed. . . The entire deck of cards is useless."

Kimberly smiles, impressed with Monica analogy.

"You know I'm right. That's why you over there cheesin."

"I don't know what time his flight leaves."

"Bitch I got you. I hit up his man Justin."

"What are you doing talking to Justin?"

Monica swiftly turns toward the closet, changing the subject. "So, which jeans are you going to wear?"

A massive smile creeps on Kimberly's face. "Did you guys?" She squints her eyes, looking at Monica.

Monica's eyes veer down to the left as she has a flashback of her and Justin at a dark night club dancing and grinding with each other. Monica drinks straight from a champagne bottle while liquor pours down her face. They both kiss passionately while dancing in the middle of the dance floor. She remembers rolling around in Justin's bed at his apartment. A shirtless Justin is straddled by Monica as she is removing her tight one-piece mini dress and Bra. He leans up, sucking on her breast as she whips her head back, moaning. He flips her over on her stomach, removing her panties, kissing her back. Justin removes his pants and underwear, pulling her rear end upward, and enters her. She closes her eyes and –

"No. You didn't." Kimberly interrupts.

Monica comes out of her momentary trance, thinking about Justin. She reaches in the closet for a blouse. “You gotta rock this blouse right here, girl.”

Kimberly shakes her head, laughing at Monica. “You really amaze me sometimes.”

Monica avoids eye contact as she hands her a pair of jeans and a blouse. “Ok, so I'm gonna be in the kitchen.”

“Fine. But when I come out there, you're gonna spill the beans. I know you slept with him.”

"Nobody ain’t say shit about sleeping. But whatever."

Kimberly pushes Monica out of the room. “You’re too much.”

Monica walks into the kitchen, opening the refrigerator to get something to drink. She starts thinking about her rendezvous with Justin and comes out of a short trance, fanning herself from the flashback. “Shit. White boy had skills.”

Kimberly exits her bedroom, grabbing her keys before putting on a pair of sneakers and a Red Sox baseball cap. Monica and Kimberly exit the apartment driving on the BQE heading to JFK Airport in Monica's Range Rover. Monica is uncharacteristically jovial this morning. She smiles, looking over at Kimberly. “This is going to be so awesome.”
“I love your positive attitude,” Kimberly replies with a hint of sarcasm.

“You know what I realized. I need to be a little more like you. I don't want to settle for crap anymore.”

“You should use some of that positive energy and talk to Camille.”

“Nah. She came at me, ready to fight. She fucked with the wrong one.”

"You didn't even let her get to tell her story before you verbally attacked her. She's aware of her predicament and is suffering in silence. She and I have both been in such a funk. It would have been nice if she had one of her friends to vent to."

"Hmm."

"And on top of that, you're not talking to Thomas. That's ya, boy."

"Yeah. We had a little argument."

"Whatever that's going on between you two, you need to fix it."

"Yeah, well, he ain't feeling me right now."

"Just call him. You two are like best friends. I swear I don't know how that happened. But, he'd do anything for you. You know that."

"Sigh. Look. I'm not here to talk about Thomas."

"Well, I am. So, just like I listened to your logic about Oliver. You're going to listen to me. You just said a moment ago that you should be more like me. Then listen."

"Ahh shit. Putting on the mom pants right now."

"Yep. Keep it up, and I'll put your ass on time out."
Monica laughs as Kimberly continues.

"You and Thomas have the weirdest friendship. I can't say I understand it, but shit, you two are thick as thieves. Whatever you did —"

"Whoa. Why do you think I did something?"

"Oh, please. Trust me. It was you."

"Daaaammmmmnnn. I get no love."

“And as for Camille. You need to call her or something. You made her feel worse than she was feeling when she started telling us her story. She didn't tell us her personal business to get judged. You haven't walked a mile in her shoes, so don't act like you know everything.”

“Yes, ma’am.”

“And don't let me have to go upside your head with my slipper.”

“Alright, alright.” Monica laughs.

They arrive at the departure section of the JFK International Airport. The deck is filled with cars dropping off people who are trying to catch their flights. Police and airport security direct the cars to move as parking is not allowed in that section of the airport.
“Ok, girl. Out.”

“What?”

"I can't wait here. The cops are going to make me move."

"If I get out, where will you be?"

"I’ll pull over somewhere. Just call me when you need me to come to pick you up. His flight leaves at 10:45. He needs to be here two hours before departure."

Kimberly exits the car closing the door. "How do we know he’s not already inside?"

"Yeah. So, Justin and I planned this. PEACE!" Monica gestures the peace sign with her fingers before she drives off.

Kimberly watches Monica drive off, shaking her head while walking to the curb, waiting for Oliver. "Stupid."

Meanwhile, Justin and Oliver are in a taxicab entering JFK International Airport.

"Remind me to pick up an iPhone charger when we get to the airport. "Justin says to Oliver.

Oliver looks out the window as they enter the departure area. "Uh-huh."

"I didn't get any sleep last night. I was anxious as hell. But I'll probably sleep through most of this flight. How'd you sleep last night?"

"I didn't."

"Didn't sleep?"

"Yeah. I tossed and turned."

The taxi pulls up to the departure terminal. Oliver gets out and walks to the back of the taxi to remove his luggage from the trunk while Justin pays the driver. Through the window, Justin can see Kimberly approaching the cab. Justin exits the taxi to help Oliver with the bags.

Justin says, attempting to take all the bags, "I got this, dude."

"What? Nah. I'll grab my bags."

"Yeah, well. Look behind you."

Oliver turns around to see Kimberly walking toward him. He smiles, opening his arms as he takes a few steps towards her. "Hey, baby."

Kimberly walks into his open arms. "Hi, baby."

Kimberly and Oliver stand in the street, holding each other for a moment as cars drive around them. Justin picks up the bags, placing them on the curb. They both cry in each other's arms. Justin watches them for a moment taking a picture with his cell phone.

"I love you so much, baby," Oliver says in her ear.

"I know you do. I didn't make this easy for you. I'm sorry."

"It's ok. I'm the one that's sorry."
Kimberly pulls back to look at Oliver. "I love you too. I'm going to miss you so much."

"I promise you. I am going to find a way to fix this."

"I know. I know you will."

"I don't want us to break up."

"Neither do I."

"We can skype. Or some other form of video chat. There's a device that actually works as a video phone between two parties. I can have the company set it up directly in your office and at home.

"Baby. Set it up."

"Really?"

"Yeah. I don't want to lose you. We don't know what tomorrow will bring for both of us. My hope is that one day in the future, we'll be telling the story of our little bump in the road. And this will be the worst thing that happens in our relationship."

"You don't know how happy I am to hear you say that."

Kimberly looks up at Oliver as tears stream down her face. "I already miss you."

Oliver pulls her closer. "I'm so sorry, baby. I'm so so sorry."

Justin walks over to Oliver. "Hey, buddy. . . Just a quick FYI. We gotta check in soon. I can take care of the bags."

Oliver shakes his head in acknowledgment. "Ok."

Kimberly wipes away her tears. "Ok, baby. I know you gotta go."

"I just want to hold you for a few more seconds."

"That's fine by me."

They embrace each other, followed by a long passionate kiss. He pulls away, taking a long look at her face before walking into the terminal. "I love you," Oliver says as he walks into the terminal, looking back at her waving.

"I love you," she says as he enters the airport. Justin waves as well, blowing a kiss at her. Oliver moves him out of the way, continuing to wave goodbye. Oliver continues through the terminal, checking into his flight. Kimberly remains standing at the curb, watching Oliver walk away. Monica circles around the airport, returning to pick up Kimberly. Monica drives up to the curb behind Kimberly. "Hey, girl. Get that big booty in here."

Kimberly enters the car and immediately begins to cry hysterically, covering her face. "This sucks!"

Monica puts the car in park and places her arms around her. "It's ok, girl."

The airport security officer notices the car park in the loading zone. He walks up to Monica's car, tapping on the window. "Ma'am, please move your car."

"Ok. One second."

"Not one second. Now!"

“I said one second."

"I SAID NOW, MA’AM!"

"I SAID ONE FUCKING SECOND BITCH! MY FRIEND IS CRYING!"

The airport Security Officer grabs his Walkie Talkie. "Control. This is 2-7. We have an unauthorized vehicle in the no standing zone at the departure ramp. An occupant is refusing to move her vehicle."

"Oh, Fuck you, you pain in the ass!! You don't even have a gun. You gotta call the big dawg."

Monica places the car in drive, pulling off exiting the airport.

Inside the airport, Justin and Oliver walk through the terminal toward the gate for their flight. Oliver stares out at nothing. "I didn't expect to see her."

Justin walks beside Oliver smiling. He turns to Oliver. "Her friend Monica called me."

"Really?"

"Yeah. We concocted a scheme to get her here. I knew that she wasn't taking your calls. We figured once you two saw each other. . ."

Oliver places his hand on Justin's shoulder. "You're a pain in the ass, but you're a good friend."

Justin laughs. "Thanks. I saw how broken up you were. It was driving me insane."

"Oh. So, you did all this for yourself?"

"Noooo. I just wanted you two to talk. Even if it was for a brief moment and look, it worked. You both are better off today than you were yesterday."

"Yeah. You're right. Thanks, man."

They both walk to the gate of their departing flight, taking a seat in the waiting area before the ticket agent begins the boarding process.

Chapter 30: Every Action Has A Reaction

After an all-day girl hangout session with Kimberly, Monica heads home to Prospect Park, Brooklyn. She pulls up to her home, parking her vehicle in the street directly in front of her house. She exits the car walking up the exterior stairs. She turns right to look around the quiet neighborhood. She can sense something is off but cannot see anything out of the ordinary. She retrieves her keys from her purse and enters the house closing the door behind her. After removing her shoes, she tosses her purse on the sofa as she walks to the kitchen, where she places her keys in one of the drawers. She walks to her bedroom taking off her clothes, tossing them on the bed, remaining in a t-shirt and underwear. Monica touches her pants, looking for her cell phone. She realizes after she doesn't find it that she placed it in her purse. She exits the bedroom stopping in place, feeling a presence to her left. Monica turns toward the guest bedroom door. Kareem appears in the darkroom, standing in the doorway wearing a dark hooded sweatshirt. She is overcome with fear as she looks down at his balled-up fist. "You send some niggas to fuck me up?"

"No. I didn't. I swear." Monica's breathing becomes heavy as she is frozen in place and doesn't say another word. Kareem steps toward her, punching Monica in the face knocking her to the floor. It's the hardest she's ever been hit. She can feel a warm sensation of blood trickle down her left nostril. She lies on the floor, looking up at Kareem standing over her. She tries to move, but someone steps on her arm, preventing her from moving. One of Kareem's friends accompanies him to ambush Monica. She looks up at the other person wearing a mask to cover his mouth. Kareem squats down, grabbing her by the shirt, lifting her head off the floor. Her eyes glaze over as she struggles to stay conscious.

"Payback is a bitch." Kareem says as he raises his fist, striking Monica again.

That evening at the home of Juan Pablo Chacon in the Castle Hill section of the Bronx, Thomas and Phoebe are attending her family's barbeque. As the barbeque ends, most of the Chacon family disperse to head home for the evening. Phoebe's father, Juan Pablo, along with her brothers and cousins, are the last remaining guest finishing a game of dominoes. Thomas looks at his watch, realizing it's getting late, and starts to say his goodbyes. "Alright. It's about that time."

"What the hell, man. We're just getting started." Says Phoebes' oldest brother Carlos.

"I know, but It's been a long-ass day for me. I had to help my dad move some furniture today. I'm beat."

"That sucks, man. But hey. Thanks for coming. This shit was fun. When we do this again, you better come."

"Definitely, man. Then I'll show you, boys, how you really play dominos."

"Yo, Phoebe," Carlos yells across the yard. "Ya man got jokes."

"Callate tonto." She fires back.

The family laughs as Thomas stands up to leave. He says goodbye to everyone as he walks up to Phoebe. "This was awesome. Thanks for the invite."

"Anytime. We enjoyed having you."

I was hoping you enjoyed my presence more than they did.

Phoebe playfully laughs. "Of course, I did. If it were up to me, I'd go with you."

"I wouldn't stop you."

She bashfully smiles, looking back at her father, who watches them talk. "I know. But I'm here with the family and all. It wouldn't look good in my father's eyes."

"I totally get it. I just didn't want to stop flirting."

"Yeah. Me too."

"Well. I'm gonna head home now."

"Ok. I'll walk you down to your car."

Thomas smiles. "That would be great."

Thomas and Phoebe walk down to his car. They stop in front of his car as he unlocks the car.

Phoebe looks back at her father's house. She is out of view of her family. She turns back to Thomas. "Ok. So..."

Thomas steps forward, placing his hands around her waist, pulling her close, kissing her passionately. She placed both hands around his neck, and they share a passionate moment. They slowly pull away from each other, staring into each other's eyes. "I've been.... Waiting all day to do that."

"So was I," Phoebe replies, smiling at Thomas. He smiles back, leaning in rubbing his nose against hers. "Alright. So, I really gotta go. I'll see you on Monday?"

"I'm off Monday. So, most likely Tuesday."

Thomas enters the car holding her hand. "Tuesday, it is. Have a good night."

"You too. Get home safe."

"I will. See you later."

Thomas drives off, heading home to Whitestone, New York.

Hours later, in Brooklyn, Monica lays on the floor of her kitchen. She opens her eyes, only able to see out of her right eye. She touches the left side of her face and feels a numb sensation. Her left eye is closed shut. She slowly stands up, leaning on the kitchen counter, looking down at her ripped shirt smeared with blood. She looks around her living room, and her flat screen T.V. has been knocked to the floor, shattering the screen. A few DVDs and CDs are scattered across the floor, along with a picture of the family. Monica turns to her left and can see her love seat is turned on its back. She utilizes the wall for support as she limps to her bedroom. She slides across the wall entering her bedroom.

Slowly Monica walks to the closet pulling a pair of sweatpants and a Rocawear hooded sweatshirt off the shelf. She sits on the bed to get dressed. Monica pulls the hood over her head while walking out of the room toward the kitchen. Feeling a little weak, she takes a break leaning on the refrigerator, hanging her head low, taking a deep breath, which causes her to cough. She opens one of the draws in the kitchen and takes her keys. She continues walking slowly over to the front door, still using the wall for support. A pair of flip flops are by the front door. She manipulates her feet to slide into the slippers without bending. She walks over to the sofa picking up her purse before turning out the lights, exiting her house, and locking the door behind her. Walking down the stairs, she stumbles, falling to the ground. A man walking his dog sees her stumble and walks over to render assistance.

"Ma'am. Are you ok?"

Monica takes a deep breath before answering. "Uh-huh. I'm good." She says as she struggles to get up. The Pedestrian grabs her arm to help. "Lemme help you."

He grabs her bruised arm. "Ouch!" She grabs her arm in pain. As she shifts her body from the pain in her arm, the pedestrian can see a small portion of her face when the hood partially exposes her face. The pedestrian pulls away in shock. "Oh, my G--. What happened to you?"

"I'm good. I'm good. Thank you so much, though." She pulls away, walking towards her car

"You're getting in that car? Do you think you should be driving?"

"Yeah. Don't worry. . . I do this shit all the time." She replies as she coughs.
She unlocks her car, slowly entering. The pedestrian watches in horror as her movements clearly indicate that she is in really bad shape.

"Please be careful."

Monica waves him off and drives away. She treks from Prospect Park Brooklyn to Whitestone Queens. She pulls up to a two-story house and parks along the sidewalk. The drive from Brooklyn has worn her out, and she has trouble gaining the energy to open the door to exit. She steps out of the car, falling to the ground. Monica takes a deep breath, using her last bit of energy to stand up using the car as leverage. She looks up at the second-story window and can see the light from a television flickering. Monica takes a few deep breaths to gather the strength to walk up to the front door ringing the bell marked the second floor. She leans on the door frame and can hear a noise as an inside door opens. The sound of someone walking down the stairs gets closer to the door. The locks click one after the other, and the door opens. Thomas is standing in front of her. He looks down at her, but the hoodie restricts the view of her face.

"Monica?" He says as he looks at her car then back at her. "What are you doing here?"

Monica raises her head, looking up at Thomas. A tear runs down her face. Her voice crackles. "Can I come in, please?"

"WHAT THE F—!" Thomas shouts as his eyes widen, covering his mouth with both of his hands, shocked and frozen in place. The left side of her face is severely bruised. Her left eye is shut. Her lip is busted open, swollen, and covered in dry blood

"Tommy. I know you're mad at me, but can I please – " Her knees start to buckle as she slides down on the side of the door. Thomas grabs her with both hands placing his arms around her before she falls. Thomas looks around outside before pulling her into the house.

"What the hell happened to you?"

"You should see the other mother fucker." Monica jokes, attempting to smile. The pain surrounding her mouth prevents her from smiling. Thomas leans her against the wall stepping back, taking a look at her face. He's speechless and can't find any words to say to her.

"I know what you're thinking. Sexy as fuck, right?" She quips, still attempting to smile but can't from the pain. She slides down the wall crying. Thomas' eyes fill with tears as he cannot believe she is standing in front of him in this condition. He grabs her before she falls, lifting her up, taking her upstairs.

"Yeah. I was about to say. I dunno if I can make it up those stairs. I'm beat. . . No pun intended." She continues trying to be humorous.

"This isn't funny, Monica. This shit isn't funny." Thomas replies. Monica places her arms around his neck, burying her face in his shoulder, and cries. She knows the severity of the situation and that Thomas is not finding anything funny.

"I know. But what else am I supposed to do?" She says as her voice cracks from emotion.

Thomas enters his apartment, softly placing her on the sofa sitting her upright. He kneels down, sliding the hood back, pushing her hair back from her face with both hands. He places his hand on her chin to raise her head. His chin begins to quiver from the sight of her face. Monica observes Thomas fighting emotion. "Please don't cry for me, Thomas. I can't take that shit."

"Kareem did this, didn't he?" He asks.

Monica hangs her head and doesn't answer, which is all the answer Thomas needs.

"Mother fucker."

Thomas takes a deep breath continuing to look at Monica's bruises.

"You need medical attention. I don't know what to do with you."

Monica panics. "Please don't call anyone. Can I just stay here?"

"Have you seen your face?! What am I supposed to do?" He replies as tears run down his face.

"Tommy, please. Can I just stay here? I just want to sleep."

"You can sleep at a hospital. I can take you and stay with you. They can give you pain meds."

"But I won't feel safe there. I already feel safe here. With you."

Thomas ponders her request staring at her. She looks up at him through her right eye. Tears run down her face as her chin quivers. "Please?"

Thomas knows this is a bad idea keeping her at his house in this condition. His police Instincts tell him there needs to be a police report filed. His Street side tells him this may be a matter best left away from police hands. But his paternal and loyal side tells him to take care of her. No matter what the consequences. "Ok. ok."

Thankful for Thomas's response, she leans forward, dropping her head on his shoulder, wrapping her arms around him. She feels safe for the moment but still fights the uncontrollable urge to cry. Thomas slowly wraps his arms around her, causing her to jump up from the pain. "Ouch."

Thomas pulls away, concerned that he may have hurt her. He notices Monica turning her body to avoid the pain on her left side. He slowly reaches for her shirt, slightly pulling it up, exposing her entire left side, which appears bruised. He pulls the shirt up higher, exposing the bruise leading up to her bra. Thomas presses his lips together, exhaling through his nose. The look on Thomas' face is embarrassing. Monica looks away as tears continue to fill her eyes.

"I'm sorry."

"Don't apologize. Why are you apologizing?"
"You look upset."

"Yes. I'm upset. I'm very upset. But I'll have to deal with my rage later. Can you take off the hoodie?"

"Can you do it? I can't lift my arm."

"Sure

Thomas removes the hoodie exposing the ripped t-shirt smeared in blood. "Let me get you a t-shirt."

Thomas runs to his bedroom and returns with an NYPD t-shirt. He assists Monica with putting it on. He runs to the linen closet, grabs a small washcloth, and a first aid kit from the bathroom. He returns with a soaked washcloth kneeling in front of her using it to clean the blood from her face. He watches her carefully as her eyes are fixated on nothing as she stares at the wall behind him.

"Are you ok?" he asks.

Monica starts to cry uncontrollably. “No!”

Thomas softly places both hands on her face. "It's ok. I’m gonna take care of you."

"I'm sorry for being an asshole to you."

Thomas laughs. "No, you're not."

Thomas utilizes a rubber band to tie her hair up, keeping it out of her face. He gives her hydrogen peroxide and water to rinse out the cut in her mouth. He uses the First Aid kit to finish cleaning her face before he places bandages on her cuts. He leans back to look at her. Thomas has done a good job cleaning away the blood. "Ok. You can't stay out here. I’m gonna carry you to the bedroom, ok?"

"No. I’ll stay out here with you."

"No. I’ll stay with you in there. You need to rest."

"I don't know if I can go to work on Monday."

"You might want to consider taking an extremely extended leave of absence."

"You got jokes."

Thomas lifts her off the sofa carrying Monica to his bedroom, placing her on the bed. She rolls over to her right side as Thomas places a few pillows under her head, pulling the sheets over her. "Can you turn on the TV?" She asks.

"Sure," Thomas says as he walks to the left side of the bed. He picks up the remote control and turns on the TV. He kneels down next to her rubbing her forehead gently. She tries to smile, but it hurts. Thomas looks her body over from head to toe. Her eyes start to fade into asleep. Fearing that she may have taken more than a beating, he hesitates to ask the next question. "Hey."

"Whassup?"

"Sigh."

"What, Thomas?"

"I can only see your face and your torso."

"Yeah, so?"

"Is there any other part of you that I can't see that may have any bruises?"

She rolls her eyes upward as she thinks. "I think my left thigh. It hurts."

"Ok," Thomas replies, hesitating to continue. "Um. Is there any other part of you, perhaps a part of you that I shouldn't look at. . .?

Monica shuts her eyes. "Nobody violated me if that's what you're asking."

"That's exactly what I was asking. I'm glad to hear that. I'm gonna get you some ice for the side of your face. It's swollen.

"Ok. Thank you."

"No problem."

Thomas walks to the kitchen and opens the freezer removing the ice tray. He places the ice in a Ziplock bag and heads back to the room. As he gets close to the bedroom door, he stops walking and heads back to the kitchen. He tosses the ice on the counter, resting both hands on the stove, hanging his head, shutting his eyes, taking a moment to gather his emotions. Quickly he shakes it off and fights tear. He takes a moment to gather himself, taking a few deep breaths.

He looks around his apartment. The TV in the living room is still on with her clothes on the floor. He walks over to the tv, shutting it off before tidying up the living room. He gathers himself before returning to the bedroom. Monica is in the same position he left her in. He places a paper towel between her face and the bag of ice holding it in place. Thomas notices Monica's body jerk as she cries. "I'm so stupid, Thomas. You told me he was bad for me, but I didn't listen. I told him to get out, and he packed up his shit and left. I thought I was done with him. He must have made a copy of the key because when I got home, he was in my house. He said, “you send someone to fuck me up?” I was like, “No. I swear,” then he punched me in the face."

Thomas listens in disgust.

"That fucking shit hurt Thomas. He hit me again, and I thought he broke my nose. I said to stop, but he kept swinging. So, I kicked him in the balls. I went to grab something to kill that mother fucker, but he had one of his fucking friends with him on the other side of the house. He came over and held me down. I tried to fight him off, but I couldn't. Next thing I know, Kareem was coming at me with his right hand balled up into a fist. I thought if he hits me again, I'm gonna pass out. Unfortunately, I didn't.".

Thomas squeezes his lips together as tears flow down his face.

"He punched me as hard as he could in my mouth. I felt dizzy. I fell to the floor. . . I felt a pain in my side, but I don't know if he kicked me or not. I don't remember much after that."

Thomas places his hand on the top of her head. "It's ok, Monica. You’re here now. You did the right thing coming here. No one is going to hurt you here."

"I know. Thank you."

Thomas remains at her side with the ice on her face, gently rubbing the top of her head. She calmly relaxes nestled on the right side of the bed, facing Thomas. Thomas reaches into his pocket and retrieves his cell phone unlocking the screen. He starts swiping side to side as he reads the information on the phone. Monica's eyes open, looking at Thomas read.

"Thomas."
Thomas raises his head, looking into her right eye. "Yes."

"What are you doing?" Monica asks.

"I'm looking up concussion symptoms."

"What does it say?"

"A bunch of stuff. But the fact that you couldn't walk is now a concern."

"I just got beat up, Thomas. My leg hurts, and I'm tired."

"It's ok. It also advises that it's pretty much ok to sleep, but I've gotta wake you up every
few hours to check for symptoms."

"Thomas. I really don't wanna go to the hospital."

"I know, but If you show a symptom when I wake you up, I'm gonna take you to a hospital."

"No. If I show a symptom, I'll just stay awake."

"Monica."

"Thomas."

"Look. I don't want you to die because I was stupid for not taking you to the hospital. You know what it's going to look like if you die in my house with these bruises?

"I took care of that."

Thomas inquisitively looks at Monica. "What do you mean you took care of it? What does that mean?"

"While driving here, I took a short video detailing what happened and where I was going for help. I saved it to my phone."

Thomas sits back, smiling, saying nothing. Monica waits for Thomas' to say something. "Monica. You're so smart. Thank you for thinking of everything. You're the best," she states humorously.
"Finally, using your head."

"I didn't want anything to happen to you. I took a peek at my face in the mirror on the way here. Not my finest hour, I must say. So, I figured I'd record a quick video detailing today's incident."

They sit quietly for a moment. Thomas removes the ice from her face and sits on the floor, staring at her face rubbing his head with both hands. Monica appears to have dozed off falling asleep.

"This is all my fault," Thomas whispers to himself.

"It's not your fault," Monica replies with her eyes closed.

"I thought you were asleep."

"Nope. I'm just laying here, not moving."

"Ok. Try to get some sleep."

"Why? so you can wake me up in two hours?"

"You have a point. But you need to rest "

"You should get some sleep too. I completely fucked your night. I can imagine how
tired you are."

"It's ok. I'm good. I figure at some point I'll fall asleep wherever I am."

"Thomas."

"Yeah."

"I heard what you said. . . This is not your fault."

Thomas hangs his head.

"I know what you did was because you care. I've never had someone fight for me before. Never. With all the shit I've been through. I can't say that anyone has stood up for me— not my family, not my friends, no one. I know I ripped you a new asshole for doing what you did. But I regretted saying the things I said to you the minute I said it. You're such a good person, and I am so lucky to have you as my friend. All the shit I said, and now you're here taking care of me. Thank you. And I mean that from the bottom of my heart."

"We were never not friends. We just had a fight. All that other shit was us just blowing off steam. This friendship is over when I say it's over."

Monica opens her arms for a hug. Thomas crawls up to her hugging her. He kisses her forehead

"Seriously. Just relax. You have a hell of a day tomorrow."

"Why do you say that?"

"Your bruises are going to be sore. And you're going to see yourself in a mirror."

"Wonderful. I'm just hoping this is a bad dream. I'll wake up in my bed and all this shit
was just a fucked-up nightmare."

Monica lay motionless, finally nodding off falling asleep. Thomas remains seated at the bedside, watching her sleep. After about twenty minutes, Thomas finds it hard to hold off sleep as his eyes start to feel heavy, causing him to fall asleep shortly thereafter on the floor beside her.

The next morning Monica wakes up, looking around the room. She opens her mouth to yawn, quickly shutting it due to the pain in her jaw. She softly calls for Thomas, who doesn't answer. She rolls off the bed in pain, standing up, walking to the bathroom. Thomas intercepts her before she enters that bathroom. "What are you doing?"

"What does it look like I'm doing. I gotta pee."

"You ok?"

"I feel like shit."

"Ok. I was going to make breakfast, but you were asleep. I can make something now."

"I'll eat whatever you make. But first, lemme go pee."

"Sure."

Monica goes to the bathroom as Thomas enters the kitchen to make her breakfast. After using the bathroom, she washes her hands, staring into the mirror. She moves her head side to side to see all of the bruises taking a deep breath. She walks out of the bathroom entering the kitchen to sit at the table, saying nothing. Thomas places a plate of food in front of her to eat.

"Thank you, Thomas,"

"It's my pleasure. How do you feel?"

"Again. Like shit."

"Sigh. I can imagine."

"They both sit quietly for a moment while she eats.

"Listen. I gotta run an errand. If I leave you here, will you be ok?"

"I suppose so. What's so important?"

"I gotta do something quick for my father."

"Ok. Can I ask you to buy me some pringles when you come back?"

"Tell you what. Text me a list of items that you might need, and I'll get it for you."

"Awesome. Thank you."

Within an hour, Thomas drives on the Bruckner Expressway, headed to the Hunts Point area of the Bronx. Thomas exits the highway, driving through Hunts Point until he arrives at Beck Street. He parks his vehicle, getting out walking toward a few unsavory types. Four massive thugs watch him walk toward them. They wear Jeans, Timberland boots, and baseball jerseys. Thomas smiles at the group and greets them with an urban handshake. "What's up, boys?"

"Sup big homie." One of the thugs says to Thomas.

"Where's E?"
"YO, E!!" One of the thugs yells into the house.

"Emmanuel, a six-foot two-inch three-hundred-and-twenty-pound Dominican man, walks out of his house looking left then right. He makes eye contact with Thomas. "Ahh shit. Whassup Wall street?"

"Nothing." Thomas laughs. "What's up with you?"

"You know me, dawg. I'm holding this shit down."

Thomas raises his right-hand, gesturing to say no more. "Well. Spare me the details."
They greet each other with a hug.

"So, what brings you all the way up here? You busy tripping over hedge funds and shit?"

"I need to talk to you about something very serious. No cell phones. No Bluetooth."

"Aight. Come in. Mom is back there, hooking up some chuletas."

"This is why I'm never leaving this city. Someone's always cooking some good food." Thomas enters the house with Emmanuel to talk.

Chapter 31: I'm Not Sure I Heard you Correctly

Early Monday morning at Plante Insurance, Isabella walks down the hallway back to her desk with a manila folder placing it on her desk. Benjamin sits at his desk, looking at his computer monitor, working on an insurance policy.

"What are you working on?" Isabella asks Benjamin.

"Nothing in particular. Why?"

"I may need you to look at an umbrella policy from 1986."

"1986? Shit. Who was the insured? Ozzy Osbourne?"

Isabella laughs. "No. It was Lisa Lisa and Cult Jam."

"Oh, baby. I loved her. I was a little too young for her, but I remember her from the video throwbacks."

"I'm sure," Isabelle says as she opens the folder removing some pages.

Benjamin stares at Isabella, turning pages in the file. He musters up the courage to say something that he's been holding on to all morning. "So, Um. I have some news for you."

"Good news, I hope." Isabella continues looking over the policy.

"Partially."

Isabella turns to looks at Benjamin. "What is it?"

"I just handed in my two weeks' notice."

"WHAT?!"

Benjamin looks around as other employees look over at Isabella. "You may want to lower your voice."

"You never told me you were leaving."

"Because I didn't know I was leaving."

"So, what happened? Why are you leaving? Are your kids ok?

"Kids are fine. It's my sister. Her restaurant in Long Island is a massive hit. She's asked me to come aboard and help her run it. She had to make some staff changes and wants someone she can trust to manage it. So, I'm going to be the general manager."

Isabella looks at him, speechless.

"She made me an offer I couldn't pass up."

"Wow. . . this sucks."

"No, it isn't."

"No. I mean for me. I'm going to really miss you."

"Yeah. I feel the same way. Actually, I was worried about telling you."

"Why?"

"I thought you would be upset."

"I am. I'm very upset. But it's family, so I get it."

"I'm sorry. I wish I could split myself, leaving one of me here to work with you."

Isabella stares at Benjamin, trying to process the news. She finds it hard to reply to his last statement. "I'm sorry. I'm just speechless."

"All good things must come to an end."

"What does that mean?"

"Well. This. Us working together. We were having way too much fun. Something had to come and break that up."

"So just like that... Our friendship is over?"
Benjamin laughs. "No. Not at all. I just meant how awesome it was to work together. We get along great, and we help each other's day go by faster. We're still friends."

The thought of losing her close friend frustrates Isabella. She stands up, walking away from Benjamin. "Excuse me."

"Hey, wait. Are you upset?" He asks while she walks towards the bathroom, not answering Benjamin. He continues staring down the hall, mumbling. "I thought she'd at least be a little happy for me."

A few blocks away at North Mutual Insurance Company, Kimberly and Camille exit a staff meeting. They walk side by side down the hall together, discussing details of a renewal meeting. "I'm not fully sure we're going to be able to retain that customer. The premium is increasing by about thirty percent. They're a high-risk company and are doing nothing to minimize the accident frequency at their job sites." Camille says to Kimberly.

"If they at least put protocols in place to help reduce those risks, it's possible that in a few years, the premiums could decrease. But they're way too stubborn. However, if they do leave, the next carrier is going to rape them on the premium. They'd best be served to stay with us. Take the beating to their wallet, and let us try to work out a premium adjustment in the coming years."

"Yeah. You have a point. You may want to put together a plan on how we can approach them with the potential price increase."

"Ok, I'll – " Kimberly shuts her eyes holding her stomach, stopping in place. "Ugh."

"Hey. What's the matter?" Camille asks.

Kimberly hands Camille her paperwork and bolts to the bathroom. Camille follows her into the bathroom, where Kimberly is in a stall throwing up. Camille stands outside the stall. "Sigh. You ok?"

"I'm just nauseous. I'm ok. I'll be out in a sec."

"I'll put some water on your desk."

"Thank you."
"Camille walks out of the bathroom, shaking her head. Her phone buzzes from a text. She looks at her phone, reading a text from Garrett *[Hey baby. I miss you.]* She deletes the message.

That evening at Thomas' house, He sits on the left side of his sofa watching TV with Monica on the right, laying on her right side with her feet close to Thomas. They both laugh at the TV show on the television. Monica switches position, laying on her back, tilting her head to the right to continue to watch TV. She looks up at Thomas

"Hey."

Thomas turns to look at Monica. "What's up?"

Monica smiles, lifting up her feet near his face. "Can you gimme a foot rub?"

"No. Get your feet outta my face." He says with annoyance.

Monica Laughs. "Come on. Be a pal."

"I'm not giving you a foot rub. "

"I'm gonna be stuck here for a bit. I'm overdue for a pedicure. Usually, after my pedicure, I always get a foot rub. I need a foot rub badly."

"Man. That's gotta suck. Tell you what I will do."

Monica sits up, smiling at full attention. "What?"

"How about I drive around to one of these many nail salons. I'm sure I'll find a family member of yours to come to do your nails and give you a foot rub."

"Awww. You would do that for me?"

"Of course."

"Kool. Before you take care of that, would you be able to give me a back rub first?"

"Monica. I'm not rubbing any part of your body."

"Sigh. You suck!"
"Oh, really?"

"You know I'm just playing. Chill out, Pops."

"I know. But on the real. You need to clip those toenails."

Monica burst out laughing. "See. I need to get my toes done. Can you take me to a nail salon soon?"

"Have you looked in the mirror? You are not leaving this house looking like that. You asked to stay here. While you're staying here, you can't leave. People will think I did that to you."

"I know. But I'm getting antsy staying here all day."

"I can imagine. But you can't leave this house, Monica. If I find out you left, I'll take you elsewhere."

"Fine."

"I take it, you spoke with Kim?"

"I told her I had an urgent family emergency to deal with."

"Ok. I didn't see her at work today. She was in a few meetings, so we missed each other."

"Hmmm."

Thomas points at Monica as he remembers he has to tell her something. "Oh. I had a locksmith friend of mine go over to your house and change the locks. He went through the house and made sure all of the windows were locked up. One of your windows was questionable, so he reinforced it. I put the keys in your purse."

"That's awesome. Thank you so much." Monica replies looking away.

Thomas notices her mood change. "You ok?"

"Yeah. I just had a flashback." Monica turns back to her right side.

"Hey. I didn't mean to –"

"No. It's not you. I just. . . I'm just trying to stay positive. It's not easy."

"Yeah. Situations like yours come with hurdles that can be tough to cross. But I've got your back."

Monica turns her head to look at Thomas and smiles before looking back at the TV. "I know. Thank you "

Chapter 32: Good Things Come To Those Who Wait?

Oliver sits behind his desk in his large picturesque office in Tokyo at 12:30 p.m. There are three computer monitors on a glass desk with glass walls. To his right is a massive window overlooking the city from the forty-seventh floor. Oliver is chatting with Kimberly via a video chatting service that his company set up for Oliver specifically. "Hi, baby," Kimberly says over the small LCD screen.

"Hello, my love," Oliver replies.

"I miss you so much."

"Nowhere near as much as I miss you. Not even close."

Kimberly bashfully smiles.

Oliver points at the screen. "That's what I miss right there."

"Well. You won't have to miss it for too long."

"What?"

"I just purchased a ticket to come to see you."

Oliver smiles from ear to ear. "Are you kidding me?!"

"Nope. See." Kimberly holds up a ticket for an Oceanic flight to Japan, placing it in front of the camera.

"You just made my day, babe. You have no idea how you just made my day."
Kimberly watches Oliver look up, waving at someone to come over to his desk. "Come here." He says.

"Who's there?"

"Justin."

Justin's face pops up on the screen, sending Kimberly into a mild frenzy. She contains herself immediately, looking through the glass door of her office to see if anyone hears her. She turns back to the LCD screen. "Hey, Justin. How are you?!"

"I'm great. Tired as shit, though. But look at you. You look great."

"I know what you did for me. I wish I'd known before. I would have given you a big hug. You're so sweet, and I totally appreciate you."

"Aww, thanks. It was no problem, Kim. I saw what he was going through, and I knew we had to do something. I was going to come to your office, but Monica talked me out of it."

"You're awesome. Thank you so much. I'm coming to visit. When I see you, be prepared for a bear hug.

"Bring it on!"

All three laugh before Oliver playfully interjects. "You're not hugging my girl. Get out."

Justin waves off Oliver continuing his conversation with Kimberly. "I can't wait to see you, Kimberly. See ya later."

"Bye, Justin," Kimberly replies, blowing a kiss.

"Ok. You need to cut that out." Oliver says while pushing Justin out of view.

"So, are you guys busy over there?"

"Yeah. But don't worry about that."

Kimberly and Oliver continue to carry on a conversation behind closed doors for over an hour.

Chapter 33: I'm Not The One.

Late evening at the Bauman residence, Dylan shuts off the lights in the living room as he heads upstairs to bed. He reaches the middle of the stairs calling out to Camille. She lifts the remote control changing the channel to a late-night talk show. "You coming up to bed, babe?" Dylan asks.

"No. You go on without me. I'll be up later."

"Camille. You say that every night. It's like you're trying to avoid me."

"I'm not, honey," Camille replies in her usual monotoned demeanor.

Dylan walks back down the stairs toward Camille, who now appears annoyed that he's returning. "Did I do something wrong?"

"No. I just want to watch TV. What's gotten into you?"

"I'm not stupid, Cami. I know something's up, and you don't want to tell me."

"Nothing is up. I just want to watch TV." She chuckles, attempting to diffuse his inquiry.

Dylan stands motionless, hovering over Camille as she looks at the TV. His presence at this moment standing over her really gets under her skin. "What?"

"You're gonna just sit there and ignore me."

Camille turns to face him with a big sarcastic smile. "There. I'm not ignoring you now. What do you need me to hear you say this late at night?"

"Don't be a bitch. I just want to know what's up with you. You refuse to be anywhere near me. It feels like when you are close to me; you're forcing yourself."

"Honey. I'm not forcing anything. However, I'm forcing myself now to listen to this." She points toward the floor.

"Is it my drinking?"

"Dammit. No babe. It's not your drinking."
"Ok. So, it's something then."

"What?"
"You said it's not my drinking. You could have said it's nothing."

"I DID SAY NOTHING A MINUTE AGO!" Camille realizes she's yelling and take a quick moment to calm down. "Sigh. You're pissing me off. Why don't you just go to bed?"

"I'll go to bed when I'm damn good and ready. You don't get to tell me what to do."

Camille calmly turns toward the TV turning up the volume on the remote control.
Dylan snatches the remote, shutting off the TV. "You're not going to ignore me any further. Talk to me."

Camille sits up, staring at the black TV screen brewing with rage.

"If it's not the drinking, is it my E.D.? Is it the trips with my friends?" Dylan asks.

Camille calmly stands up and walks toward the stairs. "This shit is getting old."

"Where the hell are you going?"

Camille talks through her teeth, "To bed.... So, you can shut up. Are you happy now?"

Dylan runs over to Camille, grabbing her by the arm, spinning her around, raising his hand to hit her. "Who do you think you're talking to?"

"A limp dick drunk fuck! Go ahead. Hit me, mother fucker! It'll be the last FUCKING THING YOU DO!!" Camille takes a step towards Dylan's face.

Dylan lowers his hand in shock. "What's gotten into you?"

"Not you. I'd ask you to finger me, but your finger probably stuck in the curved position because you're always holding a bottle. And yes. Since you asked. Your constant drinking gets on my last fucking nerve. That and when you're drunk around your stupid golf buddies, you talk too damn much about shit no one else is talking about. It's fucking embarrassing."

"Tell me how you really feel!"

"I wasn't done. You get drunk, then you come home and wanna fuck me. You get me all hot and bothered, then you can't even get up to the plate. So, I'm sitting there soaking wet, and then you decide to verbally abuse me because your fucking dick doesn't work! And then, after all of that, you leave the room to get a fucking drink."

"Why didn't you say anything?"

"Why would I have to? You keep asking me if your E.D. is bothering me. It has to bother you. So, you hope things get better rather than going to the doctor. You're such a fucking idiot."

"There's no need for name-calling."

"But you can call me a bitch? Ain't that the pot. . . Whatever."

"Calling the kettle black."
Camille looks at him very sternly. "And now you want to correct me. Correct the issues with your dick first."

"You know wh – Fuck you!"

"Yoooouuuu. You got a great choice of words. Fuck me! No! You can't. But, what I should do is go fuck myself since you're not equipped to handle anything to do with fucking me."

Dylan swings his right hand in a fit of rage, slapping her face. Camille's head jolts to the side. She turns around, looking at him, swinging her fist, landing a perfect right hook to the middle of his face. "Piece of SHIT!"

Dylan screams. "OUCH!!" As he stumbles backward. "YOU BROKE MY NOSE!"

Camille steps back, keeping her fist up, ready to fight. "You can't fuck me, but you want to slap me."

Dylan stands up, holding his bleeding nose. "You stupid bitch."

"Blow it out of your ass."

"I have a meeting tomorrow. I can't go to work like this."

"You should have just gone to bed."

Dylan runs to the upstairs bathroom to tend to his nose. Camille walks to the shiny toaster in her kitchen, looking at her reflection, talking to herself. "What the hell was he thinking?"

Camille continues standing in the kitchen for a moment, gathering herself. She walks over to the refrigerator to get a bottle of water. When she reaches for the water with her right hand, she turns her hand to see her knuckles. They are red from the punch. She continues to reach for the water. Camille takes a moment to calm down, leaning on the counter to drinks her bottle of water. A few minutes pass before she walks upstairs to her bedroom. Dylan is in the bathroom, cleaning his bloody nose. He looks in the mirror to see her standing behind him at the bedroom door, saying nothing.

"I don't think it's broken." He says as Camille looks at him with disgust shaking her head.

"I think it's time we..."

"Time we what Camille?"

"Call it quits."

Dylan doesn't take her statement seriously. "Over this? Are you kidding me?"

"It's. . . It's over, Dylan."

Dylan turns around, walking toward her. "This is bullshit. I still love you. I admit I was out of line hitting you. But that'll never happen again."

"I know... But I'm not happy. I haven't been for a while. I don't see the need to go on any further."

"No. You can't just come up here and say it's over. I love you. You just got me so mad. You've never spoken to me like that before. I'm sorry."

Camille stands motionless, staring at him. He looks into her expressionless eyes, shaking his head side to side.

"Fine. I'll make an appointment to see Dr. Leonard. I'll see someone about the drinking too. Don't just end us. I don't want to split up."

Dylan walks up to her placing both hands on her arms. "Don't leave me, babe."

Camille shamefully looks down.

"You have to forgive me, Cami. I'll never lay another hand on you ever again."

Camille knows that she doesn't want to continue their marriage. She knows that her next statement will either band-aid on their issues or be the band-aid that's ripped off violently. She goes for violently ripping off the band-aid. "I slept with someone."

Dylan shuts his eyes, taking a moment to process her statement. He takes a deep breath opening his eyes, looking directly into her eyes. "What did you say?"

Camille shakes her head, yes. "I slept with someone else."

"Why?"

"I was weak. And foolish. But to be a hundred percent honest, I didn't think about our marriage. I just acted."

Dylan's eyes fill with tears. "How could you do that?"

"I guess I'm not as perfect as you would like me to be."

"Who did you sleep with?"

She knows that honesty may be the best policy, but total honesty never helped any situation. "It didn't mean anything. It was someone I met when I was out with co-workers."

"I don't know how to process what you're telling me."

"What I did was horrible, and I'm sorry about that."

"Well, we can work through it."

"No. I don't think that would be a good idea."

"Why not?" Dylan asks.

"I don't think we should be together any longer. We're fake. We're not happy with each other

"I'm happy being with you."

"But I'm not happy with you, Dylan. I've pretty much fallen out of love with you." She pauses, looking at him. "It's over."

"How can you be so cold?"

"Dylan. We just assaulted each other what loving couple does that and is warm and fuzzy right after. I'll give us credit, were talking civilly at the moment, but what just happened downstairs is something I'm never willing to tolerate."

"Whatever then. Have it your fucking way." Dylan turns around, walking into the bedroom.

"I'm going to bed. Downstairs."

The physical fight, the emotion, and the argument have worn out an already worn Camille down. The realization that her marriage is definitely coming to an end makes her ill. She hangs her head, walking down to the guest bedroom to fall asleep. Dylan walks to the bathroom to clean his face. Camille's words hurt to his core. The idea that she was with another man brings him to tears. He falls to the bathroom floor covering his face as he cries.

Chapter 34: So, You're Saying We're Good?

The following week at Plante Insurance, Isabella returns from lunch, walking past Benjamin's desk. Benjamin talks on the phone, talking with one of his children. "Yeah. I'll pick it up before I get home, Ok? Not sure why your mom can't get it for you, but I'll be more than happy to do it for you. . . Yes, that was sarcasm–good catch on that, sweetie. I love you. Bye."

Benjamin turns to Isabella, looking at him while shaking her head side to side. "You're so good with them."

"They don't think so. My oldest finds my sarcasm humorous."

"I bet she does."

"Yeah. But every second, they either call or text me to pick up something on the way home. It's starting to get a little annoying."

"They'll appreciate it later. They know they can count on you. You're laying the groundwork for their future husbands."

"I hope so. He won't need a gym membership if he has to go to the store every second."

Isabella smirks before moving the conversation forward. "Listen."

"I'm listening."

"I would like to take you out for a quick drink after work before you leave."

"Really?"

"Of course. Why do you say it like that?"

"Ever since I told you I was leaving, you've been distant. So, I thought you were still upset."

"Oh, I'm upset. I'm not upset with you. I've. . . just grown fond of you, and I don't want you to leave. You're my friend. I can't say that about a lot of people here?"

"I know. I feel the same way. You give meaning to the term work wife?"

"How so?"

"You're a bigger pain in the ass than an actual wife."

"Look, who's talking."

Both laugh, looking away from each other.

"So.... Would you care to join me?"

"If it's just you. Yes."

"Good. Because it will just be me."

"Where are you taking me?"

"Details to be determined."

"Sounds like you have no idea where you're taking me."

"Isabella smiles, turning back to her computer monitor. Benjamin shakes his head
turning back to his desk.

Across town at North Mutual Insurance Company, Camille walks over to Kimberly's office, looking through the glass. She doesn't see Kimberly and starts to walk away when she stops in place. She walks back to the office, opening the door slowly. Kimberly is sitting in her chair, leaning forward, throwing up in the trash can. "Hey, Kimmy. Are you ok?"

"Come in. Shut the door!"

Camille shuts the door and the blinds so no one can see in. She walks over the Kimberly, squatting on the floor, pulling back Kimberly's hair. "You know what I'm gonna ask you, right?"

"You know what I'm gonna answer you, right?" Kimberly replies.

Camille laughs. "Ahhh, Shit. This just got real."
Kimberly slowly sits up in her seat. "Ugh. Life's curveballs."

"How far along are you?"

"Can't be more than a month. I have an appointment to see my doctor tomorrow. But I took a home pregnancy test."

"Izzy mentioned you throwing up at the club."

"See. I thought being upset is what made me sick. I had no clue I was pregnant until I threw up here."

"I can't even imagine what you're going through. What are you going to do?"

"I want to keep it. But I don't know whether I should or not. I'm going to see Oliver next week. I want to tell him before I do anything."

"What do you think he'll say?"

"I have no clue. I really don't. The last year, we've been so into each other that kids never really came up. Once we were in a restaurant, and a lady was taking care of her screaming baby. The lady looked miserable. Her meal was ruined. I was even like, "shut that thing up." I look over at Oliver, and he's smiling. It didn't bother him at all. He said that it's just a baby, and everyone should relax."

"I would have paid for her meal and the cab to get her outta there."

"You have serious issues."

"I don't care for children."

Kimberly holds her belly, looking sadly at Camille, giving her the guilt trip. Camille rolls her eyes. "But I'm sure I'll love your baby."

Kimberly playfully laughs. "I'm just messing with you."

"Great. Because I'm sure, I'm not going to like him."

"Whatever. But that was the moment that I thought, if we had a baby, I wouldn't have to worry about him."
"He seems the type. He's very easy going."

"I can't wait to see him. It's driving me crazy."

The smell of Kimberly's trash can has become pungent. Camille points at the trash can. "Are you gonna throw that out."

"Oh. Is it bothering you?"

Camille pinches her nose from disgust. "I'm surprised it's not bothering you."

"I'll take care of it."

"Good. And before I excuse myself. It's been well over a week, and I haven't seen Monica. Is she ok? Not that I give a shit, but it's odd."

"Yeah. She had a family emer –"

Camille cuts her off. "Yeah, yeah, yeah. I don't care. I was just curious."

"I really hope you guys make up."

"I've got enough shit on my plate to deal with. I want nothing to do with that nutcase."

"Ok. I won't press that issue." Kimberly stands up to take the trash out of her office.

Camille exits as Kimberly walks down the hall running into Thomas.

"Hey, Thomas."

"Yo. Eww. What's that smell?"

"My trash. Listen. Have you heard from Monica?"

"Last, I heard, she was up in Port Chester."

"Why?"

"I don't know. Some family crap."

"I find it hard to believe that that's all you know."
"She doesn't tell me everything, you know."

"Fine. Don't tell me."

"You need to throw that out," Thomas says, walking away toward Camille. Camille sees Thomas walking away from Kimberly in her direction. She redirects herself to talk to

Thomas, smiling, as he approaches. "You know she's pregnant, right?"

Thomas looks back at Kimberly, smiling. "That would explain the vomit sessions lately."

"I don't know what she's gonna do."

"Kim. Please. She's smart. She'll be great no matter the outcome. She's the last person I'd worry about. That baby doesn't even know how lucky it is."

"Yeah. You're right."

Thomas looks at his watch. "Shit. I've got a conference call."

"I'm sorry. Go ahead."

"We'll talk after."

"No. It's ok. Take care of your business."

Thomas heads to his office, closing the door as Camille walks past Monica's cubicle looking at the loads of pictures on her desk before she enters her office.

Chapter 35: New Experiences.

Oliver and Justin have gotten themselves acclimated to their new role at AUA Japan. Their coworkers have welcomed them with open arms. The Japanese team working on their project invite the duo out for a night of karaoke. Oliver and Justin walk through the city of Tokyo in search of Shidax Karaoke lounge to meet up with some co-workers. The skyline of Tokyo at night is breathtaking, and Justin enjoys every second of it. He walks through the city, looking up at the lights. "Dude. This is. . . Insane"

"I can't argue with you. This place is amazing at night," Oliver agrees.

"It's like an orgasm for your eyes. I can't stop looking up."

"Yeah. And we're from New York."

"New York City is beautiful day and night. But this is something much different. I want to sleep out here."

"I know. And these buildings give true meaning to the word skyscrapers."

"I just got here, but I love it here, man. Our coworkers are awesome."

"So far." Oliver laughs.

"Yeah. True. But for now, I really like it here. The ladies are treating me very nice."

"Please don't hook up with any of the women we work with."

"Wouldn't dream of it."

"I'm serious. You better not."

"I'll do my best. But I do have something interesting to tell you."

"I knew it!"

"Knew what?"

"Emiko. You made a move on her, right?"
"Did not."

Oliver points at Justin. "Justin."

"I swear. I didn't try to hook up with anyone from work yet."

"You better not."

"But."

Oliver looks at Justin.

"I hooked up with Monica back in New York."

"What? Are you serious?"

"Very serious. I gotta say. It was fucking amazing."

"I thought she didn't like you. She hates white boys." Oliver jokes.

"Chocolate seems to be the flavor of the month. But no one can ever deny a vanilla milkshake from time to time.

"You're so corny."

"Damn. A brotha can't get no love?"

"Here comes the dramatics."

"I met this girl a year ago. I tried to hook up and got rejected. Saw her a few times, and she gave me no love."

"So, what changed?"

"We had exchanged phone numbers one time. She called me before we left to come out here. She wanted to know when our flight was leaving. I said if you want that information, you gotta let me take you out."

"Are you serious?"
"Yep. She said. "Aight." You know how she talks like she's from the hood, so, yeah. She's like, "Aight. Come widdit". I had to look in my urban dictionary to figure out what the fuck that meant but google pretty much summed that up. So, I showered and shaved. Hit the road and picked her up."

"And?"

"Aside from the mind-blowing sex. We had a lot of fun. We danced, made out, and was all over each other. When I got her back to my apartment."

"Yeah."

"Phew. It was a smash session, yo," Justin says, laughing.

"You hook up with this chick once, and now you're a thug?"

"I'm keeping it real."

Oliver burst out laughing.

"I gotta tell you, though. I've always liked my women on the thin side, but she is a proper thick.

"Yeah. She is. I wouldn't have guessed you could handle all that."

"I wish I could have hung out with her again."

"There are plenty of women here. I'm sure you'll be fine."

"Yeah. You're right. But not like her. She's not like the girls here. She's not as reserved if you couldn't tell."

"Yeah. She's probably a lot more trouble than these girls. She's far from traditional than these girls here."

"This is true. But you know me. I like girls with a little edge." Justin points at Oliver.

"And if you bring up my ex. I'm gonna kick your ass."

Oliver laughs. "We're having a good time, so I won't."

As they walk through the busy city streets, they finally arrive at their destination. Justin looks up, pointing to the building. "Look. Found it."

Oliver holds Justin back. "Hey, listen. Tomorrow I'm going to a Jeweler."

"A Jeweler. Why?"

"I'm getting a ring for Kimberly."

"What? Wow. That's awesome!"

"She's coming to visit me, and I want to commit to her. I want her to be my wife."

"I don't know if I want to ask how you're gonna pull this off."

"All I know is that I can't live without her man. There is no need for me to fight this. We are perfect together, and I can't let her go home without letting her know I'm committed to our future."

Justin smiles, saying nothing.

"What's the matter?" Oliver asks.

"Nothing, man. I'm happy for you. It's nice to see two people who belong together commit to each other. If you want me to be there when you buy the ring, I'll be right there."

"Thanks, buddy. I appreciate that."

"Anytime. Let's get in here and show these people how to sing American rock and roll."

"I was thinking more R&B, but hey. You do you."

They enter the building, searching for their party. The facility is an array of rooms to match different styles of genres. The area where their co-workers wait for them has a large TV with a sofa and two lounge chairs. The employees greet Oliver and Justin with a loud cheer. They enjoy the reception before sitting with everyone to sing karaoke.

Chapter 36: That's One Hell Of A Dress

Benjamin arrives at Momma Francesca's Italian Restaurant in the little Italy section of Lower Manhattan a few minutes early. The maitre'd guides him through the busy restaurant to a high curved banquette U shaped booth for two in the far corner. Benjamin is extremely impressed with the restaurant's ambiance, especially with the selection of brat pack tunes to set the mood. The maroon and black decor is classy and sharp. Wait staff dresses neatly in all black accented with a red necktie. He nods his approval as he looks around, waiting for Isabella to arrive.

Isabella arrives about half an hour late, looking through the restaurant, making eye contact with Benjamin, who smirks at her. He does a double-take when he sees her in a close-fitting all-white short dress. She has finally let down her long wavy brown hair carrying a white clutch wearing white stiletto heels. He finds it impossible to take his eyes off her as she walks up to the table. "I'm so sorry, I'm late."

Benjamin struggles to find the words as he stares at her dress. "All is forgiven while you're wearing that dress."

Isabella smiles, touching his arm. "Thank you. But seriously. I'm so sorry."

"It's totally cool. I mean, I'm starving, so now that you're here, we can eat, but it's all good.

"Thanks for being so patient."

"You haven't learned much about me in the last year, have you?"

"What does that mean?"

"I don't care if you're late. You're here now. Better late than never. So, relax. Because after this, you'll probably never see me again."

Isabella whips her head toward Benjamin. "Are you serious?"

"Nah. I'm just kidding." Benjamin laughs.

Isabella picks up the small cocktail menu. "I hate when you say shit like that. You know it pisses me off."
"But, everything pisses you off."

Isabella turns around quickly, looking at him very seriously.

"Ok, ok. I'll stop. I was just having a little fun with you."

"Please stop."

"I will. I'm sorry."

"Thank you."

Benjamin looks around the restaurant. "I must say this is a wonderful venue. I would have been happy with a pizzeria down the street, but this is very nice."

"Why do you have to downplay everything I do?"

"What?" He says, looking into her frustrated eyes. "Why do I feel like I'm just gonna ruin the night?"

"You don't have to. But I take you here, and then you say someplace else would have been fine. I hate when you do that."

"Truth be told, Isabella. I always feel uncomfortable when people make a fuss over me: birthdays, Christmas, Father's Day. I'm very simple. That's all I was saying. If my statement upset you, I'm so sorry."

"It's ok. I know you like simple, but I wanted to do something really nice for you. I know how much you love little Italy, so I wanted to take you someplace that I knew you would enjoy."

Benjamin looks her in the eyes. "I will fully enjoy this restaurant and the company." He slowly looks down at her outfit, smirking. "I'd like to step back and fully enjoy the view, but I may not be able to get up."

Isabella playfully punches him in the arm. "Fresh."

"Alright, I gotta asks. why are you always so uptight?"

"What do you mean?"

"I imply on how hot you look with a playful flirt, and you punch me calling me fresh. A simple smile would suffice."

Their waiter comes by with water. "Oh, my goodness. I see no one's given you two a menu. I'm so sorry. I'll be right back." The waiter runs upfront to get a menu.

Benjamin looks over at Isabella. "So, as I was saying. Is it just me?"

Isabella turns to him, smiling. "No. I. . . I really like when you flirt with me. I just don't want you to know."

"Are you serious? If I had known that, I would have flirted some more."

"See." She points at him. "That's what I was trying to avoid."

"What? Compliments?"

"No. Constant flirting. It would have been a turnoff. Your flirts come randomly, and usually at times that I really need it or just like wanna hear it."

"Do you need one now?"

"If you must." She laughs as she braces herself for something potentially really naughty. She looks over at Benjamin, looking her up and down, admiring her dress.

"You look so amazing right now. . . I –" He shuts his mouth and smiles.

"I have this feeling you have more to say."

"I do. But I think I should stop there."

"My curiosity says tonight is ok. Finish your compliment."

Benjamin seductively stares at her, smiling for a moment. "If I weren't married. You wouldn't be able to keep me off you tonight."

Isabella smiles bashfully, looking away.

"Did I say something wrong?"

"Absolutely not. Honestly. There have been times I felt the same way about you."

"I'm so glad to not have known that."

"Why?"

"I would have done something stupid over and over and over."

Isabella burst out laughing.

A waiter rushes back to the table. "I am soooooo sorry that no one gave you a menu. Did you want to start with a drink tonight?"

"Yes," Isabella replies. "Um. Can you bring us a bottle of Opus One cabernet sauvignon?"

The waiters' smile can light up the room. Benjamin tries to figure out what Isabella could have said to make him smile that bright. "Excellent choice, Madame. Did you need another minute to look over the menu?"

"Well, what are the specials?" Benjamin asks.

The waiter goes over a few of the specials for the night. "So, would you like to order one of the specials or take a minute to look over the menu?"

"I know what I want right now. Do you?" He asks Isabella.

"I do. I would like one of the specials."

The waiter pulls out his pen and pad. "Great. Ok, So for the lady?"

"I'll have the Chicken Tetrazzini

"Mmmm, marvelous choice, ma'am. You're going to love that?"

"And I'll have the Capellini with Spicy Zucchini with Tomato Sauce."

The waiter smiles gleefully. "Another phenomenal choice. I'll be right back with your wine."

Isabella and Benjamin thank the waiter as he removes the menus heading to the kitchen to place the order.

"So., You were saying."

Benjamin tilts his head to the side, smiling at her as she smiles back. "I always thought you might be trouble."

Isabella leans on the table, looking at him. "I'm not trouble for anyone."

"In that dress, you are tonight."

Isabella smirks. "So.... Again... You were saying before we were interrupted."

"Why do you need me to say this to you?"

"I guess.... Sometimes.... You just need to hear certain things."

"That's fair. But I already said my peace. Do you have anything you want to get off your chest?" Benjamin says, staring into Isabella's eyes.

Isabella impishly smiles at Benjamin.

"No pun intended."

"Yeah, right." She says, sitting upright. "I guess I felt exactly the same way. I kind of kept my distance from you to a degree."

"Wait!"

"What?"

"Remember when we spent that day together, and I busted up my finger?"

"How could I forget?"

"You said that you were taking a bath thinking about me."

"Oh, boy."

"Since we're being honest and all. Did you have any dirty thoughts about me while you were home, all alone?"

Isabella's face turns beet red from embarrassment as she smiles. "You had to bring that up."

"I did. So?"

Isabella hesitates to answer. "Yeah. I did."

"I KNEW IT!" Benjamin shouts, forgetting for a moment that he is in a restaurant.

Isabella laughs, hiding her face. Benjamin turns to her. "Yeah. I'd like details."

The waiter arrives with the wine humming while he opens the bottle of wine. He looks at them, both staring at each other, smiling but not talking. "Oooh. What did I just interrupt?"

"Saved by the bell," Isabella says while looking at Benjamin.

"Don't even try it," Benjamin adds.

The waiter continues watching them as they continue staring at each other. He pours the wine into their individual glass,' leaving the bottle. "You may have to let that breath for a sec, ok guys."

"Ok. Thank you." Isabella replies, while still looking and smiling at Benjamin. The waiter walks away, smiling, shaking his head.

"I want details. Now!" He says, tapping on the table.

"I was in the tub, taking a warm bath."

Benjamin takes a gulp of the wine. Isabella watches him take a gulp. "Let it breathe!"

"This story is more important than the wine."

"Hey, That's a four-hundred-dollar bottle of wine."

Benjamin spits out the wine from shock. "WHAT?!?!"

Isabella burst out hysterical, laughing. "It's a four-hundred-dollar bottle of wine."

Benjamin looks at the spilled wine on the table.

"Shit. I'm gonna need a straw to suck this backup."

Isabella continues laughing.
"Why would you buy? You know what? Nevermind." Benjamin says, unable to comprehend the decision to buy such an expensive bottle of wine.

"Thank you. Just don't say anything."

Benjamin takes another sip of the wine and looks at the glass. "Wow. This is excellent."

"I love this bottle of wine. It's my favorite."

"I can see why. Now seriously. Tell me the story."

"Isabella takes a deep breath. "So. I'm in the bathroom in my bathtub. It's a fancy cast iron clawfoot bathtub."

"Very nice. I like those. I can picture you in there with your hair all tied up in a tight bun."

"I was just sitting in the tub relaxing. My butt was still hurting from ice skating, so when I remembered why my butt hurt. I remembered your hand was there."

Benjamin speaks softly. "Go on, baby."

"So, then I thought of you. No one was home, so I shifted positions and my lips. These lips." Isabella points between her legs. Benjamin can only smile. "Oooh. Do continue."

"When I shifted, they moved and rubbed together, and it felt really nice. Every time I moved my legs, the movement was such a turn on. Then I pictured you opening the door to my bathroom and walking in."

"And what am I wearing?" He says with a seductive tone.

"Just a pair of slacks. I could see you had an erection. So, I slid my hand down my leg, and I started touching myself. I pictured you kneeling right beside me outside the tub. You took your hands and started rubbing on my brea –"

The waiter interrupts. "Ok, guys. We had a minor hiccup in the kitchen, causing a delay with your order. It may take a little while longer."

Isabella turns to the waiter. "Oh, it's ok."

Benjamin looks up at the waiter. "You're killing me."

"I am so so sorry. Would you like an appetizer on the house, of course?"

"You know what. Yeah. I'll have the Calamari Fritti." Isabella says to the waiter.

Benjamin can't hide his annoyance. "Nothing for me. But when you come back. You can just place the order on the table. I need to hear this story she's trying to tell me."

Isabella laughs, covering her face with her hands.

"I apologize, sir."

"It's ok."

The waiter heads to the kitchen to place the appetizer order.

Benjamin turns to Isabella and smiles. "Ok. So, I was about to touch your brea–"

"I have to go to the bathroom." Isabella interrupts.

"I swear to. . . You better sit down and hold it. Finish the story!"

Isabella laughs hysterically. "I'm just fucking with you."

"You're in rare form tonight. I like that. Letting your hair down, so to speak."

Isabella leans in a little closer to tell the story. "So, I'm playing with myself, and I'm imagining you fondling my breast. I opened my legs and dropped slightly into the tub. Then you get up and remove your pants."

"This is so fucking sexy. I can totally picture this. The bathtub in the middle of the
bathroom with black and white tiles."

"You climb on top of the tub, and you're rock hard. You slowly get in the water on top of
me. I could feel myself about to climax. Then you put your – "

"Hey, guys." The restaurant owner interrupts. Benjamin becomes extremely aggravated, slapping his hand on the table. "You know what. Forget it."

"I'm sorry. What's that, sir?"

Benjamin doesn't answer and appears extremely agitated.

"I just wanted to come and express my apologies for the delay in the kitchen. Is there anything I can do to make your evening a little special?.

"Yeah. I wanted to cum too." Benjamin mumbles.

"I'm sorry. What was that, sir?"

"Um. What my friend means to say is he wanted to come here to have another bottle of this Opus One cabernet sauvignon."

The restaurant owner laughs uncomfortably. "Madame. Um, That's uh. A little excessive."

"Yeah, but it would help."

"How about a nice bottle of Joseph Phelps cabernet sauvignon?"

"We may be here for a while. Once we polish off this bottle, we will let you know."

"Ok. Thank you, Madame. We are so sorry for the delay."

"It's alright." She says before turning to Benjamin. "I'm so sorry."

"It's fine. I get the gist of what happened. You don't have to finish the story anymore."

"You sure? Reliving, it is awesome."

"Sigh. If you must."

Isabella leans in closer, placing her arms around him. "It was really good. I came harder than I've ever been able to make myself cum before. All while I was thinking of you."

"Sounds about right," Benjamin replies as Isabella laughs. He looks back at Isabella. "I'm just tooting my own horn. Don't pay me any mind."

"Hey. If that fantasy is anything close to real life. Then beep beep to you."

Benjamin smirks, taking a sip of the wine. Isabella does the same before asking him.
"Did you ever have one? About me?"

"Please. All the time. But, the best one was when I was in the office alone, helping you with your presentation. Remember when you were going to Florida?"

"Yeah."

"I was sitting at your desk, and you came around the corner because you thought you had to come in and finish your presentation. As you turn the corner, you see me
standing there, and you walk right up to me and kiss me."

"Wow."

"I wrap my arms around you, and we just keep making out. We fall to the floor and just
keep kissing."

"That's it?"

"Yeah, why?"

"I thought it would have been a little more hot and heavy."

"It could have been if I didn't answer my phone. You may have actually come to the office."

"You're right. I would have."

"Then the filth to follow after would have made it hard for you to look me in the eyes after. Because what I would have done to you on that office floor would have been legendary."

Isabella's jaw drops as Benjamin takes a sip of the wine.

The waiter returns. "Hi, Guys. I have your Calamari Fritti. Your order will be out in a few minutes."

"Thank you." They both say to the waiter.

They share the Calamari before their main course arrives. The bottle of wine gets polished off chased with over an hour of laughter. As promised, the owner provides a second bottle of wine, which they work on for the next hour. Patrons come and go as they continue enjoying their time alone together. This is the only time they've been able to spend together since their escapades throughout the city during the week of Thanksgiving. The night winds down as the wine is taking a mild effect on both of them. Isabella sits close enough to rest her head on Benjamin's shoulder. "Fuck. I'm gonna miss you."

"I'm going to miss you too," Benjamin replies.

Benjamin leans his head on her head. They sit there quietly for a brief moment. She slowly turns her head toward him. He turns toward her. Their foreheads meet.

"What am I going to do with you?" Benjamin asks.

"I'm asking myself the same thing."

The wheels turn in Benjamin's head as he and Isabella lock eyes with their nose's inches apart from each other. "We're dancing on a really fine line right now. You know that, right?"

"Sigh. I know. But at this immediate moment, I don't care."

"We don't want to do anything that we're going to regret."

Isabella hesitates to answer. "Speak for yourself."

Benjamin laughs through his nose. Isabella senses Benjamin's hesitation. "But, you're right. "We" shouldn't do anything we're going to regret."

Benjamin doesn't answer. Isabella leans upward, kissing him on the lips. He doesn't pull away. She reaches up, caressing his face. He slowly wraps his arms around her, slightly pulling her closer. They embrace in a kiss for a moment before he softly pulls away.

"I'll regret that for the both of us," Isabella says as she continues to lock eyes with Benjamin.

Benjamin licks his lips. "Was that a goodbye kiss?"

"I think so. It was a little premature because I haven't paid the bill yet."

"Well, that's gotta be the best sendoff I've ever had. So, thank you."

Benjamin looks to his right and can see that the waiter is waiting before bringing the bill. Benjamin waves at him to come over.

"I hope you can forgive me for doing that," Isabella asks.

"Forgiven."

Isabella takes the bill paying in cash as she leaves it in the black check order holder.
"Let's get out of here."

They get up from the table and walk toward the front of the restaurant. They exit the establishment where Benjamin hails a cab for Isabella. A taxi pulls up, waiting for Isabella to enter. Benjamin turns her around, pulling her in for an emotional hug. They hug each other for a long moment.

"I'm really going to miss you, Izzy."

"I'm going to really miss you too."

She pulls back, looking up at Benjamin in tears. She kisses him on the cheek before pulling away, turning around to enter the taxi. She fights the tears sitting back in the seat so he can no longer see her.

"So long, Izzy." He says from outside the taxicab.

Isabella whispers. "Te amo."

Benjamin watches as the taxi drives off, coming to a stop at a stoplight. Benjamin smiles and runs toward the taxi. He sticks his head in the window, startling Isabella. "Hey. We still have the bathtub."

Isabella burst out laughing. "Yes, we do. We certainly do."

"Take care, Izzy. I'll keep in touch."

"So, will I."

The traffic light turns green, and the taxicab pulls off, driving her home. Isabella wipes the tears from her eyes. Benjamin stands motionless, watching her taxi drive away before he sadly hangs his head. Within the hour, Isabella arrives home. She quietly enters her home hanging her light jacket on the coat rack before walking upstairs, looking at all the family photos starting with her wedding pictures. Isabella makes her way to the kids' bedroom, remaining quiet to not wake them. She stands staring at them for a brief moment smiling. She then walks into her empty bedroom. Sebastian walks out of the bathroom with a towel around his waist, smiling at Isabella. "Hey, babe. Don't you look nice."

"Hey." She says as she looks down at her dress. "This old thing?"

"That old thing looks sexy."

"Thank you, sweetie,"

"How was your day today?'

Isabella looks at Sebastian with confusion. "You really want to hear about my day?"

"Yeah. Look. Um, remember when I said all that stupid shit?"

"I remember all of it."

"I'm really, really sorry for doing that. I was being a dick."

Isabella gleefully listens to Sebastian.

"I think I was just taking you for granted. I was being selfish and not listening to you when you just wanted to talk to me. I know when I need to talk, you always listen. I know a lot of guys who have no one in their lives and would do anything to be in my shoes. I have it all, and I was horrible to you."

"You weren't horrible."

"Yes, I was. I really was. I feel really bad, and I'm sorry."

Isabella's eyes fill with tears.
"I mean, look at you. I got the hottest wife in New York. My ride or die. I got the sweetest little girls a man could ask for. Nothing else should even matter. But I gotta make sure my baby is happy."

"Isabella walks up to Sebastian falling into his arms hysterical crying. "I love you so much, honey."

"I know you do. But it's me who should be telling you that my life is worthless without you in it. I love you."

"You're the greatest husband on the planet. "

"I know that too." He replies, laughing.

Isabella pulls back, looking up at him. "And modest."

"Sebastian pulls her into the bed, lying together holding each other.

"So, go ahead, baby. Tell me about your day."

Chapter 37: Where The Hell Have You Been?

Monica stands over the counter, cutting up vegetables in Thomas' kitchen. A pot on the stove comes to a boil as she reaches over to turn down the fire on the stove. The swelling to her left eye has gone down and her face is healing very slowly. Her phone vibrates from a phone call. She looks at the table where her phone is ringing. The caller I.D. notifies her that the call is from Kimberly. She reaches for the phone. "Hey, girl."

"Monica. What the hell is going on? Are you ok?"

"I'm good. But hearing your voice right now is awesome."

"Aww. Thank you. It's good to hear your voice too. Where have you been hiding?"

"I'm up in Port Chester. I had some family shit to deal with."

"Well. One, I miss you, and two, I was getting worried. Thomas wasn't saying anything."

The door opens up as Thomas walks in, yelling. "I got you some more Pringles!!!"

Monica turns around quickly, placing her finger over her mouth to be quiet. Thomas' eyes widen.

“Is that Thomas? He’s up in Port Chester?” Kimberly asks.

Monica remains quiet, pinching the bridge of her nose. She can only imagine the graphics images that flow through Kimberly's mind. “I knew he was lying. Please don't tell me you too are fooling around.”

“Ewww. No!”

“So, what's going on then?”

“Nothing. I was in a jam, and I needed his help.”

“Shit. I didn't know. You didn't tell me anything. Do you need me to do anything?”

“Thank you. This issue I'm dealing with is pretty intense. But everything is getting resolved, so to speak.”

“Right. Ok. I guess you'll tell me what's going on when the time is right.

“Of course. It's just. . . Intense.”

"Ok, ok. Well, can you talk?”

"Of course."

“I bought tickets to Japan.”

“What? Why? Are you're moving?”

“No. But I need to see Oliver. I have news for him that I can't say over the phone.”

“What? What's the news?”

"I'm pregnant."

"GET THE FUCK OUTTA HERE!"

"I'm pregnant, girl!"

Tears of joy stream down Monica's face. "That's awesome. I'm so happy for you. I can't believe my ears."

"I wish you were here now."

Monica sadly looks down at the floor. "Me too. I'm sorry."

"No. Don't worry. But it would have been nice if you could take me to the airport before I leave."

Monica hangs her head crying. "I wish I could too. Now I feel like a bad friend."

"Seriously. If you were in Brooklyn, I would have said you had to, but it's really ok."

Monica thinks that she really should see her friend off. "Fuck this. I'll be there. I miss you. I want to see you off."

"No, no, no. Kimberly laughs. "You don't have to."

"I know. But I want to. I wanna see you before you go. My luck, you go out there and decide to stay."

"If I'm lucky, I'll talk him into coming back."

"Good luck with that."

Monica grabs a tube of Pringles walking past Thomas over to the living room, lying on the sofa, continuing to talk to Kimberly. She lifts her feet on the sofa popping the tube of Pringles continuing her conversation with Kimberly for the next two hours.

As Saturday morning arrives, Kimberly answers her cell phone while she sits on the sofa in her apartment. Monica advises her that she is downstairs waiting to take her to the airport. Kimberly stands up, walking to her apartment door. She pulls up on the handle of her rolling carry on suitcase, looking back at her apartment. She smiles before exiting the apartment, locking the door. A moment later, Kimberly exits the building pulling her carryon bag. Monica's tinted silver Range Rover Sport is parked by the sidewalk. Kimberly walks up to the car as the passenger door opens. Monica exits the vehicle wearing massive sunglasses and a lot of cover-up. Kimberly screams in excitement." Heeeyyyyy Girl!"

"What's up, boo?" Monica replies.

Thomas exits the driver's side walking around to Kimberly. "Everyone gets the news, but me, huh?"

"Oh, Thomas. That wasn't intentional. I've been hiding in my office, and I kept missing you. I'm sorry, boo." She says as they wrap their arms around each other. Thomas squeezes her extra close.

"It's ok. I just like messing with you. Camille suspected it and told me before you said anything."

"I figured she would. It's funny how we sit so close, and we kept missing each other."

"Trust me. It's all good. How far along are you?" Thomas asks.

"Eight weeks."

"I can't wait to buy clothes for him. You know he's getting a pair of Tims, Some Jordan's. My Godson is gonna be spoiled." Monica laughs.

"What makes you think it's a boy?"

"I just know these things."

"I bet you do," Kimberly replies as she notices the makeup plastered on Monica's face.
She reaches up, removing Monica's sunglasses. "Now, this."

Kimberly points at Monica's face. "What happened to your face? And what's up with those glasses?"

Thomas picks up Kimberly's luggage, placing it in the trunk. Monica's mood changes. "I don't want to talk about that right now, Kimmy."

"This is why you've been missing, right?" Kimberly asks as she looks over at Thomas, who looks away. She reaches for Thomas' tapping him. "I hope you have a handle on this."

Thomas looks at Kimberly, gesturing that everything is fine.

"Look. I just wanted to see you off. When you come back, I will tell you everything." Monica says.

"You better."

"I promise."

"Ok fine. I know Thomas is gonna handle this shit. So, I'm gonna let you off the hook." She says as Monica's mood drop. Kimberly gently places her index finger under Monica's chin lifting her face, so they are eye to eye. "You know I love you, right?" Kimberly asks as Monica shakes her head up and down. "I don't want to beat a dead horse but seeing you like this..."
"I know. I know," Monica replies.

Kimberly pulls Monica in, hugging her kissing her face. She pulls away inches from Monica's face. "Now, let's go. I don't wanna miss my flight."

Monica's face lights up from excitement for Kimberly. "This is the shit I'm talking about. This is inspiring. You're off to see your man on the other side of the planet."

"I know, right. I wish I had a girlfriend like me."

"We can all dare to dream," Thomas adds.

All three laugh as they enter the car driving off towards JFK International Airport. They arrive at the departure section exiting the vehicle. Thomas walks around the rear of the vehicle to remove Kimberly's luggage from the trunk. Monica and Kimberly embrace each other in a long affectionate hug. Kimberly takes a deep breath. "I can't wait to see him."

"I can imagine. I'm so happy for you. Have fun."

"I will."

Thomas places her luggage in front of her. "Come here, girl."

Kimberly and Thomas embrace in an affectionate hug lifting her off her feet.

"Thank you for seeing me off."

"My pleasure," Thomas replies. "Have fun.”

"Yeah. And tell him we say hi." Monica interjects

"I will. I’ll see you guys in a week, ok" Kimberly replies as she grabs her carryon.

"Ok. Bye!" Monica replies.

"Bring back some sushi," Thomas yells.

"You're so stupid," Kimberly says to Thomas.
"Hey." Thomas' says to Kimberly, who looks up at Thomas, pointing at her. "Be careful, ok."

Kimberly looks up with a big smile. "You know me."

Kimberly walks into the terminal, waving goodbye as she continues to the ticket counter. Monica watches Kimberly leave with hopes of love. "I love those two."

"Yeah. They're cool. . . Come on. Let's go." As they turn around, the same security officer from two weeks earlier stands in front of them. "I'm gonna need you to move your car."

"This dude again. Yo. You gotta get a better paying job." Monica says to the security officer.

The security officer walks up to Monica abruptly. "I remember you. You and your foul mouth."

"Yo. My man. Get away from her so she can get in the car, please." Thomas interrupts.

Monica smirks, looking the security officer up and down. "You heard the man."

The security officer steps aside, allowing Monica to enter the car. "That's what I thought," Monica says to the security officer.

"Get in the car!" Thomas yells at Monica. Monica and Thomas get in the car driving off.

"I swear. . . It's like you look for trouble."

"No. He was being a bitch last time. Acting like a jerk."

"Sometimes in life, you gotta just let some things go. You waste your energy with bullshit like that. Trust me."

"I guess," Monica replies.

Thomas, sensing a potential argument about to start, changes the subject. "You wanna find a diner and go get some breakfast?"

"Wait. Did I get a furlough? So, I can go out in public and mingle with regular people?"

"Yep. All on your dime, Ms. Money Bags."

"Seriously. You want me to pay?"

"What? You can't take me out for breakfast. It's the least you could do." He expresses playfully."

"Of course, I can. But when this was all said and done, I was going to take you to that Puerto Rican restaurant by the Queens borough bridge."

"Wait. El Porron?"

"Yeah. That's it."

Thomas smiles from ear to ear. "Yo. It's on."

"It is the very least I could do to thank you. You're such a good friend to me. I will never forget everything you did for me, Thomas. Never."

Thomas looks over at Monica, smiling. "Anytime, pretty lady."

They continue driving through traffic, exiting the airport.

Chapter 38: Woulda, Coulda, Shoulda

Oliver sits at a Starbucks in the Narita International Airport, waiting for Kimberly's flight to arrive. He Is drinking a large flavored latte while watching a video on his cell phone. The plane should have arrived by now, and he is getting a little antsy. He walks up to the flight board to check on her flight. It reads, “Delayed.” He walks back to the Starbucks and sits there looking at his phone. After a few hours pass by, he grows impatient. He walks to the information desk to speak to one of the representatives. "Hello. Um. Do you speak English?"

"Yes. How are you?" The Japanese representative says to Oliver.

"I'm ok. I’m waiting for a flight to arrive. The Flight information board says delayed. But It's been like that for hours."

The representative leans in to listen to the other representative speak to a member of leadership over the phone. She turns back to Oliver. "Which flight are you inquiring about?"

"The Oceanic Flight from San Francisco”

The representative looks at her monitor. "Yes. There is a delay with that flight."

"I know. But is there any way you could find out what is causing the delay?" Oliver reaches in his pocket to grab his cell phone. Caller

ID notifies him that Justin is calling. He sends the call to voicemail and places the phone back in his pocket. The representative's eyes move left to right as she reads data on the monitor.

"Ok. It looks like we have not been given an update of the status of that flight."

"Is there anyone you can call to find out what's going on?" Oliver feels his cell phone vibrating in his pocket.

"At this time, we are also waiting for that information."

"It's been three hours, ma'am. There's gotta be someone you can call to find out what's going on with that flight." Oliver grabs the phone out of his pocket and sends the call to voicemail again.

"When we get the information, it will update the flight arrivals board."

"I'm sorry, but that's not really good enough. Would you be able to get me your supervisor?"

"My supervisor will tell you the same thing, sir. He has access to the same system."

Oliver's phone vibrates again. "Dammit, Justin." He answers the phone. "What!?"

"Have you seen the news?" Justin asks.

"Justin. I'm at the airport waiting for Kimberly. No, I haven't seen the news."

"Sigh. Dude. There was a plane crash in San Francisco moments after takeoff. It's the Oceanic flight that departed the same time as Kimberly's flight."

Oliver takes two steps back from the information counter. "Kimberly's flight."

"I know. I turned on the TV, and it was the first thing on the news."

"Maybe she missed her flight," Oliver says, clinging to hope.

"I hope so, man."

Oliver looks up at the representative. "Did you know the plane crashed?"

"No, sir. We are only being advised that the plane is delayed."

"It crashed. Right after taking off."

"We were not informed of a plane crash, sir. I'm sorry."

Oliver redirects his attention to the phone call as his mouth becomes dry. "I - I."

"Stay there. I'll be right there."

"Ok," Oliver replies as he ends the call and tries to call Kimberly via a mobile app. There is no response. He checks her Facebook status. It reads that she checked into San Francisco International Airport. He scrolls down and views another post with a selfie of her sitting on the Oceanic flight. The caption reads "Tokyo. Here I come to see my boo" with a check-in status that reads Oceanic Air along with the date and time. He begins to panic and places both hands on his head. His knees buckle, but he reaches for the information desk to prevent a fall. "Sir. Would you like a seat?" The representative says to Oliver.

"I don't – I don't feel so good."

The representative rushes to his aid preventing him from fainting. She grabs his arm and walks him to a seat.

"Would you like a bottle of water?"

Oliver doesn't reply. He is in shock. Breaking news on the airport television sets sends a few people in the airport Starbucks into a panic.

Some of those people rush to the info desk to get any information. Oliver looks around and can see a woman screaming in disbelief. The representative leaves him to talk to the screaming woman. Oliver sits motionless, saying nothing for a while.

Chapter 39: Let's See Where We Go From here

Thomas and Phoebe enjoy a romantic evening at Rye Playland, NY. Thomas does well at the basketball game, making a majority of his shots in his attempts to win a big prize for Phoebe. "I think those hoops are smaller than regulation."

‘Excuses, excuses."

"No, seriously. You gotta get the ball directly in the hoop. If not," Thomas' shoots the ball and misses. "Boing. That happens."

Phoebe laughs hysterically. "Hey. If you can't get it in."

"Oh, I can get in it. Trust me." Thomas takes another shot and makes it. "Told you."

"Nice shot, sir. You win a prize for the beautiful lady." Says the Carney.

Thomas points up at the massive stuffed animals. "Now, can I have that, Garfield?"

"Yes, sir. Here you go." Carney grabs the massive stuffed Garfield and hands it to Thomas.

"Thank you, my good man," Thomas says as he hands the stuffed animal to Phoebe.

"My man got me the biggest one in the park," Phoebe replies as she kisses Thomas.

"Anything for you, baby."

"No one has ever won something like that for me before. I'm honored."

"I pretty much paid for it. I just dropped liked fifty dollars playing that game."

"I know, but I really appreciate it. Thank you." She kisses Thomas on the cheek several times.

"If you're happy, I'm happy."

"I'm happy, baby, trust me."

"What do you want to do next?"

"I'm tired. Do you want to head back to my place?"

"I would love to. Let's go."

Phoebe and Thomas drive back to her home, where he stays for the night. The next morning, Phoebe opens her eyes to Thomas lying beside her. She leans over, kissing Thomas' neck, waking him up. They both smile at each other.

"Good morning." She says playfully, covering her mouth.

"Good morning, little lady."

"How'd you sleep?"

"Great." Thomas thinks. "I had a great dream."

"What about?"

"I dreamt that I spent the night with you. It appears dreams do come true."

Phoebe laughs, continuing to cover her mouth. "You're a nut."

"This much I know."

"I gotta brush my teeth." Phoebe gets out of bed, walking to the bathroom.

"Phoebe. Do you have a spare toothbrush?"

"I do. One sec."

Thomas sits up, taking a look at his phone, which was placed on silent. He has twenty two missed calls and text messages. He opens one of the texts from Monica. He reads the first sentence. "What the hell?!"

Phoebe sticks her head out from the hall closet. "What's the matter?"

"There was a plane crash?"

"Yeah. I saw an alert on my phone last night."

"I think my friend Kimberly was on that flight."

Phoebe walks over to Thomas. "Are you kidding me?"

"No."

"Your friend Kimberly from work? Is there any way you can verify?"

Thomas sits frozen in place, looking at his phone, saying nothing.

"Thomas. Is there any way you can find out if she was on the plane?"

Thomas continues reading a text from Monica, indicating that Kimberly's Facebook status placed her on the doomed flight. He covers his mouth and stands up.

"What? Are you ok?" Phoebe asks.

"She posted a selfie on social media stating that she was on board that flight to Japan to see her boyfriend."

"Oh, my goodness Thomas. I am so sorry." Phoebe says as she reaches over, touching his arm."

"I can't believe this. I just saw her. I took her to the airport yesterday morning."
"I remember you telling me. I'm sorry, Thomas."

"Um. I—I—think I need to go."

"Do you need me to go with you?"

"No. Really, no." He picks up his pants and shirt, wandering through her bedroom, aimlessly.

Phoebe watches with concern. "I want to help you. Is there anything I can do?"

"No. I just need to go. I'm sorry."

"No. Don't be sorry."

Thomas gets dressed with a look of distress on his face. Once dressed, he walks to the front door kissing Phoebe before he exits. He enters his car sitting in the driver's seat before he breaks down crying. Phoebe watches Thomas from the window before she runs out in her robe, tapping on the window.

"Thomas. Opens the door." She yells from outside the car.

"I'm ok."

"Baby. Please open the door and let me in?"

"Thomas unlocks the door allowing Phoebe to enter his car on the passenger side. She reaches over and comforts Thomas. They remain in the car for several minutes while
Thomas cries in her arms.

The day appears to be horrific for all of Kimberly's friends. They all take the news of the flight extremely hard. Monica sits on her living room sofa alone, hysterical crying while watching news coverage on the plane crash.

Sebastian stands in the kitchen, consoling an emotionally broken Isabella. The Kitchen TV is on CNN for continuous coverage of the horrific plane crash.

Camille sits on the kitchen floor, crying uncontrollably. Dylan runs to her side to console her. He sits with her on the floor as she buries her head into his shoulder.

Oliver and Justin sit together on a flight from Tokyo to San Francisco. Tears run down an emotionless Oliver's face. He leans his head against the window staring out into the bright blue horizon. As he begins to doze off, Justin places a pillow between Oliver's head and the window covering him with a fleece blanket. As Oliver sleeps, Justin rests his head on the seat in front of him, quietly crying, covering his face.

At a makeshift morgue near the San Francisco coastline, Oliver is escorted to a facility to Identify Kimberly's body. Justin waits in another area as authorities have made an exception for Oliver since he is not family. Justin is surrounded by family and friends of the deceased passengers that were on board the doomed flight. Oliver enters a frigid bright, lit room with multiple body bags. His stomach is in knots as he walks calmly, following the coroner, trying not to look down. They arrive at a body bag marked with a seat number and passenger name. His breathing becomes heavy at the sight of her name. The coroner leans forward, opening the bag revealing Kimberly's face, which is covered in bruises and cuts. The right side of her face is severely burned. His breathing becomes erratic as he whimpers, fighting tears. Oliver Immediately shuts his eyes as tight as he can, grabbing his chest, trying to escape his present reality.

He escapes to a reality far from where he is right now. He can see Kimberly in a Boston Red Sox baseball cap laughing while they are at a baseball game at Fenway Park enjoying a hotdog and a couple of cold beers. She is lying next to him in all white, trying to wake him up on an early Sunday morning so they can have breakfast. He grabs her, pulling her under the covers playfully kissing her face. They snorkel in Key West on a beautiful clear summer day, holding hands, and enjoying the marine life underwater. He is on bended knee, asking her to marry him as she cries, nodding her head up and down. They run out of the church, waving goodbye to their family and friends. They kiss each other good night as she turns to look him in the eyes. "I love you." Their life is what dreams are made of. He opens his eyes, and it's not a dream. It's his worst nightmare. Catching another glimpse of Kimberly's battered face sends him over the deep end. His scream is heard by everyone in the facility. Justin drops back in his seat, crying as he hears his friend screaming in agony. Oliver is carried out of the area as he cannot stop screaming. He is taken back to Justin, waiting outside the morgue. Oliver's eyes are filled with tears as he is inconsolable. Justin wraps his arms around Oliver as he continues to scream hysterically. The crying becomes contagious as Justin cries hysterically with him. Other family members of the flight victims lose their will to be strong and cry right beside Oliver and Justin. A Japanese man walks up to them, both placing his hand on Oliver's shoulder, expressing his condolences in Japanese. Oliver reaches out to the crying man holding his hand as they all cry together.

Days later, on a mild cloudy afternoon, Oliver, Justin, Camille, Dylan, Isabella, Sebastian, Thomas, Phoebe, Monica, and all of Kimberly's family and close friends attend her funeral in Brooklyn, NY. Monica sits beside Camille, both hysterically crying while consoling each other. Funeral attendees walk up to the podium to read passages from the Bible and share their thoughts. Thomas walks up to the podium, taking a moment to gather himself looking out at the nice gathering of family and friends.

"I look out at all of you. Kimberly's family and friends. And us. Her work family. And I don't have anything profound to say. But Kimberly was blessed. Kimberly loved everyone. It was hard not to love her back. I can't say how many times I hear people say that their loved ones were so happy and pleasant to be around. But Kimberly personified happiness. Those of us who were lucky enough to be in her presence were lucky to get a whiff of her life. Being in her presence meant constant laughter, joy, and happiness. I don't remember many days being in her presence and not laughing at something. This is why I can't understand why someone like her could be taken from this world. . . Our world can be so ugly. People like Kimmy made it beautiful at times. . ."

He takes a moment to gather himself, fighting tears. His chin quivers as he looks up at everyone in attendance, struggling to fight tears as well. He takes a deep breath.

"I heard a quote. . . 'They say you die twice. One time when you stop breathing and a second time, a bit later on, when somebody says your name for the last time.'"

Oliver's whimper can be heard by everyone, as Thomas pauses.

"I will never stop saying Kimberly's name. I have too many precious memories and funny stories to tell. I know she is here looking down on us."

He looks upward. "This isn't goodbye, Kimmy. . . Until we meet again."

Thomas walks back to his seat passing Oliver, who sits beside Kimberly's mother. Thomas places his hand on Oliver's shoulder. Oliver is a mess but trying to maintain his composure while holding Kimberly's mothers' hand. The funeral comes to an end, and everyone follows the hearse to the cemetery in Long Island, where Kimberly is laid to rest. Oliver stands motionlessly, unable to speak, staring at the coffin. Isabella and Monica stand next to him, consoling him. "This is all my fault."

"This is not your fault," Isabella says, rubbing Oliver's arm.

"If I didn't take that stupid position in Japan, she would be here right now. We'd be together doing something random. I'd be happy. She'd be happy. Nobody would be in pain."
"Sigh. I can't compare my loss to yours. But I do know one thing for sure. She would want you to go on. She would not want you to live the rest of your life in sadness."

Oliver slowly walks away from Isabella, mumbling. "I can't picture my life without her."

Justin walks up behind Isabella and Monica. "I'm not going to lie. I'm extremely worried about him."

"What's he doing?" Isabella asks, turning towards Justin.

"He said he needs to be with her now. He's not sleeping, not eating and not talking."

"We all feel that way. I wouldn't even know how to help him. I don't know how to help myself."

"My heart is just broken. I can't picture her being gone. It's unreal." Monica interjects.

"I just don't know how to process any of this," Isabella says as Sebastian walks over, escorting her away from the grave.

Monica hangs her head crying. "That was my girl."

Justin places his arm around Monica, pulling her in to hug her as she buries her face into his shoulder. "I'm so sorry, Monica." They remain at the cemetery as the rest of Kimberly's family and friends slowly disperse, exiting the cemetery.

Following the burial, Kimberly's close friends from North Mutual Insurance Company, along with Oliver and Justin, gather at the Maldonado residence. Isabella lays out coffee and finger foods.

Thomas, Phoebe, Monica, Camille, Dylan Justin, and Oliver sit around listening to her coworkers reminisce about Kimberly. Thomas relives intimate moments with his lunch breaks. "Our lunches, we're off the chain. I never liked being loud, but you could never put us in a restaurant together. We would make so much noise. The patrons would complain to the wait staff."

"Yeah. I remember. I used to be the butt of many of those jokes." Camille says before Standing up, walking to the kitchen.

"Oh yeah. Even when you left the table, we still had jokes about you." Thomas says to Camille as she walks to the kitchen.

"You guys are a piece of work."

"Yeah, but you loved it. And one thing we ever did was talk about work during lunch."

"That must have been very difficult to do," Phoebe adds.

"Does anyone want anything from the kitchen?" Camille yells from the kitchen.

Both Thomas and Phoebe ask Camille for bottled water. Thomas turns back to address Phoebe. "The idea of having lunch without talking about work was her idea. She said it helped her recharge. She could do the next few hours without stressing."

Phoebe nods in agreement. "I guess that makes sense."

Monica stands up, walking to the kitchen. She stands in front of Camille as she reaches into the refrigerator, grabbing a few bottles of water. "Hey, Mon. Do you want water?"

"No. I'm good. But I have something I want to say to you."

Camille turns around to look at Monica. "You ok?"

"No. I'm not. But I just wanted to say I'm sorry for the way I treated you the night at the club. I was being judgmental, and I should have been more of a friend to you."

"That's water under the bridge Monica. It's Ok."

Monica starts to cry. "I'm such a shitty friend."

Camille opens her arms to Monica. "No, you're not. A shitty friend wouldn't be here now, apologizing. None of us are perfect."

They both remain in the kitchen, embracing each other. Oliver sits in the living room, listening to everyone reminisce as he grows irritated. "Was anyone of you going to tell me she was pregnant?"

Everyone stops talking, looking around the room at each other. Justin looks around at everyone as he learns of this news for the first time.

"She was pregnant?" Isabella asks.

"Yes. The coroner told me that she was pregnant."

Everyone looks around at each other.

"So, no one was going to tell me about that?"

Monica overhears Oliver from the kitchen. She pulls away from Camille, walking from the kitchen to the living room. "What does that matter now?"

"I got an impersonal note advising me that she was pregnant."

"Yeah. She was pregnant. She was coming out there to tell you she was pregnant. She was going to Japan." Monica points at Oliver. "Where you were."

Tears stream down Oliver's face. "I was going to ask her to marry me."

"A lot of good that did," Monica says under breath.

"Alright, Monica. That's enough. Don't start your shit." Isabella interrupts.

"I'm not allowed to grieve. This shit is partly my fault. I'm the one that went to her house to get her to the airport to see him off." She points at Oliver. "If I had left this shit alone, she'd still be here."

"I know what you did. I fully appreciate that?" Oliver says to Monica.

"I'm so glad YOU appreciate that. But all I did was help my friend realize that you meant something. Now she's gone because of that realization. I should have just left well enough alone. You already made your fucking decision. Now my friend is six feet under because of it."

Oliver listens as Monica's words only add more guilt to his conscience. He looks down, fighting emotion, unable to defend himself.

"If you would have stayed here and not gone to Japan."

"Monica. Enough!" Thomas yells.

"She wouldn't have been on a plane to Japan. What the fuck is in Japan for her to go see?"
"You're heartless," Oliver says to Monica.

"No. I'm in pain. That was my girl. I loved that like my sister. And I loved both of you together. She was so happy with you. And you had to fucking go to Japan. I hope it was worth it." She says as she starts to cry.

Thomas stands up to stop Monica. "That's enough. Stop it!"

"Monica. Please stop?" Camille says from the kitchen.

"We are all in pain," Isabella adds.

"I know. And I feel like I'm in the most pain because this is partly my fault. But I'm not gonna cosign with his bullshit. I know you feel bad." Pointing at Oliver. "But you need to come to grips with the fact that she wouldn't be dead if you didn't move to Japan."

"You're a cold-hearted. . . I was going to ask her to marry me." He says before tightly pressing his lips together.

Justin stands up. "Look. I know that Kimberly meant a lot to everyone here. I can't deny that. I got to know her, and she was truly amazing inside and out. Let's not embarrass her memory by fighting. I would imagine that she wouldn't want that."

"He's right," Isabella replies.

Monica walks back to the kitchen, passing Thomas. Thomas speaks softly to Monica. "What's the matter with you?"

"I'm angry, and I'm hurt. I want to take it out on someone."

"You can't take it out on him, Monica. He's going through hell."

"So, what about what we've been through?"

"Our road to recovery is going to be a long one. Everyone loved her." Camille says.

"Yeah, but she was my favorite. I loved her like a sister."

"I'm not taking that from you. All I'm saying is everyone here is suffering in their own way."
"I just feel like it's worse for me." Tears run down Monica's face.

"I'm sorry, honey. Come here." Camille says, opening her arms to Monica, who walks directly into her embrace. Monica feels an unfamiliar feeling of maternal warmth and security in Camille's arms.

She snuggles her face into Camille's shoulder, squeezing her tight, taking a deep breath. "I think I'm going to go home."

"Are you sure?" Camille asks.

"Yeah. My emotions are raw. If I stay here, I'm going to say something far worse to upset everyone."

"I'm actually gonna head home shortly myself. Why don't you just come to stay with me?"

Monica's eyes widen as she keeps her face buried in Camille's shoulder. "Are you sure?"

Camille smiles, leaning her head on Monica's head. "That's what friends are for, sweetie.

"Yeah. I've gotta take Phoebe home as well." Thomas says as he looks at his watch.

Isabella enters the kitchen looking over at Camille and Monica holding each other. The picture itself is worth a thousand words. She looks over at Thomas before looking back at Camille and Monica. "You guys, ok?"

Camille nods, yes. "Just trying to keep our emotions tranquil."

"I know," Isabella replies as she looks back at Oliver in the living room. "Oliver is going to be tough to deal with. He can break at any moment."

Thomas turns to look at Oliver as well. "Yeah. You noticed that too, huh?"

"Can you imagine what he's going through?"

Thomas turns back to Isabella, staring at her sarcastically. "No. I can't imagine that."

Isabella realizes the severe ignorance of her statement. "Shit. Um, I didn't mean–"

"No. Don't apologize. I didn't mean to come off sarcastic like that. I'm sorry."

"I'm still sorry. If anyone of us understands the severity of a loss like this...."

"Izzy. You're good. You don't have to say anymore. I'm not upset."

Monica pulls away from Camille, looking over at Thomas and Isabella. She turns back to Camille. "I'm gonna head out."

"Ok," Camille replies to Monica. "I'll head out with you.

Monica walks through Isabella's house, passing everyone on her way to the front door. She hugs everyone before she gets to Oliver. Oliver stands up to address Monica. "I'm sorry for what you're going through. I know it's hell. But if it means anything to you, she loved you like a sister."

Monica takes a deep breath making eye contact with Oliver. She flips a proverbial coin in her head, deciding whether to just walk away from Oliver or take the high road. "Thank you for saying that." Monica looks down at the floor as she heads for the front door. Oliver watches Monica exit before turning to face everyone left in the house.

"I'm gonna put myself in all of your shoes for a second. And I can only imagine what you guys are going through. I know what she meant to you all. For that, I'm truly sorry. But you guys can't fathom what I'm going through. I was going to ask her to marry me. I was prepared to leave my job. I know you might blame me for being on that flight to Japan. I blame myself for that too. But I can't tell you all how sorry I am for causing this much grief to this many people."

Isabella steps forward. "No, Oliver. You don't have to apologize to us."

"I do because I have to come to grips with my decision to move to Japan. Monica was right. She would be alive if I made a different decision. I feel like I fucked up my future because she was supposed to be in it."

Isabella walks up to Oliver, hugging him. "I'm dying inside. I wish it were me instead of her."

Everyone stands around quietly. The silence is deafening. Phoebe stands up, walking over to Oliver, giving him a hug. "You just need time to heal. A lot of time."

"Thank you," Oliver replies as he looks around the room at all the somber faces. "I'm going to leave now."

"You don't have to," Isabella replies.
"Yeah. You can stay here, man." Sebastian adds.

Justin interrupts. "He's staying with me. My folks don't live too far from here. They have a guest room ready for him."

"Either way, you're both welcome to stay here if you ever need to," Sebastian says to Oliver and Justin.

"Thanks, man. I may take you up on that one day." Justin replies to Sebastian.

Oliver turns around, walking toward the front door as Justin joins him, waving goodbye to everyone left in the house. Shortly thereafter, the group of friends leaves Isabella's home one after the other.

In the days to come, Oliver stays with Justin at his parents' home on the Upper East Side of Manhattan. The days are long drawn as Oliver is at his lowest point. He won't talk, eat, or engage in any form of communication. Justin realizes that taking on the responsibility of looking after Oliver may be more than he can handle, especially since Oliver refuses to say anything. The only glimmer of hope is Oliver's has been seen using his laptop.

Ten days after the funeral, Justin wakes up in the guest bedroom at his parents' house. He walks over to the other guest bedroom to check on Oliver. He peeks into the room to see the bed is made. The morning sunrise lights up the tidy room. Oliver's luggage is nowhere to be seen. Justin enters the room, looking around for anything. On the night table is an envelope labeled "Justin." Justin opens the envelope to read the letter inside.

"Justin. I can't tell you what a valuable friend you have become in my life over that past few years. You have proven that people do not have to have the same mother to be family. I will never forget how you were there for me at the absolute worst moment in my life. Thank you for everything. I love you."

"Right now, I feel like I'm going to hurt myself. I hate life without Kimberly, and I just don't know what I'm supposed to do with myself. I can't close my eyes without seeing her beautiful face. I know that the road to healing will be hard, but this road may never end. I am heading to a facility to enroll in complicated grief treatment. It's an inpatient treatment center that will allow me to stay there for an extended period of time. I don't know if or when I will come back. But once I settle in, I will call you."

"So long, brother."

Justin sits on the bed, lifting his head, looking out the window at the sunrise. He is unable to find the words in his head to put anything into perspective. He takes a deep breath falling back into the bed.

Chapter 40: Time To Heal Those Wounds

That same afternoon at North Mutual Insurance Group, Monica sits at her desk with plenty of makeup to cover the yellowing of her skin from the bruise on her face. Thomas walks out of his office and turns to the left, looking into Kimberly's office. He drops his head, releasing a loud sigh. Monica looks up at him as he raises his head, making eye contact with each other. They half-smile as Thomas walks toward the legal department. He walks through the hall, passing the small kitchen in the legal department where Phoebe is eating a snack while looking at a magazine. "Hey." He calls out to Phoebe

Phoebe looks up, smiling happily to see him. "HI!"

Thomas returns the smile. "What are you doing?"

"Just having a quick snack. How are you feeling?"

"Hollow."

"Sigh. Is there anything I can do?"

"You've already done enough. You've been awesome during this. . . Tragedy."

"It must be hard coming in to work and not seeing her."

"Not seeing her is one thing. Knowing that she's gone is the part that's hard to deal with."

Phoebe reaches out, grabbing his hand. "I know what she meant to you. I'm so sorry."

"Thanks."

Camille walks past Thomas and Phoebe in the small kitchen back towards her office. She stops by Monica's desk. "Hey, kiddo."

"Hey, Cami."

"What are you doing for lunch?"

"I dunno. I may go pick something up from outside."
"You wanna grab something together. I made lunch, but I think I need to get out of the office."

"I'm in the mood for a chicken wrap. What did you have in mind?"

"I don't care. A pizza may just do it today."

"You know me and pizza. I'm in."

Thomas slowly walks back from legal with both hands in his pockets. Camille turns to see him walking in their direction.

"Hey, buddy," Camille calls out to Thomas.

"Thomas looks up at Camille. "Hey, Cami. What's up?"

"Pizza?"

Thomas looks at Camille then Monica. "Sure."

"If you want, you can bring Phoebe," Camille suggests.

"She's working through her lunch. She's got a deadline to meet.

"Oh, ok. I like her. She's really nice."

"So do I."

"That's her boo, daddy." Monica jokes with Thomas.

"You're always trying to be funny."

"What else am I supposed to do?"

Thomas looks at Monica, smiling. "I guess you're right."

"So, lunch in ten minutes?" Camille states, while pointing at the both of them.

Monica and Thomas nod. "Yes,"
As Thomas turns around to walks to his desk, Camille places her hand on his shoulder. "I miss her to pieces too."

"Sigh. Yeah, me too."

Thomas walks back to his office and sits behind his desk. The ladies continue to talk at Monica's desk

Chapter 41: Unfinished Business

Kareem walks through his neighborhood, arriving at a building in the projects in Queensbridge. As he walks across the street towards the project building, he notices a pearl white Cadillac Escalade with the Dominican Flag on the rear window parked right in front of the building. A large thug exits the rear door of the Escalade making eye contact with Kareem. The thug walks in the same direction behind Kareem. Kareem continues walking, looking behind him at the thug, who appears extremely menacing. Kareem picks up the pace getting to the building door quickly. He notices another man standing in front of the building peeking through the glass into the lobby. Kareem retrieves his keys quickly from his pocket, unlocking the door entering the building. He attempts to close the door as the man peeking in prevents the door from closing. Kareem pushes the door as hard as he can when the first thug pushes the door knocking Kareem to the floor. Both men enter the building looking at Kareem on the ground.

"You're a funny little bitch. You might as well just get up." Thug one says to Kareem.

"Just make this shit easy." Thug two reiterates.

"What da fuck yall bitches want?" Kareem asks.

Thug one and two look at each other, laughing. Thug one turns to Kareem. "I'm gonna enjoy this shit. GET UP!"

Kareem stands up in front of the thugs. They escort Kareem through the elevator door.

Kareem enters pressing the sixth floor. Both thugs look at each other, laughing again. Thug two reaches over, selecting the right floor.

"This little nigga thinks we're stupid." one thug says to the other before turning to Kareem. "Your mom lives on the eighth floor. Don't play yourself."

They ride the elevator to eight. The elevator door opens, and everyone exits. Thug one takes the lead walking down the hallway. Kareem walks between both thugs noticing that another thug is standing in front of his mother's apartment door. Thug one gestures with his head for Kareem to enter the apartment. Kareem passes the third thug entering the apartment. Inside his mother's apartment, He sees another large Dominican man smoking a cigarette sitting at the breakfast table waiting for Kareem. The strong smell of cigarette smoke fills the entire apartment. The large man waves at Kareem to come and sit down in the only chair available in front of him. Emmanuel, Thomas's acquaintance from the Bronx, points at the chair. "Come on, man, sit down. I don't bite."

"Where's my mother?" Kareem asks, still standing.

Emmanuel takes a drag of his cigarette. "Your mom?"

"Yeah. Where is she?"

Emmanuel gives Kareem a friendly smile to take the stress off Kareem. "My name is Emmanuel. . . Please, take a seat."

Emmanuel locks eyes with Kareem while he sits down. "I take it that you're Kareem, right?"

"Yes."

"The pussy that likes to beat on women. That Kareem, right?"

Kareem doesn't answer. Emmanuel looks up, nodding at the first thug who charges behind Kareem, grabbing his arm, placing his right hand on the table. In a quick downward motion, Emmanuel stabs Kareem's hand. The knife goes through his hand, entering the table. Kareem's scream is muffled by the thug's hand over his mouth. Kareem's mother calls out to her son from inside her bedroom. "Kareem. Baby, are you ok?!"

Emmanuel turns to face her bedroom behind him, yelling. "He's good, Ma!"

"Please don't hurt my baby?" Kareem's mother yells.

"I can't make that promise, Ma." Emmanuel turns back to Kareem. "He's gonna remove his hand from your mouth. It would be in your best interest to not scream. You understand me?"

Kareem shakes his head yes in acknowledgment of Emmanuel's statement.

"So. The reason why I'm here. . . You like to beat on women. . . I don't care for mother fuckers who beat on women. Unless there's a reason. Wouldn't you agree?

Kareem's chin quivers, and doesn't answer. Emmanuel looks up at the Thug again, who charges behind Kareem, grabbing his other arm placing his left hand on the table. Again, In a quick downward motion, Emmanuel stabs Kareem's left hand. The Thug covers Kareem's mouth as he screams into the thug's hand. Emmanuel pulls the knife out. "I'm gonna need you to verbally answer me. Ok?"

The thug removes his hand from Kareem's mouth, allowing him to answer.

"Yes." He replies, struggling from the sharp pain to bother hands.

"So. Like I said before. I don't care for mother fuckers who beat on women. Unless there's a reason. Wouldn't you agree?

"Yes."

"Your mom is in her bedroom chillin. Now I could just walk in there and beat her to a pulp just to teach you a lesson. To me, that's a legitimate reason to hit a woman. It might not be a good reason to you, but to me, It has a legitimate cause. Feel me?

"Yes. But she didn't do anything to you."

Emmanuel smiles, pointing at Kareem. "Monica, right?"

"What?"

"Monica. What did she ever do to you?"

Kareem delays answering. Emmanuel looks at the Thug. Kareem freaks out and answers. "Nothing! Nothing! She didn't do anything!

"So, why'd you hit her?"

"I don't know."

"I know why you did it. . . You wanna know why I think you do it?"

"No."

"I'm gonna tell you anyway. You're a bitch nigga who feels big when you beat on someone weaker."

Kareem looks at Emmanuel. "I won't go near her again."

"Really?"

"Yes. I won't go anywhere near her. I promise."

Emmanuel sarcastically smiles as if he knows something that Kareem doesn't. "You promise?"

"I promise."

Emmanuel's smile fades as he stares at Kareem. The silence gets awkward. Kareem can hear his own breathing. Emmanuel playfully taps his knife on the table. "See. Funny thing is you got roughed up a while back and was given specific instructions to stay away from her. But you didn't listen." Emmanuel points the knife in his face. "So, I was sent here to handle shit my way. Funny thing is I was asked to not hurt you. Apparently, I don't listen either. . . I might get in trouble for stabbing you."

"Look, I–"

Emmanuel prevents Kareem from finishing his sentence. "In most cases, a situation like this would call for masks. But, I have all kinds of impulse issues, as you can clearly see."

Kareem raises his blood-soaked hands. "Look. I get it now. I swear, I do. I will stay as far away from her as possible. And I'm sorry."

Emmanuel and Kareem look at each other. Emmanuel says nothing as Kareem finds it hard to look into Emmanuel's eyes. The silence is awkward, as Emmanuel leans in.
"How's your sister Yolanda?"

Kareem starts to panic as his face turns white. "What?"

"Yolanda. You're sister. She lives in a dorm at Virginia Tech, right?"

"Come on, man. She ain't do nothing!" He yells as he starts to cry.

"Bitches like you only learn lessons the hard way. I have no problem teaching hard-headed mother fuckers the lesson of a lifetime. Know what I mean?"

Kareem continues crying, not answering Emmanuel.
Emmanuel looks up at the thug, who pulls Kareem's chair backward. Emmanuel raises his hand over his head, stabbing Kareem violently in this thigh. Kareem screams as the thug covers his mouth.

"See. You don't listen. I just told you to answer me."

Kareem cries from the agony of the pain. "I'm sorry." He says through his covered mouth as saliva streams down his chin.

"It's all good, dawg. Next time." Emmanuel extends his hand as a Thug hands him a hammer. "I'm gonna smash fingers and toes."

"Ok. Ok"

Emmanuel looks up at the thug. "Bring his mom out here."

The thug walks to the back to get Kareem's mother. Kareem attempts to stand up, yelling at the thug. "No. Leave her alone?"

"Are you telling me what to do?" Emmanuel says to Kareem.

"No. No. I swear. I'm not. I just think this would be better if we keep this between us.

The thug returns with Kareem's mother. She sees him bleeding and starts to cry. "Please leave my baby alone. He's a good boy. What did he ever do to you?"

"Nothing," Emmanuel replies as he looks toward Kareem. "He did nothing to me. He just happened to fuck with the wrong person. He likes to beat women. Right, Kareem?"

"No. He would never do that. You have the wrong man." Kareem's mother yells.

Emmanuel turns to Kareem. "Tell her what you did."

Kareem doesn't hesitate to answer, fearing Emmanuel's impulsive behavior. "I hit Monica."

"No. Tell her everything." Emmanuel interjects.

Kareem hangs his head in shame, unable to look his mother in the eyes. "I beat her bad, mom. Really bad. I always beat her."

"Why?" She asks.

"I don't know."

"You raised a bitch ass nigga. That's why." Emmanuel adds as mom says nothing. Everyone in the apartment remains quiet, waiting for Emmanuel to say something. Kareem's mother tends to her son's bleeding hands.

Emmanuel picks up his knife, closing it. "Here's what's going to happen. Me and my crew is gonna get up outta here. Kareem will stay the fuck away from Monica or any other woman for that matter. Feel me?"

Kareem is hopeful that this ordeal is coming to an end as he releases a sigh of relief. "Yes."

"So, here's the rules. If Monica trips on the subway and twists her ankle. I'm coming here to kill her." Emmanuel point at Kareem's mother. "If after that, Monica catches the flu. I'm gonna fuck you up just because I want to."

Every member of Emmanuel's crew laughs. Emmanuel can't help but snicker himself as he leans back in the chair. "Nah, seriously, though. If she walks into a door and bruises her arm. I'm gonna have your sister's hands removed and mailed to you express mail. Feel me?"

"Yes."

"Then there's your grandmother. And your father."

"We get it!" Kareem's mother yells. "Please stay away from my baby."

"Of course. We won't lay a hand on her. As long as this bitch follows the rules. Right, Kareem?"

"Yeah, man. I promise."

Emmanuel stands up to exit the kitchen. He stops walking and turns to look down at Kareem. "Oh. I saw Monica's face. You got a mean right hook."

Kareem takes a deep breath. "I'm really, really sorry."

Emmanuel looks at Kareem with disgust. He looks at one of his thugs and nods over toward Kareem. The thug grabs Kareem's right hand, placing it back on the table. Emmanuel slams the hammer down on Kareem's hand several times. Kareem screams in agony. Emmanuel pulls out a pistol from the back of his pants, pointing it at Kareem's mother's head.

"SHUT THE FUCK UP!!!"

Kareem fights the urge to scream as he begins to hyperventilate. The pain to Kareem's hand is overbearing.

"If I find out one of your homeboys tries to hurt her. Everybody dies. Do you understand?"

"YES!!!!" He screams while nursing his hand. Emmanuel pulls the gun away from mom, tucking it in his jeans. "Good."

Kareem's mother goes over to Kareem, kneeling in front of him, nursing his hand. She looks at the blood-drenched table as Kareem tries to fight the pain. Emmanuel and his crew exit the apartment taking the elevator to the first floor. Kareem's mother runs to the hall closet grabbing a few clean towels and tends to her son's injured hands. Fearing for the rest of her family, she makes no attempt to call the police. Kareem falls to the floor, looking at his severely bruised and impaled hands, trying not to scream from the pain.

Chapter 42: A Start of Something New

Nine months later, on a warm sunny spring afternoon at Bryant Park in midtown Manhattan, Thomas and Phoebe sit outside together at a table for two near a garden of flowers. Their bond has grown into an exclusive relationship. The one thing they've learned throughout their relationship is to take full advantage of every possible moment. On any given day, they can be found outside having a meal enjoying the moment. Today is no exception. Thomas closes his eyes, tilting his face up toward the warm afternoon sunlight. Phoebe turns to Thomas. "What are you doing?"

"Taking in the sun. It beautiful out today."

Phoebe looks up and around at the Manhattan skyline squinting from the bright sunlight. "It sure is. I'm glad you asked me to take the day off.

"Seize the moment. I figured since I'm going to be working at the midtown office, we won't be able to have our lunches like normal."

"I know. I'm going to miss seeing you around the office, baby."

"Yeah. Me too. But we can do these types of lunches every now and again. You know me and my extended lunches?"

"Yeah. I could take a half-day, or we can just spend a weekend day out here. You know how much I love the city."

"Trust me. I know." He replies as he crumbles up his lunch bag and places it on the table. The bag rolls off the table onto the ground next to Phoebe. Thomas squats down to pick up the bag next to Phoebe. He remains on the ground picking up the paper looking up at Phoebe. Phoebe turns to see what he is doing. Thomas is on bended knee with a ring box in his hand. "What the–" Phoebe says in shock as she looks at the box before looking into his eyes in shock.

Thomas picks up from Phoebe's recent statement. "Yes. I know how much you love the city. Which is why I planned to do this here."

Phoebe laughs, covering her mouth. "Are you crazy?"

"Yes. You chose the right words. Because I'm crazy in love with you."
Phoebe's voice cracks as she starts to cry. "Baby, what are you doing to me?"

"I'm telling you that I love you. I'm telling you that I love spending every moment with you. I'm telling you that I want to spend the rest of my life with you. And I'm telling you that my life became more meaningful when I let you in. I love you so much."

"I love you too."

"I know. I can feel it when you hug me. I can feel it when you kiss me."

Thomas continues holding the ring leaning in with his other hand touching Phoebe.
"I've had an unusually rough few years. And I thought I would have to coast through the rest of my life feeling a sense of hopelessness, especially when I was alone. I always felt like there was such a massive hole in my heart."

"I'm sorry, baby."

"It's ok. I had to go through that grief get to where I am today. But once I met you, things started to change. Being with you has revitalized my existence. I'm just happy to see the caller ID on my phone when you call. I'm happy when we see each other after a long day apart. I want to have that feeling always. It's not often a guy like me is lucky enough to find a woman like you. But when he does, he shouldn't wait to start the rest of his life with her.

Tears stream down Phoebe's face.

"Phoebe. . . Will you marry me?" He asks as her as he remains on bended knee.

"Absolutely, baby," Phoebe answers, dropping out of the seat onto the ground, hugging Thomas. She places both hands on Thomas's face taking in the moment while looking into his eyes before kissing him passionately. People sitting in their proximity watch in awe. Some record the encounter; others just observe the beautiful moment. Thomas pulls away, smiling at Phoebe. "Can I put the ring on you?"

Phoebe laughs from embarrassment. "Oh. I was so caught up in the moment. I forgot about that."

Thomas places the ring on her finger. "There you go."

Phoebe admirers the ring. "I love it, baby. I love you. Thank you."
"No. Thank you for making me the happiest guy on the planet."

He pulls her closer, kissing her passionately while onlookers clap with excitement. The excitement of people clapping brings more curious spectators who arrive to see them kneeling on the ground with their arms wrapped around each other. Thomas has closed a chapter in his life, moving toward a whole new book with Phoebe. Though his courtship with Phoebe had outside obstacles pulling at his loyalty to his close friends, he allowed himself to find love that no heart can deny. He found his soulmate.

The end. . .

I May Have To Change My Outlook

A chilly late fall moonlit Friday night at an upper east side apartment building in the Murray Hill section of Manhattan. A young woman exits a taxicab wearing a tan trench coat and black high heels. She enters the building behind an older gentleman who walks over to the mailbox as she trots over to the elevator. She enters the elevator pressing fourteen. As the elevator door is about to close, the man checking his mail shoves his hand into the elevator preventing the door from closing. He enters the elevator making eye contact with the young woman wearing the trench coat. He extends his hand, pressing twenty. As they ascend uninterrupted to the fourteenth floor, the older gentleman looks over at the young woman's pretty face. They make eye contact as she bashfully smiles before the elevator comes to a stop on fourteen. The young woman exits the elevator, turning left.

The older man peeks out of the elevator to watch the young woman strut down the hall. Realizing that the elevator door did not close, the young woman stops walking, turning around to look behind her. She makes eye contact with the smiling man who sticks his head out of the opened elevator door. "Are you enjoying the view?" She asks sarcastically.

"Very much, thank you. I'm on the twentieth floor if you want to come up for a nightcap." The older man replies.

The young woman smiles before turning around, heading to her destination of 14G. She rings the doorbell with her right hand, holding a bottle of champagne in her left hand behind her back. Justin opens the door wearing a t-shirt and basketball shorts. He smiles as he recognizes his visitor. "Hey Monica"

Monica whips the bottle of champagne from behind her back. Her trench coat opens up, exposing her black satin bra and panties. "What's up, white boy?"

Justin's eyes widen as he looks at Monica's curvy body underneath her coat. He leans on the door bringing his eyes up to Monica's eyes. "Nothing yet. What brings you to this part of town?"

Monica leans in, getting closer to Justin. "You and I started something a while ago that we didn't finish."

"Well, you've come to the right place then. Because I'm all about a good finish." He replies with an impish grin. Monica wraps her right hand around Justin's head, pulling him toward her kissing him passionately. He reaches down, placing his hands around her waist under her coat, pulling her into him. She pushes Justin backward into his apartment, closing the door behind her. . .

Now it's over.

Special Thank You

I'd like to thank my parents for, well. . . being my parents. All those times, they watched me play with my action figures for hours and letting my imagination run free and never complained about my toys all over the imaginary city, which was the entire house that has come a long way. Thanks to my brothers, whose words of encouragement only help fuel the passion to want to continue writing.

A most special thank you to my wife Maritza, mi mejor amiga, mi amor, the mother of our beautiful children, my constant partner in crime, my ride or die, my final beta reader, and the sexy voice of Camille. Being able to put up with my personality makes you more special than you know. It takes a very extraordinary woman to be married to me, and you are by far an exceptional woman, wife, and mother in my eyes. Your input on the final draft was vital to the changes made to this story. I look forward to your input when I continue with the remaining stories in this series. Thank you for always being honest.

Thank you to my kids Jonathan Blake and Victoria Blake, for all of your support and help with a multitude of my different projects.

To my favorite coworker, friend, and sister that I never knew existed, Sabrina Mojica. Thank you so much for always believing in my stories. You are so important to this journey. You've spent hours upon hours reading and re-reading my manuscripts on your long train rides, breaks, and lunches. Thank you for the hours of feedback dissecting each chapter, and every character nuance that you either disliked or loved. I truly hope that every reader appreciates my writing the way you do because if they do, I will be a success.

Liz Martinez. Thank you so much for taking the time to read this book along with the other stories in this and my other series. You took reading my manuscripts very seriously and made it a joy listening to your feedback months after a story was complete. You carry your emotions on your sleeves and would allow yourself to become so immersed in these stories that you would become visible distraught when something didn't go as you expected. You cried, you laughed, and sometimes you were downright aggravated with certain parts of the story. But through all of that, you always maintained a positivity, knowing that I would be here someday. Thank you for your support.

To the man who is forever looking way beyond the outside of the box. Ricardo Rampersad. Thank you for always keeping it real and honest. You've opened my eyes in more ways than one on the best ways to move forward in this venture and everything else. The tidbits of information on how to get around, over, under, and through his industry was heard, and I plan on taking your advice. I know in life, we can often feel unappreciated by those who should be showing us the most gratitude. But I want you to know that I value and appreciate you, my brother. Thanks for being in my corner.

Joanne Skribis, we haven't spoken in a while, but I've always wanted to put together a story either on the silver screen or in a novel that would be worthy of your time. Your support when I told you that I wanted to write was just the positive response I needed to push forward. Thank you for reading my two very first manuscripts and taking the time to provide honest feedback that I needed to hear. It was through your feedback where are started to learn that I needed to become a little thicker skinned. Your brutal honesty made me realized that a rewrite is not a bad thing if it makes the story better. Thank you so much for your honesty and support.

To Tracey Salvodon. The real reason why I started writing again. You shared your script with me that you wrote when you were sixteen years old, and I couldn't believe that a high schooler wrote such an awesome script. You became someone I looked up to because you knew what you wanted to do, and you started working at it at such a young age. It is still one of the best stories I've ever read. After reading it, I became so inspired that I just sat in front of my PC and started writing. And as you know, I kept writing and writing and writing. And here we are now. Thank you so much for inspiring me and challenging me, and always being the voice that said, "when this happens" when I would say "If this happens." Thank you for all your support.

Thank you, Arielle Reed, for all of those small pep talks when I had doubt in myself. You would always stay honest and tell me that this isn't something that may or may not happen. You always said this would happen, and you will be successful. Every pep talk was needed and made me thankful to have someone like you in my corner. Thank you.

To my editor Mariah Jackson, I found you by luck and put my faith in you, and you didn't disappoint. You took on this project, and you've been on point with communication while maintaining a friendly and professional disposition. I wish nothing but the best for you and your career. Thank you for being in the right place at the right time.

To my book illustrator/cover designer Jun Aceres. Words cannot express how impressed I am with the cover you put together for my manuscript. I thought my idea was nice until you took the lead and came up with the cover that left me speechless. It's fair to say that I love it. Thank you for staying on top of things and always keeping me updated. Thank you for giving me a visual to let me know that this was really happening.

Thank you to Safa Shaqsy and Patricia Bates, whom I met in Writers' Group on Facebook, for being gracious enough to take time away from your personal journeys and provide information to help me on my self-publishing journey. You both were so positive and more than willing to provide information that I needed to move forward to self-publish my manuscripts. People in these types of forums can be so negative and hateful. It was very uplifting to meet you two, who were so pleasant and easy to talk to. I hope you both do well with your writing journeys.

And I didn't forget those who took the time to give feedback on various scenes and chapters from this and other manuscripts, providing valuable feedback. I'd like to extend a thank you to Vicky Mack, Phary Cotrell, Jonijah Latta, Amy Bogdahn, Nathaniel Hagood, Justin "BluJD" Davis, Paula Mendoza, April Irving, Manny Tate, Janell Coleman, Brittaney Short, Sonia Valero, and Angela Mills, Gina Nguyen and Melissa Morales, Stephanie Deaton, Fannie

Marzouka, and Carolyn Wasielewski.

Made in the USA
Columbia, SC
29 November 2020

25817892R00202